Between

By Cyndi Tefft

To Cheryel,
I hope Aiden
MacRae brings you
joy! :)
Cyndi Tefft

Dedication

This book is dedicated to Ryan Tefft, Lisa Surdyk and Jamie Schlecht Knapp, who know for sure whether there are Transporters waiting for us on the other side.

Acknowledgments

This book would not have been possible without the loving support of my husband, Dave Tefft, who took the kids out so I could write, who suffered my tossing and turning as I worked out scenes in my sleep, and who has always encouraged me in whatever creative endeavors strike my fancy. You are my soul mate in this life and whatever comes next.

Thanks to Dyan Kirkpatrick who was such a help with reading, editing and offering her valuable insight. I love you, Mom!

A big thanks to Teresa Velasquez and Korene Pearson who read the book in its infancy and prodded me to finish. Lindsey has green eyes because of Teresa!

Love to Sue Martin and Jan Wigen as well, for giving me their honest opinion once I'd reached the end. Thanks to Beth Isaacs and Linda Ge for being brutal critique partners, too!

Clare and David from EditingandDesign.com are the wizards behind the breathtaking cover. You guys rock!

For support and encouragement, a big squeeze from me to Jim Gill, Robin Mickelson, Paul Ahrens, Tim Surdyk, Tim and AnneMarie Kuhnau, Steve Scott, Maria McCrackin, Q Jackson, Saskia Kidd, Pam Horton, Karin Nelson, Stephanie Hance, Paula McClure, Tammy Tegge, and Camay Wells.

And lastly, thanks to Diana Gabaldon for creating such a delectable character in Jamie Fraser that I had to create my own version. I will always be indebted to Diana for introducing me to the wonders of Scotland, the land of my heart.

Chapter 1

Ravi's lips were soft and familiar against mine, but my mind was elsewhere. I was so not ready for my history final and should have been back at the dorm, studying.

"Lindsey, you're so beautiful," he said, pressing me against the seat of the car. His mouth trailed over my jaw to my neck, his breath warm in my ear.

"I love you," he whispered.

That snapped me back to reality.

Damn. I liked Ravi, I really did, but not as much as he liked me. The kissing was nice, but I didn't feel IT, the connection, the zing. *The L word? Ugh.* I didn't want to lose him as a friend and I did love him, in a way. Just not that way.

"Ravi…" I began and he stiffened.

"You know what, never mind. Just forget I said anything, okay?" He jerked away, his voice tight with embarrassment. He turned the key and the engine roared to life.

"No, really, it's just…"

He flicked on the high beams. "Let's just go."

Fat droplets of rain splattered on the windshield and built into a steady drumming on the roof. The swish of the wipers and the hum of the heater echoed in the chasm between us and I struggled to think of a way to alleviate the tension. He flipped on the radio and the sound of screeching guitars raked my nerves.

The highway was deserted and we hadn't seen another

car pass by us for miles. As he started around a corner, I touched him on the arm.

"Ravi, I'm sorry."

He turned to me with a frustrated sigh, giving minimal attention to the familiar road. "No, it's my fault. I shouldn't have said it. I know it's only been a couple of months, but I feel like…"

"Look out!" I yelled.

The sedan in front of us was creeping along and we came screaming up behind it. His eyes snapped forward and he slammed on the brakes. My chest seized with panic as the car started to hydroplane, the tires sliding across the slick asphalt. He wrenched on the steering wheel and pumped the brakes, trying to regain control. The sickening crunch of metal mingled with my screams as we rammed into the other vehicle.

The headlights flung streaks of light like fireworks in the driving rain as we spun out of control. We sailed off the roadway and the car hung in mid air before the hood smashed into the ground. Distorted acid rock pounded in my ears as the car rolled down the embankment. Ravi's body floated over mine, his face contorted in fear. The pine tree outside my window beckoned with relentless persistence until the car door wrapped around me in a vicious embrace, squeezing the air from my lungs.

Chapter 2

I awoke with my knees drawn to my chest. Shaking with fear, jaw clenched in anticipation of searing pain, I took an experimental breath and waited.

Nothing hurt.

Relief flooded through me and I breathed to try and still the tremors in my flesh, still dreading the moment I'd be wracked with pain. Slowly unfurling, I reached out, expecting to feel the cold metal of the car door.

It wasn't there. My hand landed on soft, dry grass and my eyes snapped open in confusion.

Where am I?

Completely disoriented, I scrambled to my feet. Birds flitted between the tree branches at the edge of a meadow, their sweet melody floating through the air. Wildflowers tickled my knees as I stood with my mouth agape.

What the—? I must be dreaming.

Energy hummed—building, bubbling inside—and the air caressed me with its warm, honeyed scent. I walked along the bank of a stream, sunlight sparkling on its surface, then knelt for a drink.

A shadow appeared over the water.

Shielding my eyes with my hand, I turned and peered up at the towering figure. Illuminated from behind, his wavy blond hair shone like a halo around his head. He wore a cream shirt and pants, and couldn't have been much older than me, but he looked like a Greek god. When he smiled, a dimple appeared on one cheek.

"Weel, hallo there," he said in a thick accent. My eyebrows shot up in surprise.

Without thinking, I blurted, "You're Scottish."

Brilliant, Einstein.

He threw his head back and laughed—a rich, joyous sound that bounced off the water. "Aye, that I am, indeed. Aiden MacRae of Eilean Donan. Very pleased to be meeting you." He bowed with a grand sweep of his arm, and straightened with an upright carriage that cast an air of royalty.

"Wow. Um, I'm uh..." I struggled to think of something impressive to say in return, but gave up. "I'm Lindsey. Lindsey Waters."

He repeated my name carefully with a sweet lilt I'd never heard before. "It's a lovely name." He tipped his head and smiled, his blue eyes crinkled at the corners.

I wanted to say something witty, but I just stood there, absorbing him with my eyes. He knelt beside the water and took a drink. I couldn't help but stare at the strength of his movements: swift and fluid in one way, but filled with an underlying power, like a lion at rest.

"You look like an angel," I breathed.

Oh man, did I just say that out loud?

"Thank you kindly, lass. But no, angels are incredible beings, fierce and dangerous, and so beautiful you can barely stand to look at them." He fit the description pretty well, but I kept my mouth shut. "No, I'm not an angel. I'm what you might call a Transporter. I'm here to take you from earth to heaven."

My brows furrowed as if I'd just realized I'd forgotten something important. I shook my head. "From earth to heaven? To go to heaven, I'd have to be... dead." The word lay on my tongue, heavy and tasteless, as I tried to absorb exactly what that meant. The meadow dissolved around me, replaced by a rainy night. The wind whipped my hair around my face and I stared in horror at the crumpled car wrapped around the pine tree before me.

A man at the edge of the road slid down the bank toward us. Upon reaching the mangled car, he shouted, "Are you okay?"

Ravi choked out a sob. "Help her. I think she's hurt."

"I'm here! Over here!" I yelled, but the man didn't react.

The stranger moved over to the side of the car by the tree and yelled, "Miss? Miss, are you all right? Can you hear me?" When he got no response, he gave up and moved back to Ravi. "I called 9-1-1. Help is coming. Don't worry, man, she's going to be fine." I ran over to him, panic welling up inside me.

"What are you talking about?" I said. "I'm right here! I must have been thrown from the car. I'm not—" A bloody, lifeless arm lay on the ground, sticking out through the shattered window.

My hand flew to my mouth.

NO!

My throat tightened and I swallowed hard in a vain attempt to tamp down the surge of grief. Aiden appeared at my side and touched my shoulder. I bit my quivering lip, jerking away from him. Choking back the tears, I wiped my face, blinking fiercely and trying to get a breath.

A cold wall of denial solidified inside me.

It can't be true.

I took a tentative step and peered inside the car. My broken body lay in a pool of blood, unmoving. Dead.

I couldn't contain it anymore, and great hiccupping sobs broke free. Aiden's arms came around me in a tight embrace and I didn't resist. He stroked my hair, whispering comforting words in a language I didn't understand, and held me until no more tears would come. Resting my forehead on his chest, I tried to slow my breathing to match his. Peace radiated from him.

"Better?" he asked, all traces of the earlier amusement

gone. I nodded and he wiped a tear from my cheek, the warmth of his body enveloping me. A siren's piercing wail was coming toward us and I turned to watch with bleary, stinging eyes. The paramedics came down the bank and worked to free the driver. The door wrenched free with a piercing screech of metal and they pulled him out.

"Ravi!" Agony shot through me at the sight of his bloodied face. I frantically scrambled over the wet earth to him.

He was barely conscious. "No, leave me. Help Lindsey," he repeated.

"We've got our top paramedic working on her. Let's worry about you," the EMT said. Ravi's eyes rolled back in his head and his breathing became labored.

"Help him! Do something! You can't let him die!" I screamed at Aiden, reaching out to Ravi, but my hand passed right through.

Aiden's eyes held a deep compassion but his voice was resolute. "He will not die, Lindsey. I've only come for you."

"But I can't..." I began, but then stopped upon seeing the determined set of his jaw. "It's really over, isn't it?" I asked, though I already knew the answer. He nodded and held out a hand. I felt hollow inside, knowing there was nothing I could do. A tear slid down my cheek as I stole a glance back at the car where my body lay, surrounded by people working earnestly to save what I knew was already lost.

"Goodbye," I breathed to my former self, then turned to Aiden and what lay ahead.

Chapter 3

The instant my fingertips touched his, the rainy night melted into a picturesque scene. I looked out over a lake toward green, rolling hills dotted with purple heather. The setting sun reflected pools of orange in the water's mirrored surface. Behind us, wreathed in mist, a stone castle dominated the small island where we stood. A narrow bridge spanned the distance to the mainland. There were no sounds or signs of modern day: no electric lights or lampposts, no familiar hum of traffic.

Aiden moved to stand beside me, his presence as tangible as a supportive embrace. All at once, the despair that had been choking me suddenly dissolved. Aiden exuded a supernatural peace that chased away my grief like a warm blanket blocks out the chilly night. I felt like I was supposed to be sad about something, but I couldn't quite remember what. Overwhelmed, I stared across the peaceful water.

"I just can't believe it… dead." I rolled it around in my mind, considering. "I always thought that death was something to be afraid of, you know, something terrible. And yet, now here I am in this beautiful place." He smiled, his eyes filled with understanding. "And I feel more alive than I ever did before. It's crazy," I said, shaking my head in awe.

"Many folk say they believe in heaven, but more often than not, they're surprised to find out God wasn't lying after all."

I noted he was no longer wearing the cream shirt and

slacks, but a red and green kilt, white linen shirt and black boots. With his hair pulled away from his face in a braid, the glowing light of the sunset danced off the sharp angles of his cheeks and jaw.

"If you don't mind, I'll make us a wee campfire to warm your toes." He set to work gathering sticks from the sparse woods around us. I sat down and tucked my arms around my knees, enthralled by his accent and fascinated by the sight of him in his native dress. I'd never seen a guy in a kilt before but I had to admit I really liked it. My gaze traveled up his bare calves and over his back. His muscles flexed as he bent to arrange the twigs and limbs for the fire. The kilt covered his legs at one moment, then revealed them anew as he stood up. All my earlier thoughts seemed to wash away as I watched him, drinking in his strength and beauty.

Damn, he is gorgeous.

I suddenly remembered the saying that Scots don't wear anything under their kilts and pushed back a crazy impulse to see for myself. Afraid that he might notice me checking him out, I cleared my throat to break the silence.

"Do you want some help?" I asked.

"Thank you for the offer but I've done this a thousand times if I've done it once. No fear, I've a flint in my sporran." He reached into a small pouch tied around his waist and pulled out the flint. A spark lighted from the metal, and he deftly turned it into a flame that lapped at the kindling hungrily.

"Where are we? This place is so beautiful and yet it seems almost surreal. Is this heaven, then?" I asked.

He added more substantial wood to the fire and stood up. "I'm glad that you like it. But no, it's not heaven. Not really. It's my home, Eilean Donan." He swept his arm out in front of him to include everything in view. "The castle, the land, the sea, the cottages, the stables. It all belonged to my family, the MacRaes and the MacKenzies. I lived here as a lad. Once upon a time, that is." His voice had a wistful quality to it, of a great sadness reconciled long ago. Wanting to comfort him, I reached out and touched his arm. His hand closed over mine with a brief squeeze.

"Tell me about yourself. We've enough time yet." He sat down and I settled in next to him.

My mind was a blank. "What's there to tell? I just started college a few months ago. My parents got divorced last year and have used me as a pawn in their tug of war against one another." I frowned and tried to come up with something more cheerful to talk about. "Let's see... I like to sing."

"Sing me a song then. I'd love to hear you sing."

I shook my head, embarrassed that I'd brought it up.

"I promise I won't laugh. Go on." His blue eyes danced with the firelight and my heart sped up. His smile was wreaking havoc on my insides, so I closed my eyes and took a breath to calm my nerves. I sang the first verse of "Amazing Grace," the only song that came to mind. To my surprise, my voice came out rich and full, pulsing with a soothing energy. The sound relaxed me and spurred me on so that I built with confidence to the last verse.

When we've been there ten thousand years
Bright shining as the sun
We've no less days to sing God's praise
Than when we'd first begun

The final note hung in the air like a delicious scent and when I opened my eyes, he grinned and clapped enthusiastically.

"Bravo! That was beautiful. You've a very lovely voice." I returned his smile and thanked him, thrilled with his praise. "A perfect song, too," he said. "'Tis true, that. A man could stay here for ten thousand years and it'd be just as if one day had gone by. And yet other times, the days speed by faster than you want them to." He looked at me with a curious expression and I wondered what he meant.

"You said you're here to take me from earth to heaven,"

I said, "but that this isn't heaven. You also said you'd seen an angel but that you aren't one. Have you met God as well? Are we going to go to heaven, then?"

The last question seemed to subdue him, as if he'd been expecting it but not looking forward to it. "No, I haven't met God face-to-face yet, though I feel His presence with me all the time."

"What do you mean you feel His presence? What does it feel like?"

"It's hard to explain. My uncle taught me about something called gravity that pulls you down to the ground and keeps you from flying off into the sky like a bird. I guess God is like that. His presence is a tether that keeps me and holds me," he said with a shrug.

"Have you always felt God's presence?" I asked, fascinated.

"Aye, God's always been with me, even when I was a wee lad." His eyes narrowed with a far-off remembering. "My father died when I was six years old. I remember crying in my bed at night, missing my Da. Mam had told me that he went to be with God, and I thought God must be pretty terrible to take a young lad's Da." He gave me a crooked smile and continued. "I lay there weeping and praying, 'God, give him back. Give my Da back!' and then He was there."

"God?"

He nodded. "I was lying on my back, staring up at the roof and it started to glow—a beautiful soft, yellow glow. It spread from the roof down over the room like a waterfall. It washed over me and through me, into the floor and then it was gone. I never cried for my Da again after that, and God's presence has been with me ever since."

"Wow." Excitement fluttered in my stomach at the thought of meeting God. "So let's go meet Him together."

His face fell and he breathed a deep sigh. He attempted a smile, but the sadness in his eyes broke my heart.

"I'd like nothing better than to go to heaven with you

and meet our Creator. But alas, I cannot do that. You'll go on to meet Him, but I..." He broke off and turned away so I couldn't see the emotion there. I touched his leg in unspoken support and his hand closed over mine.

"Why can't you come, too?" I asked. "I don't understand."

He regarded me for a moment, like he wanted to say something, then shook his head in frustration. "It's a long story." He stood up and started walking along the edge of the water and I followed, but his stride was so long, it was a struggle to keep up with him. I started to jog a little and was surprised at how easy it was. After picking up the pace, I sped past him, giggling at his startled expression.

"Race you to the church," I challenged, spying the stone structure with a cross above the door. Aiden grinned and broke into a sprint behind me. I hastened my pace to stay in front but made it to the church mere seconds after he did and fell into his arms, laughing.

"That's amazing!" I gushed. "I could never run like that on earth because I've always been too fat."

Aiden stiffened in surprise. His face creased in a frown as he looked me over. "You're not fat. Your body is soft and feminine, with curves like a wild rose. In fact, I'd say you're fair beautiful."

"Yeah, right." I dismissed him with a wave of my hand. I had some admirable qualities, I supposed, but beauty was not one of them. My roommate Jen was tall, blonde and athletic, her tanned body seemingly carved from marble. Now *she* was beautiful.

"No, it's true," he insisted. "You've this wild, curly hair like the stems of a grape vine. And it dances when the wind touches it, with a mind of its own." He playfully ruffled my hair and it obligingly set off in multiple directions. I tried to flatten it with my hands and fixed him with a glare. His gaze grew thoughtful as he continued. "Your skin is like the finest silk, so thin and smooth."

He ran a single finger down my cheek and under my chin. My pulse quickened and I swallowed hard in an effort to contain the shivers dancing down my spine.

"And your green eyes are the color of the hills—the color of my home." His voice dropped to a whisper. "Aye, there's something about you, Lindsey Waters."

His eyes focused on my lips with a flicker of hunger and my heart raced at the thought of his kiss. He leaned forward, his lips merely inches from mine. My breath caught in anticipation, but he sighed and abruptly moved away. "Come. I'll show you the kirk," he said, his voice more gruff than before.

Stung, I hesitated as he held the door open for me. I brushed past him as I entered the church, unwilling to meet his eyes. Soot from the fireplace darkened the walls and filled the room with a rich, peaty scent. The afternoon light streamed through warm hues of stained glass, illuminating the Virgin Mary and her child. My chest squeezed in response to the image of the tightly wrapped infant.

"I'll never have a baby now," I said, transfixed by the love in Mary's face. I never really knew I wanted one until that moment, and now it was too late. A crushing weight pressed down on me with the realization of all the things I'd never get to do. A sob caught in my throat. I sensed Aiden's movement behind me and was struck with a wild desire to know what his child would look like, bouncing on my father's knee. My hand flew to my mouth in horror.

"My parents... I mean, my dad is all alone now. My mom moved in with her boyfriend and now Dad... with me gone..." I struggled to explain, to help him understand what my death would mean to them. "Do you know what will happen to them? Will they be all right?" I asked, but he shook his head.

"I cannot tell the future. I'm sorry." He frowned, but the compassion in his eyes was sincere. I nodded and wiped my wet cheeks, trying to get a hold of myself.

"I'm sorry I keep doing that. It's just a lot to digest." Buffeted by emotion and the waves of comfort that radiated from him, I plopped down on the front pew and tried in vain to work it out.

"I understand," he said, sitting down beside me. "And if you want to know the truth, I don't think you're daft at all. You're a tender-hearted woman with a caring spirit. Not everyone I meet sheds a tear for those left behind."

"They don't?" I asked, perplexed. "Well, to be fair, I was crying for myself, too. I didn't even know I wanted kids. Did you?" I blurted out the question before I realized he might have had children once upon a time. The thought was unsettling, but he was quick to respond.

"No, I did not have any bairns of my own, though I've taken a fair number of them to heaven."

"Oh, I'm sorry," I said. "I can't imagine how awful that must be for you."

"For me?" he said. "Why would you say that?"

"Well, you know, to have to take a baby from its parents, to know how much they'll grieve its death. That must be heart wrenching for you. I couldn't do it."

He stared at me like his world had suddenly slipped on its axle and he was seeing me for the first time. A flicker of hope crossed his face before he clamped his jaw and shook his head as if to clear it. His voice was unsteady when he spoke.

"I cannot count the number of years I've been here and never once has someone cared about what it's like for me." His blue eyes locked onto mine for a moment, then I dropped my gaze to the floor, a blush heating my cheeks. He took my hand and lifted it to his lips. Tingles shot up my neck at the soft press of his mouth against my skin.

"You're an uncommon woman, Lindsey." He let out a heavy sigh. "But I should not get so attached to you."

I snapped my head up. "What do you mean? Why not?"

"You cannot stay here. You must go on to heaven. We

have some time yet, but I don't know how much." I bit my lip as fresh tears threatened to start. He put his arm around me, cradled me against his chest and stroked my hair. I was suddenly exhausted, overwhelmed by all that had happened.

"Come, rest your head. You've had more than enough for one day."

"I'm afraid to fall asleep," I protested weakly, my eyelids already starting to droop. "What if you're not here when I wake up?"

"We've a bit of time yet. I promise I'll be here when you wake, lass."

Chapter 4

The feather bed cradled me in its soft embrace and I nuzzled my face into the pillow, afloat in the sensation of waking. Yawning, I rolled over and my gaze settled on a full-length cheval mirror, its reflective surface sending rays of sunlight dancing across the room. A hand-woven rug covered most of the hardwood floor, and a golden railing disappeared behind a green chaise lounge. Leather bound books lined one wall from floor to ceiling, their spines perfectly straight like soldiers in formation. A nobleman on a majestic white horse looked down his nose at me from a tapestry on the wall. An empty pallet with a blanket and a flat pillow lay tucked under the window.

As my mind dimly struggled to make sense of the unfamiliar surroundings, I suddenly remembered Aiden and panic seized my throat.

"*Bon matin*. Good morning, Lindsey."

Aiden came through the door, carrying a breakfast tray piled high with fruit, cheese and biscuits. Relief flooded through me.

"Good morning to you, too. Where are we?"

He set the tray down next to me. "Would you like some breakfast, *ma chérie?*" The smell of warm honey wafted through the air and my stomach growled in appreciation. I mumbled a thank you as I tore off the corner of a biscuit and popped it in my mouth. Aiden took an apple slice and sat next to me. "I was thinking you might like to go someplace

15

new, and this is the most beautiful place I remember, aside from home."

Above the fireplace hung a large, ornately framed portrait of a beautiful woman and her two young sons. Curly wisps of blonde hair escaped from her bonnet, softly framing her face, and her eyes shone with a serene smile as she sat with one hand draped over her youngest child. The boys wore stern expressions and looked very serious in their fancy outfits. I couldn't help but smile as I imagined the painter trying to capture the scene before the kids got bored and became completely unmanageable.

"She's lovely, no?" he asked in a wistful tone.

Nodding, I helped myself to a cluster of grapes from the tray and picked them off the stem, one by one. "Who is she?" I asked.

"My mother."

"So this little boy in the front, that's you?" I walked over and reached out as if to touch the child, though the painting was out of my reach, high up on the wall.

"'Tis me and my brother Duncan. I don't remember it well, just that the clothes she made us wear were bloody uncomfortable." He winked at me. "My uncle Alex Fraser had it painted as a gift to my Mam. This is his château in Versailles," he explained.

"Versailles? France?"

"Aye. I spent three years here as a lad, studying under my uncle, learning how to be a proper gentleman and taking care of his horses." My eyes welled up with tears and he looked at me quizzically.

"I'm sorry... It's just... I always..." I sputtered. He pulled a handkerchief out of the sporran around his waist and handed it to me as I stammered nonsensically. "I took French classes in high school and was still taking them in college when I..." I took a deep breath and gave him a brave smile. "I always meant to go to France someday, and I thought my 'somedays' were over. And now here we are, and it just... it just means a lot to me. Thank you."

He didn't say anything, but nodded as if he understood. I remembered that I'd heard him speaking French earlier, though it hadn't registered before. "You speak French? *Parlez-vous français?*" I asked. He bowed deeply in response, sweeping his arm out and down.

"Oui, mademoiselle. Je parle français très bien. I think, milady, that you might like to see the grounds. Perhaps we'll go for a ride on one of Uncle's prized horses. But you cannot go outside in your shift."

A long nightgown of lightweight linen hung loosely on my shoulders, and by the feel of it, I had absolutely nothing on underneath. I racked my brain to try and remember changing out of my jeans and sweater—let alone my underwear—and wondered how I had gotten into this outfit. My eyes darted around the room, looking for my discarded clothes. Aiden saw my confusion and laughed.

"Don't fret, I haven't undressed you. Not that I wouldn't like to, mind." He gave me a wicked grin. "But if I had, I wouldn't have been sleeping on the floor, aye?" I felt my cheeks go hot at his comment. Wrapping my arms around my chest, I asked where my clothes had gone. He shrugged. "You can wear them again, if you like, but I thought you might like to dress like a lady for our outing."

At his words, a strange sensation passed through me and the edges of the room blurred for a moment, like I was viewing it underwater. When I blinked my eyes a few times, the room snapped into focus once again. My ribs were slightly compressed as if someone were hugging me. Aiden eyed me with appreciation and said with a smug smile, "Mmm, that'll do." My breath caught as I glanced down to find myself clad in an elaborate dressing gown from the 18th century.

"Go on, take a look," he said.

The dress made swooshing sounds as I walked to the mirror, the billowing pink skirt silken under my hands. With my hair miraculously pinned up, soft ringlets bounced against the back of my neck. The dress scooped low in the front, its dark pink bodice pressing my breasts upward. A corset constricted my ribs in a tight embrace, accentuating the smallest part of my waist before flaring out at my hips. The long skirt, a few shades lighter than the bodice, ended in a white lace trim. Delicate pink roses dotted the puffy sleeves that gathered at my elbows. A shawl made of the same material as the gown rested on my shoulders. I pulled the skirt up slightly and stuck out a foot, admiring the laced white boots underneath. Aiden watched me with a wide grin and I gazed at him in wonder.

"How did you do that? I look like a fairy princess!" I spun around with my arms out wide. "I love it, really I do! But how did you change my clothes and pin up my hair without even touching me?"

He chuckled and twirled me around with one arm. "I'm glad you like it. You're as bonnie a princess as I've ever seen." He gave me an admiring smile and I giggled, then bowed to him ceremoniously. "And now I'd best be changing as well, I suppose," he said.

Again the edges of the room became blurry, and I felt that same shimmery sensation, but the room came back into focus quickly. He stood before me in a dress kilt and a cream-colored linen shirt with long, flowing sleeves. A cloak of matching plaid rested atop his broad shoulder, secured with an ornate gold brooch. Knee-high socks with a criss-cross pattern covered his calves and his black leather shoes laced above the ankle.

"Wow, you look amazing," I said, awed.

"I was just thinking the same about you," he replied and lifted my hands to his lips.

"But you still haven't told me how you're doing all this," I protested, trying to ignore the zipline of tingles from his touch. He tucked my hand into the crook of his arm and led me outside, explaining as we walked.

18

"So I haven't. Well, I call it 'casting.' If you can see it in your mind, you can make it real here. You just have to think of it and cast it out from your head and then it appears around you." He shrugged, like this was commonplace and a pretty simple concept. "If you want to change location though, it's best if you've been there before because it's easier to remember details than to imagine them."

"So anything I can think of, I can just project it out and it comes true?" I asked.

He paused for a minute and shook his head. "Well, not just anything, really. You cannot cast people. Animals, yes, but not people."

"But what about the car accident? There were definitely people there."

Out in the courtyard, rows of manicured hedges framed a meticulously edged lawn with a large fountain in the center. "There were, but that's different. You can cast a memory, somewhere you've been and the events will play out again before you. But you can't change anything, and you can't interact with the people. Or you can cast a place you know without any people, and then you can control everything in it."

I thought about it for a moment as we walked along. "Hmm... so if it's a memory of something that's happened to me, then the people can't see or hear me, but if it's someplace I've been before and I don't include any people, I can imagine it and the atmosphere changes to what I am picturing. Is that right?"

"You're a quick study," he replied.

The humid air of the stables enveloped us with its warm, earthy smell when we entered through the gate. A dry bed of straw crunched under our feet and rows of horses whinnied in welcome as we approached. Aiden spoke to them in a foreign language, scratching each one affectionately.

"Uncle Fraser raised them especially for the royal court, mostly Andalusian and Lusitanian. The cream-colored

beauties with the blue eyes were a favorite of King Louis."
When I gingerly reached out to one, it sniffed at me and
turned its head. "He likes you," Aiden said. "Scratch him
behind the ears and pet his face. Just go slow and you'll be
fine."

I'd never seen a horse with blue eyes before, and I could
see why the king would be enamored with them. His pale
coat twitched as I ran my hand down the top of his muzzle.
He sidled a bit, shaking his head as he snorted. I squealed,
pulling my hand away, my heart suddenly in my throat.
Aiden chuckled and came over to pet the horse himself,
much more firmly and confidently than I had.

"You've naught to fear with him, lassie. He will not hurt
you. Would you like to take him for a ride?" he asked. My
eyes opened wide as I imagined myself falling off the
backside of the horse, a crumpled mass of pink silk. "You've
no need to be afraid, *mo chridhe*. I'll ride with you and I
won't let you fall."

He slipped his arms around my waist in demonstration
and pulled me close, his fingertips trailing along the edge of
my corset. A soft breeze played with the tips of his blond hair
and our eyes locked for several heartbeats. He began to lean
his face toward mine when the horse to my right suddenly
blew a loud breath through its lips and broke the spell.

I stepped out of his warm embrace and mustered a little
bravery. "Sure, why not? I'll give it a try," I said. "It'll be
fun. I've never ridden one before."

"Truly? You've never ridden a horse? Now that's a
crying shame." He opened the gate to the stall and made a
clicking sound with his mouth. He pulled a saddle down from
the wall and with a few quick movements, attached the
saddle to the horse and led it out into the gardens. He held
out a hand to me and frowned down at my frilly dress. "The
safest way to ride is in front of me, but in that dress, you'd
need to ride sidesaddle behind."

My earlier vision popped back into my head. "No way

am I riding sidesaddle behind you. The very idea scares the crap out of me." He raised one eyebrow but kept silent. "Maybe I could try casting and change my outfit to something more suitable for riding," I suggested.

"All right, then. Give it a try."

I closed my eyes and pictured the outfit in my mind: beige slacks with brown loafers and a short-sleeved top made of the same pink silk as the dress I'd been wearing. That wavy shimmer passed through me. I opened my eyes hesitantly and looked down.

"Hey, it worked. Sweet!"

He helped me up onto the saddle. "You kept the pink silk for a blouse. Very clever." He hoisted himself up in one fluid motion, then called out something to the horse and it took off like a shot through the gardens. His arm tightened around my stomach and I leaned against him, holding my breath, but it wasn't long before I relaxed and began to enjoy the wind on my face.

Aiden's chest pressed against my back and his thighs held me firmly in place. We moved together as one, gliding in the saddle as the horse slowed to a steady gallop. The trees blurred with our passing and wisps of my hair tickled my cheeks. It was like riding in a speedboat with the wind swirling around me, but I felt a connection with the horse and the earth as we moved, something innately satisfying. The ride was over all too soon as we slowed to a walk at the edge of a clearing.

"I thought you might like to stop here and have a picnic," he said, his breath warm on my cheek. He swung down easily and offered me his hand. I wasn't nearly so graceful as I dismounted, but he caught me in his arms. He stopped me halfway down with my breasts pressed tight against his chest. My heart caught in my throat at the sudden flame of passion in his eyes. His lips hovered before mine for a moment too long, but then he loosened his grip and let me slide the rest of the way to the ground.

"Well, did you enjoy it?" he asked, his voice a shade deeper than usual. I wasn't sure if he meant the horseback riding or the fact that I had been pressed against him, but the answer was an emphatic 'yes' regardless.

"I loved it."

Chapter 5

The horse had wandered to the edge of the clearing and stood munching grass, uninterested. Aiden unpinned the plaid that hung over his shoulder and swung it onto the ground as a picnic blanket. The now-familiar shimmer passed through me and a basket of food miraculously appeared on his cloak. He'd cast a scrumptious collection of bread, cheese, salami and fruit. I sat down on the blanket and nibbled at the food, trying to still my racing pulse.

"So you said you stayed here for three years with your uncle when you were younger," I asked. "What was that like?"

"Alex Fraser was married to my mam's sister, and when I turned fourteen, they took me under their wing to get proper training. The Frasers were quite wealthy, not only providing horses for the royal court, but also shipping in silk from China. Besides the château, Uncle Alex also had an office in Paris. He took me with him a couple of times, but mostly I stayed here in Versailles." He broke off a piece of the baguette.

"What were they like, your aunt and uncle?"

He pulled a small knife from his knee-high sock and sliced off a chunk of cheese. "Well, they were a fair bit older than my parents. Aunt Margaret was a right pistol and kept the house in order like the captain of an army. Nothing slipped by her and she had a nasty temper if you crossed her. Which, mind you, never happened more than once." He waggled his eyebrows and I laughed. "But she was also very funny, with a quick wit and a dry sense of humor.

"Uncle Alex was a practical man with a keen mind for business. He was highly esteemed in the royal court and wanted to pass on his legacy but with no children of his own, he'd only us MacRae lads to hope for. It was hard at first because he insisted we only speak French and I didn't know a word of it before I came. He spoke fluent Gaelic and English, so that wasn't the issue. He just wanted me to know French and that was the fastest way to learn. I couldn't even find the privy on the first day!"

He laughed heartily at the memory. "Luckily, a servant took pity on me and showed me the way. I used a great deal of body language in the beginning to communicate, but it didn't take long before I could understand conversations. I had tutors who taught me to read and write as well, and I was fully fluent by the end of the first year. I guess Uncle Alex knew what he was doing, aye?"

I found myself jealous of his intense language training but pushed the thought aside. "Wow, fluent after just one year? That's amazing. I took French in school for four years and I wouldn't consider myself anywhere close to fluent."

His eyebrows went up in surprise. *"C'est vrai? Je peux peut-être t'apprendre le français moi-même."*

"Oui, s'il vous plaît!" I nodded, proud to have understood his offer. "But I don't think I'd want you to teach me by only speaking French until I caught on. I mean, what if I had to use the 'privy?'" I reached over and poked him in the ribs.

"Hey!" He caught me by the wrists and made a big show of defending himself. In our teasing, he ended up pulling me forward until I was nearly sitting in his lap. The heat of his body warmed me through my light pink blouse. I opened my mouth but promptly forgot what I was going to say, I was so distracted by the closeness of his lips. He cleared his throat and I straightened so that I wasn't all over him anymore. An invisible spot on my thumbnail became suddenly fascinating as I worked to avoid his gaze.

"No, actually," he continued. "You'll never need to use the privy here." I glanced up, surprised.

"What? Why not?" It was true, as I thought about it. I'd been here for—how long?—and hadn't once had the urge to go to the bathroom.

"Well, I think it's because we cast all the food ourselves, so it's not really there. You don't actually have to eat at all. We just do it because we enjoy it, not because we need to."

"But when I woke up this morning, you offered me breakfast and I was starved. How could I have been hungry if my body didn't need it?"

He shook his head and tsk'd at me like I was a student who'd gotten the answer wrong.

"I'll bet that you only felt hungry after I asked you about breakfast or once you'd seen the tray. Am I right?" he asked. I thought about it and nodded, confused. "Your mind responded to the suggestion of food or the sight of it, if you saw the tray before I mentioned it," he explained. "In truth, I can't say we have bodies here at all, not in the earthly sense anyway."

My gaze swept from his face over the flat expanse of his chest and a rebellious thought took hold. With a smirk, I reached out and trailed a finger down the length of his bicep and peeked up at him through my eyelashes.

"So this… isn't real?" I asked.

"I'm warning you, lass. You shouldn't tempt me," he said, though his voice was unsteady.

"What do you mean?" I teased. "If it's not real, what difference does it make? Does it even count as touching after all?" I dragged my finger across his chest and flicked my lip with my tongue, enjoying the look of indecision on his face.

"God help me," he whispered. Then he snaked a hand behind my neck and pulled me toward him, covering my mouth with his own. His kiss was everything I wanted it to be: hot, exciting and sensual, sending off a rampage of tingles down my spine. His other arm rested on my hip as we kissed, radiating waves of heat across my stomach. I tried to press closer to him and he let himself fall backward, pulling me on top of him as he went.

His fingers wound through my hair as the kiss deepened. My heart was pounding so hard, I was sure it was going to explode.

"*Ah, ma minette.* You slay me," he groaned. His lips met mine again, but this time they were different, his kisses tender and soft. He pulled away and gazed at me in adoration, his hand cupping my cheek. "*Tu es très belle, Lindsey.*" He blew out his breath and shook his head, then pulled me down onto the blanket beside him.

Tucked in the crook of his arm, I ran my fingers over his chest and marveled at how badly I wanted to keep going. I'd kissed a few guys before, but nothing even came close to this. I hadn't ever gone all the way, but it felt so right with Aiden that I didn't want to stop. Everything in me ached to be closer to him.

His breathing evened out and I slowed mine to match, trying to reign in my lustful thoughts. Curled up against him, I closed my eyes and inhaled his clean, woodsy scent, feeling as if I'd finally found where I belonged.

As I lay there with my eyes closed, a warm light washed over me, as enticing as the scent of freshly baked bread. It beckoned to me and the compulsion to follow was overwhelming. Joy flooded through me as I began to move toward it. Aiden's voice called to me from far away.

"Lindsey! Oh, don't leave yet, lass. Stay with me a little while longer," he pleaded. I wanted so badly to follow the light but I turned and fought my way back to him. The sensation ebbed away and I found myself standing, gripped tight in Aiden's arms. I stared at him, confused and afraid.

"What was that? I almost went after it, but then I heard your voice."

His arms relaxed but he didn't let go. "It's heaven calling you. I told you that you cannot stay here forever. You must go on, but I didn't want to lose you... not yet." His face was etched with a sadness that made my heart ache. I threw my arms around his neck and hugged him close.

"I don't want to go. I want to stay here with you." I searched his face for answers. "Why can't you come to heaven with me? I don't understand!"

He hung his head and sighed with the weight of a condemned man. When he looked up again, his face was closed off, his jaw set in a hard line.

"I've never shown this to anyone," he began, his voice barely audible. "But you deserve the truth, Lindsey. You just may not want to stay once you've seen it."

Chapter 6

"You remember how I told you that my family, the MacRaes and the MacKenzies owned the castle and all the land around it?" I nodded and he went on, resigned but determined. "It was the month of May in the year of our Lord 1719 and I'd just had my twentieth birthday. I lived at the castle with my mam, my older brother Duncan, my younger brother Willie and many other relatives. The Clan MacRae had guarded the castle for generations, keeping her safe from warring clans who might try to overpower her. Strength and power ran in our blood, and we were warriors when we needed to be, to protect our lands and the castle."

As he spoke, the pasture around us melted away and then we were standing in a banquet hall. The early morning light streamed through vertical slits into the stone walled room, which was filled to bursting with heavily armed men in kilts. The air was thick with the scent of sweaty, unwashed bodies, soot, smoked meat and ale. I covered my face with my hand in a convulsive attempt to block out the stench.

A long dining table ran the length of the space, and a majestic fireplace spread its warmth throughout the room. Half empty steins of whisky and beer littered the table, though it was barely dawn. The men were packed in around the table, a few of them seated and eating, but most of them standing and talking, waiting for something. The atmosphere hummed with the men's hostility and excitement.

The leader of the group addressed them from an upstairs

pulpit overlooking the great room. "My brothers in arms!" He held out his hand and a hush fell over the hall. "*Fàilte!* Welcome, friends. I, William MacKenzie, Earl of Seaforth, have asked you here today to defend this castle and this country. The Spanish fleet that was to be joining us hit stormy weather and had to port in England. Now the bloody Sassenachs know we mean to march on Inverness and they've sent three warships to try and stop us."

The crowd began to murmur in agitation at his statement.

"They are powerful, with more men than we have here, and with many a cannon. If you stay and fight, some of you in this room will die today." He waited, watching with narrowed eyes as this statement rippled through the crowd. The men turned to each other in mumbled displeasure, shifting uneasily back and forth. The Earl's booming voice called them back.

"Men! Let me remind you that our rightful king has been dethroned and the redcoats' *King George"*—he said the name with disgust and spat on the ground—"seeks to take away our freedom and impose his rule on our land, this land that our fathers have passed down to us. They have raped our women and tried to make us English slaves, and they hang those who won't pledge allegiance to the traitor king!"

The men responded with roars of indignation, several pulling out their weapons and emitting war cries. The Earl's speech gained momentum with their fury.

"Will we let them? Will we let our brothers' deaths go unavenged? Will we bow down and let the bloody redcoats steal our land because we were afraid to fight?"

The crowd was boiling now, men waving their weapons and shouting with barely-contained blood lust.

"No! We are Highlanders and we will fight for our freedom!" Cheers of agreement rose up from the men, some clasping arms or pounding their neighbor on the back.

The Earl held out a hand to silence the crowd. "If you're

with me, friends, come forward."

Men from each clan stepped forward one by one, calling out their allegiance.

"The MacKenzies of Glen Shiel are here! The MacRaes of Kintail are here! The Frasers of Lovat are here!" The list went on and on, including the Spaniards who had come to join the fight. Once the last man had declared his loyalty, the Earl bowed his head for a prayer and the men followed suit.

"Blessed Saint Michael, be with us this day. Let your light shine upon us and deliver our enemies into our hands. In the holy name of our savior, Jesus Christ, amen." He raised his head and scanned the room, making eye contact with a specific handful of men. "Lairds, prepare your men to your posts. The battle is on! *Tulloch Ard!*" The leaders of each clan took their men off to receive their assigned posts. The Earl descended the stairs and addressed his own group. He barked orders, all pomp and circumstance gone from his speech now.

I saw Aiden in the back of the line, waiting to come forward and receive his assignment. He was as riled up as the rest of them, standing tall with his chest puffed out, eyes wild with excitement and ferocity. His older brother Duncan received his orders to man the bridge, nodded sharply to the Earl and strode out of the room. Aiden stepped forward to receive his station and the Earl paused. He looked Aiden up and down, considering.

"Aiden MacRae, you will take Señor Delgado," he gestured with his head to a pale, thin man with stringy black hair who was standing against the wall, "and guard the entrance to the cellar."

Aiden's face fell and he shook his head in pleading protest. "But Uncle, I am ready. I can do more than guard the door! I am a man now and I want to fight! I…"

The Earl backhanded him hard across the face and all conversations in the room stopped. Aiden turned to look at his uncle, his face unreadable. The Earl said, "A man knows when to speak and when to be silent. I have given you your post. Go."

Aiden turned on one heel and stormed out. Señor Delgado scrambled wordlessly after him. He didn't slow his pace for the Spaniard to catch up, but threw a venomous glare at the direction of the bridge where his brother had gone. He swore and spat on the ground as he made his way to the rear of the castle and down the stone steps to the cellar.

The entrance to the cellar was a heavy wooden door with a metal handle. Aiden strode back and forth, muttering under his breath in a language I didn't understand. The Spaniard clearly didn't understand it either and sat on the wooden chair next to the door, waiting for him to calm down. Finally, his anger dissipated enough for Delgado to risk conversation. His accent was thick, but it was obvious he was going to great pains not to upset Aiden further.

"Excuse me, sir, but what is in this cellar that is so important it takes two grown men to guard it?"

Aiden's glare made it clear he thought this a stupid question. "The gunpowder," he barked and resumed his pacing.

Delgado's eyes flittered around the small space and he shifted his weight in the chair. "Surely it can't be that much, can it?" he asked.

Affronted, he retorted with pride, "Aye, we've collected 343 barrels of powder and 52 barrels of musket shot for our march on Inverness. Those bloody lobsterbacks will get what is coming to them!" Delgado's eyes grew wide and Aiden went on, boasting. "We've another stash in the kirk down the hill so we can hit them from both sides." Convinced that he'd impressed the Spaniard enough, he went back to pacing.

The battle had begun outside and faint cries wafted down the staircase. Occasionally, the walls and ground would shake as a cannon ball struck the outside of the stone walled castle. Delgado fidgeted nervously, not speaking, and Aiden paid him no attention, lost in his own thoughts.

Another shot rattled the enclosure. The Spaniard leapt to his feet. "I must relieve myself."

Aiden waved his hand absentmindedly. "The privy's out behind the stable."

Delgado looked ready to flee, but turned and asked, "Will you be all right while I am gone?"

"I think I can bloody well manage to guard the door while you take a piss!"

Delgado streaked up the stairs and out of sight without another word. Time seemed to crawl by as Aiden paced, then sat, then kicked the cellar door, all the while muttering to himself. The sounds of battle and firing cannon from outside seemed to agitate him further. We heard light footsteps approaching on the stairs and he sprang into action, sword at the ready. His eyes danced with fury and anticipation as he prepared to finally meet the enemy. With his back pressed against the wall, he listened, waiting for the moment the English soldier would come into the clear.

He caught movement out of the corner of his eye and lunged forward with a cry, *"Sgurr Uaran!"* A split second before his sword came down, he stopped and jumped back.

A thin, red-haired boy screamed. "It's me, Willie!"

Aiden's face went white as a sheet. "What in the name of God are you doing down here? You're supposed to be with Mam! I could have killed you just now, ye wee fool!"

Willie held out a loaf of bread and flask of whisky to him and his stomach growled in response. "You shouldn't be here. Does Mam know that you've gone?" he asked, though his tone had softened.

Willie smiled mischievously. "I told her I had to use the privy and then I snuck down to bring you some food."

At the sound of the word 'privy' Aiden's head snapped up. His face froze in horror as the realization sank in that the Spaniard had never come back. "Holy mother of God," he whispered. Willie looked at him in confusion and fear. Aiden took a dagger from his belt and pressed it into the boy's hands. "Take my dirk and guard the door. If anyone comes, remember how I showed you. One stroke with all your strength, under the breastbone and push up."

He mimicked the motion on his own chest, pointing out exactly where the knife should penetrate. Mustering all his courage, Willie drew himself up tall and nodded. Aiden hugged the boy tightly, then pulled away and held him by the shoulders. "You'll do fine. I love you, lad." Then he turned and bolted up the stairs. He ran full bore, scanning the grounds and water in search for the Spaniard.

Acrid smoke filled the sky and the walls of the castle were badly damaged from the battle. Three English warships were in plain view; the sound of their belching cannons was deafening. He spotted Delgado streaking across the other side of the loch. It was too late to stop the traitor. He cried out in anguish and fell to his knees in shame. The Spaniard would tell the English of the hundreds of barrels of gunpowder and shot stored within the castle, a fact that he himself had made known in his boasting.

A soldier from the closest ship spied him and fired a musket. The ball struck Aiden in the left shoulder and knocked him backward. I watched in horror, unable to do anything to help. Blood began flowing freely from the wound and he scrambled to the stables for cover. Within minutes, a longboat carrying six Englishmen was launched, covered by heavy cannon fire.

Aiden ran down low and took cover behind a boulder near the water's edge. He waited until the boat had drawn close to the shore and fired his pistol. One man went down and the rest turned to see where the shot had come from. Aiden ducked behind the rock and waited as the shots from the boat whizzed past him on either side. Realization crossed his features and he breathed in horror, "Willie. Oh, blessed Jesus."

The longboat landed on the shore with a thud and the men splashed into the water to pull it onto land. Aiden dropped his empty pistol and came streaking out from behind the rock, screaming a war cry with his sword held high in the air. He swung the heavy sword across the neck of the first soldier coming toward him. Blood spurted in a stream as his head flew away from his body. Bile rose in my throat and I stifled a scream.

Two other men converged on him, wielding bayonets as they scrambled onto the shore. He ran his sword through the guts of one soldier and spun around to face the next. The Englishman thrust his bayonet through Aiden's upper thigh. His face clenched with pain as he sliced the man through the chest with his massive sword. The soldier made a sickening gurgling sound as he fell dead.

Two of the redcoats remained near the boat and one took aim, but his musket misfired. He swore and instead swung it with both hands and cracked Aiden in the skull with the butt of the gun. He crumbled in a bloody heap on the ground.

The soldier drew his sword to strike the killing blow, but the officer swore at him impatiently. "Leave him! He'll either die where he lies or we'll circle back to hang him later. Move out!" The soldier spat at Aiden, then broke into a run behind the officer, disappearing into the castle.

Tears streamed down my face as I imagined the scene inside with Willie bravely guarding the door against the two Englishmen. He was only a boy and I knew he had no chance of survival. The waiting was gut wrenching and I breathed out a mournful sigh when I saw the English officer running full-tilt away from the castle. He was alone and I realized with a surge of pride that Willie must have been successful in carrying out his brother's instructions with the dirk he'd been given.

The vibrations of the Englishman's footsteps as he passed stirred Aiden into consciousness and he moaned, trying to sit up. The officer jumped into the boat and bent down to pick up the oars. Aiden took a small knife from his sock and flung it with all his might at the man. The blade stuck cleanly into the base of the man's skull and he fell forward into the boat with a thud. Aiden collapsed with the effort. With an ear-splitting roar, the barrels of gunpowder caught fire and the castle exploded around us. Aiden's limp body was blown across the grounds and against the rock where he'd been hiding before.

He reached out, grasping blindly and finally closed his hand around the pistol he'd left there earlier. He loaded the pistol with his eyes closed and cocked back the hammer.

To my horror, he pointed it at his head and pulled the trigger.

I shrieked and covered my mouth with my hand. I turned to Aiden standing next to me to see his eyes filled with pain, searching mine for forgiveness and understanding.

"Oh my God, Aiden." I wrapped my arms tight around him and held him so close I could hardly breathe. His stiff body relaxed in my arms and then shook as he quietly sobbed, his head on my shoulder. I kissed his temple and whispered words of comfort, wishing I could hold him tight enough to somehow make it right.

Slowly, our breathing fell into synch, our chests rising and falling together. Strength from my body flowed into him, then returned to me. The air caressed us, binding us together. When I opened my eyes, we were standing in the clearing where we'd had our picnic. He took a deep breath and straightened, then pulled away and wiped his face with his palm. I stayed close by his side, holding one hand, unwilling to let go.

His voice trembled as he continued his story. "And then an angel stood before me, blazing white and gold, with eyes like flames and a sword made of fire. I fell down on my face, shaking with fear at the sight of him. His voice was the sound of a raging thunderstorm and it filled my head so as it would explode. He said 'Aiden Alexander MacKenzie MacRae, God is not pleased with what you have done. But do not be afraid, for you have found favor with the Almighty One. You will not enter heaven now but instead, you will transport God's chosen ones to join Him there.' And that's what I've been doing every day since."

"For three hundred years," I breathed.

He raised his eyebrows, and then made a grunting noise in his throat. His eyes locked onto mine with brutal honesty. "I am so ashamed of what I've done that I can never forgive myself. My family was killed and my home was destroyed because of my pride. I knew it wouldn't be long before the English found me and I'd be hanged as a rebel. I didn't want anyone to know it was my fault. I was a fool and a coward."

He dropped his gaze to the ground and his shoulders slumped in defeat.

"No!" Shock and defensiveness sprang up in me at his words. I grabbed him by the shoulders and forced him to look at me. "Aiden MacRae, you are neither a fool nor a coward. You were shot in the shoulder and stabbed through the leg, and you still killed five men by yourself, for crying out loud!"

All my pent-up emotion took over and I pounded his chest with my fists as if to beat my words into him. He didn't flinch.

"That damn Spaniard was the coward, not you. He was the one who betrayed your family, not you. You gave everything you had to try and save them. You're a freakin' hero! Do you hear me, dammit? You are NOT a coward!" He gently pulled my arms down so I couldn't hit him anymore.

"Thank you." His voice was solemn and quiet.

As quickly as it had come, my anger dissipated at his words and I let out a deep breath. A smile played across his lips as he watched me deflate from my puffed up state.

"You're fair beautiful when you're angry."

His statement caught me off guard.

"Shut up!" I punched him on the arm and he winced playfully. But then he shook his head and grinned, gathering me into his arms. I struggled for a second, but quickly relaxed in his embrace.

"I didn't say it was a bad thing. I like it when you're angry. You're like a mother cat protecting her litter." He squinted and made a hissing sound, his hand curled like a cat's claw. I smacked him again out of principle.

"Stop it, you." I gave him my best glare, but I couldn't hold it and finally let loose a giggle. He bent his face to mine and lifted my chin with a curled finger. I pressed myself into him and pulled him close. His hands caressed my neck up and down as we kissed. Melting into him, I couldn't tell where I left off and he began.

Thank you, my sweet.

The words formed inside my head and I heard them in his voice, yet I was certain he had not said them aloud. I gazed up at him in surprise, the unasked question on my face.

Eyes filled with a mixture of relief and adoration, he smiled down at me like he'd finally trusted his best friend to keep his deepest secret. I shook my head in confusion and started to say something but he put a finger to my lips.

"I asked the angel if I would ever see heaven. He said, 'There is one whose love will redeem you.' I asked him how I'd know that one, and he said, 'You will know.' And I do."

I felt as if my heart would burst, entranced by his gaze. Air was not moving in my chest, and I uttered weakly, "How do you know I am that one?"

His brows drew together in a slightly pained expression and he took a deep breath, closing his eyes. "When I showed you my death, my shame. And you held me. I heard your sweet voice in my head. You said everything would be fine, that you were here now and that you'd never leave me."

I froze, remembering that I'd willed those very words to him in my mind. And he'd heard them, in his head, the way I'd heard him just now in mine. I was suddenly reminded of exactly what I'd wanted to do with him on the picnic blanket. I jerked back from him, my cheeks aflame.

"You don't hear all my thoughts, do you?"

He threw his head back with an uproarious laugh and I narrowed my eyes in my most menacing glare, which made him laugh harder. "Gracious, woman, what kind of thoughts have you been thinking that you don't want me to know?" His eyes danced with naughtiness and I turned away from him in an embarrassed huff. He reached out and grabbed my arm, pulling me easily to him. He stroked my cheek, his eyes tender.

"Ah, my brown haired lassie, I cannot give you heaven, at least not with me. But I can show you the most beautiful palace in all of France. You can even see the king of France himself, King Louis XIV, if you like." One corner of his mouth curled up in a satisfied grin. He'd caught me hook, line and sinker with that invitation and he knew it.

"*La Palace de Versailles?* You've been there? And you've met King Louis XIV?"

"Aye, I have. Did ye want to go?" he asked in a casual tone. I squealed and flung my arms around his neck. He lifted me easily in his strong arms and swung me in circles, laughing as I grinned at him with unrestrained enthusiasm. When he set me on my feet, I was practically dancing with excitement.

"When can we go? Should we ride back to the château?" My eyes darted around the clearing, looking for the horse. I found him still munching grass and he glanced up at me and shook his mane, whinnying.

"We can go anytime you like, love. I can just cast the memory and we're there. Still…" his voice trailed off as his gaze swept over my pink shirt and beige slacks. "Maybe we should get ready for the ball first, aye?"

Chapter 7

The clearing washed away like a ruined painting—blanket, basket, horse and all. I blinked to focus my eyes and the château appeared, with two majestic black horses standing patiently before an old fashioned carriage. I glanced up at Aiden and my hand flew to my mouth as a giggle escaped me.

He was wearing a forest green jacket, ornately decorated with golden embroidery. Shining buttons ran down the front and the sleeves flared in wide cuffs at his wrists. A white scarf was tied around his neck and tucked into the front of his coat. Billowing culottes peeked out from under the heavy coat, tied at the knees with elaborate bows. His legs were encased in tights that matched his jacket and ended in black shoes with square toes and two-inch heels.

The *pièce de résistance* however, was the curly powdered wig that flowed over his shoulders. He looked completely regal and absolutely ridiculous. I struggled to stifle the giggles and he glared down at me, his eyebrows drawn together in a frown.

"What's so funny? Don't you like my *costume*? This is very fashionable, *haute couture*, I assure ye!"

Pulling myself together, I glanced down at the outfit he'd cast upon me and my laughter turned to amazement. "Oh, my goodness, Aiden, it's beautiful!" Vertical rows of opalescent pearls adorned the bodice of my deep green ball gown, and my breasts floated above the corset in silk pockets like white candles in water. The tight sleeves ended at my elbows in ruffles of lace. White satin gloves covered the length of my forearms and an exquisite emerald bracelet encircled my left wrist.

My hair was pulled up and cascaded in bouncy ringlets down the back of my neck. The gown flared at my waist while the green silk skirt split in the front to reveal a ruffled white taffeta petticoat underneath. I twirled around, enjoying the swishing sound of the skirts, and beamed up at Aiden, no longer finding his costume quite so funny. He smiled down at me, obviously pleased at my reaction to the gown.

"Hmm... You're missing something." He reached into his suit jacket and pulled out a strand of iridescent pearls. An emerald hung from the center of the necklace, set into a golden replica of the sun. He affixed the necklace in place and I gazed up at him in wonder.

You are amazing.

I spoke to him with my mind and he bowed his head in acceptance of my compliment. He held out one arm to me in invitation and opened the carriage door.

"Mademoiselle?"

With a giggle, I did my best curtsey then looped one gloved hand around his arm. Stepping through the door of the carriage was like being transported back in time as the scene changed from one he was casting now to one from his memory.

I glanced up and gasped.

A younger version of Aiden sat directly across from us, anxiously tapping his fingers on his knee. An older gentleman, whom I guessed to be Uncle Alex, sat stiffly beside him. He was somewhat portly, with squinty eyes and a bulbous nose. Yet he had an authoritative air that demanded unquestioning respect. I liked him instantly.

The carriage jerked to life and Aiden reflexively reached out an arm to steady me. The movement quickly mellowed to a bouncy, rolling gait. Uncle Alex spoke in quick bursts of

French to young Aiden, who responded as if he were reciting answers to an exam. Though I didn't follow the conversation fully, I gathered that Alex was quizzing him on appropriate behavior and what to expect once they'd arrived at the palace. I caught the name Marie Hélène de Saint-Simon as they were talking and leaned over to Aiden.

"Who are they talking about?" I whispered as if they could hear me.

"She was the daughter of the Duke of Saint-Simon. My uncle wanted me to make a good impression on her so that I might court her and win favor with the Duke."

My eyebrows shot up in surprise. I hadn't expected a former love interest and I found the thought both intriguing and unsettling at the same time. "And did you?" I asked.

"Hmph. You'll see," he responded with a shrug.

We rode in silence while Uncle Alex peppered young Aiden with questions in French. I watched out the window in wide-eyed wonder as the carriage pulled into the palace gardens. The landscaping was completely different from the countryside, with lengthy rows of hedges and meticulously manicured bushes. Grand canals of water reflected the moonlight like mirrors. Statues of King Louis peered down at us from every angle as we proceeded toward his dwelling place. An immense fountain with a golden statue of a god-like figure on a chariot spouted water thirty feet in the air. Hunting dogs encircled him, shooting water from their mouths into the center. It was all incredibly surreal and my heart raced at the thought of what the palace itself must be like. I'd never seen anything so massive and struggled to imagine how many people lived in this palace, catering to the king's every whim.

I can't believe I'm really here. In Versailles.

The carriage jerked to a stop and the door was opened from the outside as we reached another set of gates. A palace guard peered inside and inquired in gruff French about our identity and business. Uncle Alex stated his name and

Aiden's and that they were guests of the king for the ball in honor of the ambassador of the Shah of Persia, Mohammed Reza Beg. It was eerie the way that the guard looked right through me as if I weren't there. I had to remind myself that he couldn't see me since this was simply a memory of Aiden's projected out for me to enjoy. Satisfied, the guard waved us on and the carriage started off again.

Finally, the carriage pulled to a stop and we got out, people streaming all around us in the equestrian parade of carriages. Royal guards escorted us into the lobby, which was decorated in golden patterns covering the walls and ceiling. A magnificent marble staircase led up to the king's quarters on one side and the queen's quarters on the other. I thought it rather sad actually, that they had separate bedrooms. Threads of orchestral music floated over me, the violins and flutes sweetly welcoming us.

We moved with the throngs of guests and I gaped unabashedly at the splendor of the rooms, knowing no one could see me anyway. Aiden detailed the history for me as we were swept through the interior of the palace.

"King Louis likened himself to Apollo, pagan god of the Sun, so everything is golden and reflects the sun."

I nodded, enchanted by the statues of naked cherubs frolicking along the walls. The domed ceilings were painted with exquisite detail, some depicting heroic battle scenes of the king's triumph over his enemies, others displaying peaceful harmony with angels and Rubenesque naked women fawning at the king's feet. The crowd seemed to settle in as we came to *La Galerie des Glaces*—the Hall of Mirrors. My eyes welled up with tears at the beauty of the vast enclosed terrace, with its mirrored arches on one side and matching windows on the other.

The firelight from the gardens outside streamed in through the windows, reflecting in the mirrors and casting a radiant glow throughout the room. An empty throne stood at the south end of the long hall, tucked into a closed archway, stationed high on a podium overlooking the gallery. The room buzzed with excitement as the courtiers anxiously awaited the presentation of the king. My own pulse beat rapidly in anticipation, caught up in this extraordinary exhibition of wealth and power. The orchestra abruptly stopped and a hush fell over the crowd.

The king's guards entered in a single file, assuming their places around the throne. With a grand flourish, the symphony sprang to life. King Louis appeared through the doorway and made his way up to the throne. His outfit was similar to Aiden's, but with a fiery red coat and a brilliant blue sash across his chest. A curly brown wig reached to the middle of his back. He commanded the room with ease and I held my breath, entranced by the spectacle of the king's power.

A murmur rippled through the crowd, and I turned to look down the opposite end of the hall. The orchestra fell silent again as a small group of men in deeply colored turbans and flowing garments appeared. I remembered Uncle Alex's comment to the guard about the Persian ambassador to the Shah. The leader of the group had olive skin and a closely cropped beard. No hair peeked out from under his red turban. He wore a floor-length orange cloak with a fur collar. He had a majestic presence of his own, wordlessly commanding the small group of men behind him. They carried ornate shields and sabers on outstretched hands.

The crowd parted like the Red Sea, drawing to either side of the hall. A long, empty pathway stretched between the ambassador and the waiting king at the other end. All eyes followed the six Persians as they slowly made their way down the spacious room to kneel before the king. I couldn't hear their exchange but the Persian presented several gifts, one of them a hand-woven sash. King Louis nodded grandly in acceptance and the room seemed to collectively let out its breath, relieved by the successful presentation.

The orchestra took its cue and broke into a processional

march. Courtiers and noblemen in the crowd lined up behind the ambassador's group to present themselves before the king. Uncle Alex and young Aiden took their places in the procession and we waited our turn to be seen by the king. I entertained myself by admiring the room and the period dress of the courtiers in line with us, but the progress was painstakingly slow. Both versions of Aiden looked equally bored with the queue. My ears perked up as I heard the name Marie Hélène de Saint-Simon being presented to the king several rows in front of us. Craning my neck, I tried to get a glimpse of her. Aiden glanced at me and rolled his eyes.

As she and the Duke made their way out of the hall, I caught a wave of shiny black curls sweeping out the door. I sighed, frustrated that I hadn't been able to see her face. Aiden chuckled and shook his head.

"Don't fret, you'll get to see her soon enough, though she's not that much to see, mind ye."

I'll be the judge of that.

I cocked one eyebrow at him as I sent the message in my mind. He laughed heartily and squeezed my hand. I knew it was just a memory but I still found it strange that no one turned to look at us when he laughed out loud.

Finally, it was our turn to meet the king face-to-face. My pulse raced with giddy excitement. Alex bowed deeply, then presented young Aiden who quickly followed suit. The king nodded slightly from his throne, looking bored. Though I knew no one could see me, I found myself curtseying to the king and smiled as I saw Aiden bow as well, out of the corner of my eye.

The moment was over far too soon and I felt Aiden's hand on my arm, pulling me toward the door. Reluctantly, I turned my attention away from the king and we moved into the adjoining salon where long buffet tables were piled with mountains of food. The scent of roasted meat greeted me and my stomach growled in response. I reached out to steal a piece of cheese and my hand passed right through it. I grunted in frustration.

"We've gone from heaven to hell, where I can see and smell the food, but not touch it!" I complained.

Just then I caught sight of those shiny black curls again and lost all interest in the buffet. Marie Hélène was watching young Aiden with interest as he arranged bites of food onto a silver plate. She had beady eyes and a beak-like nose with thin, pale lips. Her gown was richly detailed and undoubtedly expensive, but she was very skinny and had no breasts to speak of. Relief washed over me.

She stopped next to Aiden at the buffet table. "The King is wonderful, isn't he?" she asked in flowing French, giving him a toothy smile. Surprised, he looked up and agreed in his easy, charming manner. "*Je suis Marie Hélène de Saint-Simon*," she introduced herself with a slight curtsy and held out her gloved hand to him expectantly.

His face fell and he froze for second in recognition of the name but then quickly regained his composure. "*Enchanté, mademoiselle.*" He bowed slightly and introduced himself, then placed a light kiss on her outstretched hand. While his head was down, her eyes lustily perused his frame and I felt a pang of jealousy.

She lowered her eyes quickly and batted her lashes at him. He took a deep breath and inquired in perfect French if she would be so kind as to dance with him at the king's ball, since he did not have a partner. Her face lit up with excitement and she nodded enthusiastically.

As if on cue, the orchestra changed from the processional march to a lively ballroom dance tune and young Aiden offered Marie Hélène his arm in invitation. She readily accepted and they moved through the crowd back toward the Hall of Mirrors. Aiden held out his arm next to me with a smile.

"Shall we dance, *ma chérie*?"

"*Bien sûr. Allons y!*" I agreed and placed my hand on top of his arm.

The Hall of Mirrors was now full of activity as couples twirled on the patterned hardwood floor, their arms locked in stiff circles, ladies' skirts swishing with the movement. Music from the flutes and violins rose and fell in waves, mimicking the graceful dance of the courtiers and mistresses in front of the mirrors. Aiden and Marie Hélène made an odd-looking couple since she was almost as tall as he was. She flirted outrageously with him, laughing too much and sending him sly looks. I had to bite back a groan. He held his back erect and looked quite regal while keeping as much distance between them as his arms would allow.

I struck a similar pose with Aiden myself and lost myself in the dance as he masterfully led me around the room. The reflections of the other dancers in the mirrors swirled around us. I wished I could catch a glimpse of us, but it wasn't possible. Instead, I looked up at Aiden and saw my reflection in his eyes.

"You are the most beautiful woman in this room tonight and your eyes dance like the twinkling stars on the loch at night."

My heart was in my throat as he gazed down at me and I couldn't speak. It was true; I had never felt so beautiful in my life, and being here with him, twirling gracefully to the rise and fall of the music was like a fairytale dream come true. We danced late into the night and I was drunk with the sound of the classical music that filled my head and swam through my veins. I wanted nothing more than to stay in this hall of candlelight and mirrors, dancing with Aiden in my arms.

I almost didn't notice it—I was so captivated by the joy of the dance—but Marie Hélène leaned forward and whispered something to young Aiden. His eyebrows rose up sharply in surprise. With a mischievous smile, she glanced around the room to ensure no one would notice and forcefully pulled him by the hand out of the hall. We followed, my curiosity piqued, as she led him through the masses of guests.

She paused, bidding a good evening to a passing nobleman and pretended like she was just taking a short break from the dance. Aiden followed suit, looking increasingly uncomfortable. When no one was looking, she grabbed Aiden's hand and stole through a narrow door at the back of the room.

The hidden room was actually quite large and looked to be a resting chamber of some sort. The décor was light blue and gold, with a grand chaise against one wall. Once inside, Marie Hélène flung her arms around young Aiden and pressed her lips to his with wild abandon. He instantly stiffened at her embrace, apparently trying to decide what to do, but she would not be deterred. She spoke rapidly and huskily to him in French and I caught his frown of indecision. He looked right through me as I stood watching with a mixture of horror and excitement. I realized he was checking the door to make sure they would not be overseen. Satisfied, he closed his eyes, took a deep breath and kissed her back. She made a haughty, guttural noise in her throat and proceeded to undo the buttons on his jacket. She slipped her hands inside to stroke his chest. Careful not to mess her hair or dress, he ran his hands over her shoulders to her waist as he kissed her.

I was transfixed by the spectacle, emotions warring inside me. Part of me was completely affronted by seeing another girl kissing Aiden and another part of me was completely turned on. Heat sprang to my cheeks and I didn't dare look up at Aiden next to me. I startled guiltily when his hand caressed my neck and his fingers wound in my hair at the base of my skull. I peered up at him sheepishly and his eyes danced with amusement.

Really? You like that?

His teasing tone was clear even in my mind's ear and I turned away in embarrassment. I let out a small squeak as he forcefully swept me up in his strong arms and pressed his lips to mine. My breasts bobbed in the front of my gown like balls of soft dough as his kisses ran over my neck and chest. I closed my eyes in bliss, entranced by the sounds of passion echoing in the room.

A loud noise made the four of us jump and all eyes turned to the door in fear of discovery. Aiden set me down and I giggled, feeling completely naughty and loving it.

Young Aiden and Marie Hélène quickly composed themselves, straightening their clothing while still breathing hard. No one came in but the scare had taken its toll and the moment had passed. Young Aiden held out his arm to Marie Hélène and asked in fluent French, "Shall we go see the fireworks? I believe they will be starting soon." She nodded and they quickly snuck out through the door.

The sound of fireworks streamed in from the gardens and we hurried outdoors to watch the show. The Duke of Saint-Simon stood talking with a small group and Marie Hélène bid Aiden *adieu* with a flirty smile, leaving to join her father. Aiden's eyes scanned the grounds in search of his uncle and he shook his head, muttering to himself.

"Well, Uncle Alex said to entertain her. Aye, I can at least say I've done what he asked."

The parade of horse-drawn carriages returned just as dawn broke over the palace grounds. Like magic, Uncle Alex appeared from behind one of them and called to him in French. Once we climbed in, the carriage lurched forward and set off toward the château. I leaned against Aiden with a sigh.

"We don't have to ride all the way back," he said. "Nothing interesting happens. You look as if you're ready to drop."

"Thank you," I said, enraptured. "For the gown, for the ball, meeting the king, the hidden room—for everything. It was incredible." I never wanted the evening to end and my chest ached with longing as our eyes locked.

"I love you," I whispered, my heart breaking into pieces. I knew it sounded crazy because I'd just met him, but in my heart, it didn't matter. The angel had said when he met the one, he'd know. And now I knew it, too.

"Oh, lass," he breathed in response, his face pinched with pain.

I closed my eyes and the familiar wave of his cast swept through me. He held me in his strong arms and I buried my face in his chest, feeling only his thin linen shirt, the heavy jacket gone.

"I love you too, my dove. I don't know how much time we have but it doesn't matter, in truth. My heart is yours just the same."

He kissed me lightly on the mouth and I melted into him, exhausted. He scooped me into his arms and carried me to the soft bed in our room at the château. I sank into the feather mattress.

I was wearing the thin white nightgown he'd called a shift and my hair flowed loose over the pillow. He reached down and smoothed a stray curl away from my face. He pulled the covers up over my shoulders and tucked me in with a kiss on my forehead.

"Sweet dreams, *mo chridhe*. I'll be here when you wake. I promise you that much." He walked over to the pallet on the floor where he'd slept before and took off his sporran and dirk. He set them on the floor within arm's reach and pulled the linen shirt over his head in one fluid motion, left wearing only his kilt. I peered over the top of my pillow at his naked chest and bare stomach, drinking in the beauty of his skin and the strength of his muscles just beneath the surface.

Lord, what are you doing to me? I can't ever let him go.

My silent prayer was filled with agony. He lay down on the blanket and I ran my eyes over his body until I couldn't keep them open any longer, then let sleep overtake me.

Chapter 8

Awakened by the sun streaming in through the windows, I blinked sleepily and rubbed my eyes. The delicious, homey smell of breakfast called to me. I rolled over in the bed and smiled at Aiden across the room, who was already dressed in his kilt and linen shirt, tending the fire.

You are too good to me.

I reached out to him lazily with my thoughts. He didn't turn around, but I heard the smile in his response nonetheless.

Not possible, my love.

I grinned and swung my legs off the edge of the bed. My legs and feet were bare under my shift and I wiggled my toes out in front of me, frowning at their unpolished state. Closing my eyes, I imagined them a soft rose-petal pink and felt the shimmering sensation pass through me. When I peered down at my newly painted toes, I giggled with girlish glee. Aiden turned to me with a raised eyebrow, obviously wondering what I was up to, having felt the wave of change himself. I tucked my feet up under my shift and batted my eyes at him innocently. He just shook his head and laughed.

"*Bon matin, ma chérie.* Would you like some breakfast?" he asked, bringing over a tray of oatmeal, honey and fruit. The feather bed sank with his weight when he sat down next to me. I drizzled some honey over my oatmeal and scooped up a big spoonful. It was thick and tasted like it had been sitting in the pot too long.

"What is that?" I made a face, wrinkling my nose with

distaste.

"Have you never had parritch before? I ate it nearly every day as a lad. It's good for you."

"Well of course it is. Anything that tastes like that has to be good for you!" I gave him a gentle shove with my shoulder and he harrumphed. I popped a piece of fruit in my mouth and he changed the subject.

"Have you any idea where you'd like to go today? We could go to the Highland Games and dance to the bagpipes. There's a weapons competition as well that's great fun to watch. That's where Uncle William first taught me to fight with a sword." His words were filled with pride, but my last experience with his uncle in the castle before Aiden's bloody death was still too fresh, and I wasn't eager to go back. I tried to think of an alternative so as not to hurt his feelings. An idea came to me and I brightened, excited at the thought.

"You mentioned that your Uncle Alex had an office in Paris for his shipping business. Could we go there?" I asked hopefully. He scratched his head, considering.

"Paris, eh? Well, I guess we could go there, though I'm not exactly sure why you'd want to. It wasn't a very nice place, that."

"Why I'd want to? Because Paris is the romance capital of the world! *Nôtre Dame, La Musée du Louvre, L'Arc de Triomphe, Les Champs-Élysées,* the Eiffel Tower. I mean, what's not to love?"

He furrowed his brow in confusion. "I'm aware of *Nôtre Dame* and *Le Grand Louvre*, but I am unfamiliar with the others."

I realized some of the Parisian sites I'd read about might not have been around back in the early 1700s. "Oh. Well, they must have been built later." I waved a hand in dismissal. "Can we go, please?" I implored, giving him my most pathetic puppy dog eyes.

"All right, but only because I know you cannot get hurt in my memory," he said in a warning tone. I hugged him and planted a kiss on his lips. "You're a foolish wee lass, but God help me, I can't deny you anything when you look at me like that."

I gave him a flirty smile and jumped off the bed. "What should I wear? Another dress, I suppose. Women didn't get to wear pants then, did they?" I wrinkled my nose in irritation. Aiden shrugged in mock disinterest, though I could see the playfulness in his eyes.

"Aye, that's true. Women in Paris during my day didn't wear breeks. You're free to wear whatever you like though, if you'd prefer to wear the trousers. I don't think I'd look quite so lovely as you in my gown, though."

I shrieked in outrage and threw myself onto the bed, flinging the pillow at his head. He rolled backward, laughing, and easily dodged the blow, then gathered me into his arms.

"You brat!" I glared at him and he raised his eyebrows innocently as if to say "Who, me? What did I do?" I struggled to get free of his grasp and his arms tightened around me like a vise, his fingers tickling my ribs. I jerked and squealed in protest, giggling and kicking, while he laughed at my vain attempts to free myself.

In one fluid motion, he flipped me onto my back and laid on top of me, his body pressing mine deep into the feather mattress. My giggles abruptly stopped and I grabbed him by the hair, pulling his mouth to mine. He responded with a sigh of satisfaction and ran one hand over my shoulder, down my side.

A fire ignited within me and my body twitched with pleasure at his touch. He pressed his hips against me and I arched my back as his kisses moved down my neck, suckling my jaw and earlobe. My nightgown fell away as I raised my leg against his body and he caressed my naked thigh.

"Oh, God in heaven, have mercy," he breathed in my ear, his voice trembling. Then he made a painful groan and stopped moving entirely. My hopes sank as he lay there holding me, breathing hard, his head on my shoulder.

"Don't stop, Aiden, please." My blood was on fire and my body felt like a rubber band pulled taut and ready to snap. I was on the edge of something, but I wasn't quite sure what. I just knew I needed him to keep going.

He lifted his head and looked down at me with intense longing, yet I could see he was held back by a deeper conviction he did not explain.

"Ah, my love. You've already convinced me of one thing today against my better judgment. We'd best not make it two."

My shoulders slumped in disappointment and I turned my head away so he couldn't see the emotional turmoil there. He sighed and rolled off me, then moved across the room. I lay there quivering and stared up at the ceiling, trying to choke back the tears. I wrapped my arms around my chest, feeling suddenly cold and rejected.

Don't you want me?

He growled in frustration and crossed the room in quick strides, then grabbed me by the shoulders. "How can you even think that? Gracious, woman, it takes every ounce of strength I have not to take you right now in this bed. The touch of your hair, your soft breasts, your arse…" His gaze poured over my body and he moaned in frustration. "I'm killing myself to safeguard your purity and you…"

His face fell suddenly and he scowled at me, eyes filled with suspicion. "But maybe you're not an honest woman after all. Have you already given yourself to another man, then? Is that it?" My mouth fell open in shock at his accusation. "Well, is it? Is that why you want to go further, because you've already warmed another man's bed?" His words were acidic and blunt, but his hands trembled as he waited for my response.

I shook my head and sputtered incoherently, "No, I… I just… I've never…" But the look of distrust I saw in his eyes made me defensive and the frustration I felt earlier blossomed into anger.

"I am a virgin, but what if I weren't? What if I had slept with someone else on earth? Does that mean that I wouldn't be good enough for you? You said you love me but if that's all that matters to you, you might as well take me to heaven right now, Aiden MacRae."

He stiffened as if I'd slapped him. Silence hung in the air between us, heavy with fear and doubt. His eyes drilled into mine until I had to look away. His voice was quiet when he finally spoke.

"If you ask me to take you to heaven, I cannot deny you, Lindsey. So tell me honestly now, for I am bound by your answer. Do you truly want to go?"

The pain in his voice broke me. "No, I don't," I said, my voice wavering with emotion. "I want to stay with you. I'm sorry. It's just... I don't know how much time we have and I wanted to know what it's like before I go. Is that so wrong?"

He sat next to me on the bed and held my hand. "No, it's not wrong of you to ask, but I've sinned enough and I won't add defiling a maiden to the list."

I reached up and stroked his cheek, wanting him to feel the strength of my love. Pressing his palm to my chest over my heart, I concentrated on the rhythmic beat, slowing my breathing in time. I stared into his eyes, baring my soul.

"Aiden, I have never loved anyone but you. You are my first and my last."

"I do believe you, my sweet. And I can promise you the same." He leaned toward me and lightly touched his lips to mine. When he pulled away from the kiss, I sagged against him, exhausted. We sat in silence for a while, watching the fire.

"You know," I said, "now that I think of it, you may be right about the oatmeal. I probably could use something good for me right now, even if it does taste like cardboard." I gave him a feeble smile and he cocked an eyebrow at me.

"What's cardboard?" he asked.

I started to giggle, softly at first but then giddily, which made him laugh and before we knew it, we were both laughing with tears in our eyes, thankful that the moment had passed.

"So you really want to go to Paris, eh?" He looked down at me, checking to see if I'd changed my mind. I nodded earnestly and he sighed in resignation, then stood up. He reached out one hand and pulled me to my feet. "Well, all right then. You asked for it. Let's go to Paris."

Chapter 9

The sunny bedroom dissolved around me. We were standing on a cobbled street with gray clouds overhead and a drizzly mist in the air. I shivered and pulled my arms around my body, the coarse wool of my overcoat scratchy under my fingers. My hair was pulled up under a floppy bonnet, and the long, gray cloak hung heavy on my shoulders.

Aiden's outfit was a scaled-back version of the one he'd worn to the ball. His light blue jacket was knee-length and had modest silver buttons down the front. His tan trousers underneath fit snug against his legs, buttoning at the knees, and he wore heavy white tights underneath. His hair was pulled back and tied with a small ribbon and he wore a hat that pulled up on the sides and sat low in the front.

Tall brick buildings loomed over either side of the narrow street. Uncle Alex and young Aiden walked briskly through the skinny passage and I struggled to keep up with them. A beggar sat with his hand out in front of a row of apartments. He was hardly more than a pile of bones: his tattered clothes hanging on him loosely, his beard scraggly and unkempt, his eyes devoid of hope. My heart reached out to him in compassion as we passed. Young Aiden looked back at the man and said something to Alex who jerked his head in distaste and continued on. I looked up at Aiden next to me, but he was staring straight ahead with his jaw locked in concentration.

We turned the corner onto a wider street where men and

women milled about, talking quietly with their heads down. The buildings all had bars over the windows and I watched with interest as an old woman opened one of the windows in the top story.

"Garde a l'eau!" she shouted and then dumped a pot into the street below. Realization struck me and I stopped mid-stride, pulling on Aiden's sleeve and pointing up at the window.

"Ewww! That woman just dumped raw sewage into the street!" My eyes widened in horror as I peered down the rows of windows in the building to see the scene repeated further down.

Aiden shrugged, nonplussed. "They don't have the luxury of a privy here in the city with so many people in tight quarters. So they dump it in the street and wait for the rain to wash it off into the river." I made a gagging face and shook my head, understanding a bit more why he didn't want to bring me here.

As we walked, another beggar on the street reached out and grabbed the hem of young Aiden's jacket, pleading for bread. Aiden shook his head at the man sadly, brushing away his hand, and kept walking alongside his uncle. My mind was reeling, seeing the filthy, miserable city after having just spent such an indulgent evening at the king's palace.

"Come on, then." He took my hand and pulled me toward a pub down the street. The small tavern seemed to be the only lively thing in sight, with bawdy music spilling out the doors and shouts of drunken laughter coming from within. I relaxed and smiled, grateful for the evidence of life in this dank and gloomy memory. Aiden squeezed my hand, his face drawn.

Just then I heard a woman's piercing cry for help and my heart leapt into my throat. Young Aiden looked quickly at his uncle with a question in his eyes and Alex nodded, almost imperceptibly. Aiden took off like a shot down the side street, the woman's cries becoming louder and increasingly frantic. We came upon two men brutally attacking a girl, their eyes full of malice and their tongues hanging out in drunken lust.

One man held her by the wrist and was crouched over her, fondling her, while the other pushed up her skirts with one hand and tugged at the front of his pants with the other. The girl's blouse was ripped open, her breasts exposed and tears streamed down her battered face as she writhed underneath them, begging them to let her go.

Young Aiden grabbed hold of one man and jerked him to his feet, then punched him hard in the stomach. He wrenched the man's head backward by his hair and pounded him squarely in the jaw. The blow sent him flying and he landed in a heap on the ground, unmoving.

"Hey!" the second called out, scrambling to his feet in a wild rage. He drew a knife from his belt and lunged at Aiden.

Instinctively I screamed, "Look out!"

Aiden whirled around and caught the man's arm, twisting it up behind his back. I heard the bones snap and the man groaned in pain, dropping his knife to the ground with a clang. Aiden's own blade was at the man's throat, a thin line of blood trickling down from the tip of it. He growled something under his breath in French to the assailant, who promptly wet his pants. The first man finally came to and took off running. Aiden tossed the man away in disgust and kicked him in the backside as he did, making the rapist tumble and fall to his knees. He hastily pulled himself up and scampered off with his arm bent at an unnatural angle.

Aiden took a deep breath and turned to the girl, who was shaking in fear on the ground and clutching her woolen cloak to her chest. He picked up the man's knife and held it out to her, hilt first.

"Pour vous, mademoiselle." He bowed to her and waited. Her eyes shone with fear and awe. She hesitantly took the knife from him and tucked it into her skirts.

"Merci, monsieur. Merci beaucoup." She scrambled to

her feet and fled.

Aiden walked back to his uncle and approached him with a nervous look. Alex steadied him with a hand on his shoulder, his eyes boring into Aiden's with intensity. He said something in Gaelic to Aiden who drew in his breath and pulled himself up tall. They stood for a moment, staring at each other wordlessly as thoughts seemed to pass between them, and then turned together toward the tavern. Aiden reached down and took my hand as we walked behind them, his eyes moist.

"What did he say?" I whispered, not wanting to ruin the moment.

"He said 'Well done, my son. I am proud of you.' And he said it in the tongue of our fathers, which he'd never spoken to me before," he replied, his voice cracking with emotion. My heart swelled with affection for Alex.

The noise from the pub hit me with a tangible force as we entered, along with the yeasty smell of ale and sweaty, unwashed bodies. The tavern was packed with patrons, the men laughing loudly and playing cards, women sitting on their laps. The open sensuality of the women surprised me: ample cleavage spilling out of their frilly dresses and girlish ribbons in their hair. A blonde woman refilled a customer's drink and he pinched her butt as she passed. She giggled and batted her eyelashes at him in invitation.

"Whores," Aiden said with distaste. The man took a swig of his drink and grabbed the blonde's hand. She smiled and led him up the stairs at the far end of the pub. Uncle Alex and young Aiden sat at the bar, ordering whisky and some type of stew I'd never heard of. Occasionally a prostitute tried to approach them but would quickly move away after getting a terse word from one or the other.

Aiden spoke next to me, looking out over the tables of men. "It's a pity that the pub was such a filthy hole because I did love to play cards." He winked at me to lighten the mood and I smiled, thankful to be safe in his memory so that none of the men could reach out and pinch me.

They finished their meal in silence, then headed out into the rain. I let out the breath I'd been holding as we left the pub and inhaled deeply, hoping for fresh air. Instead, I coughed as my lungs filled with the acrid stench of human waste lining the streets.

"Is there much more to this memory?" I asked. He stopped walking and took both of my hands in his.

"Not really, no. This is the Paris that I knew. I'm sorry it's not what you were hoping for."

"No, it's not your fault. It was stupid of me to insist. We shouldn't spend what little time we have reliving unpleasant memories." The thought of being separated from him was like acid in my stomach and I had a sudden urge to share my memories with him before it was too late.

"Aiden, I want to go home."

"Aye, I'll take you back to the château. Maybe you'd like to see my uncle's library. He has books in French, Latin, English, Gaelic—thousands of them."

"No, I mean I want to go home, back to America, back to my time. I want to take you to the most beautiful places I know, like you've done for me."

"Well, you can cast a memory or a place just as sure as I can. So, why not? I'd love to see your home."

Chapter 10

Closing my eyes, I concentrated on a happy memory from my childhood, imagining I was there again. The familiar shimmer passed through my flesh like a ripple in a pond and I knew I'd been successful. The cold, drab backdrop of Paris gave way to a beautiful, sunny day in Seattle.

Outside the blue split-level house where I grew up, the garage door was open with our black Chevy Blazer parked inside. My parents shouted to one another from within the house, asking if she'd remember to grab this or where he had last seen that. My 14-year-old self kicked rocks in the driveway, humming songs and trying to stay out of the frenzy. I relished the familiar surroundings but felt a piercing loss, knowing I'd never see my parents again.

Aiden checked out the knee-length shorts and t-shirt I'd cast him in. He lifted up one foot in examination of the flip-flop sandal with a curious expression. But when he saw my shorts and sleeveless tank top, his eyebrows furrowed in disapproval. "You can't wear that out in public. Why, you're half naked!"

"No, I'm not. Everyone dresses this way. Just wait, you'll see."

My mother came out through the garage door and pulled open the hatch on the Blazer. Her long blonde hair was pulled back into a ponytail with a red bow and her oversized dark sunglasses covered half her face. Her white sundress with red flowers matched her sandals. Her signature perfume enveloped me and I felt a pang of love and regret.

Mom.

Aiden heard and replied with a teasing tone.

Ah, I can see where you get your lovely round arse from.

"Ewww!" I shrieked in outrage and smacked him on the arm. He laughed and shrugged innocently, pretending he hadn't said anything at all.

"Gary, let's go! Come on!" Mom bellowed at the top of her lungs, slamming the trunk shut. She climbed into the passenger seat and pulled down the visor mirror to check her lipstick. Dad came bumbling out the door, dressed in his usual weekend garb: stark white legs poking out under blue shorts, a Hawaiian print shirt flowing over his round belly. He walked to the car, muttering to himself.

"Wallet, check. Keys, check. Phone, check. Sunglasses…" He stopped mid-stride, patting himself on the chest and thighs, then touched his hands to his head and found the missing item there.

"Check." He smiled and climbed in through the driver's side door.

Taking Aiden's hand, I led him into the backseat and made him climb in before me. "You go first. I want you to be able to see out the window."

He hesitated. "I've never been inside one of these. Most of the ones I've seen before were crumpled like…" He stopped before he could finish with, "like the one you were in," but we both knew what he'd started to say. I tried to lighten the mood.

"It's okay. Cars are kinda like horse-drawn carriages but without the horses. Don't worry; nothing's going to hurt me now," I said with a reassuring smile.

My younger self leaped in next to me and slammed the door, then began dancing in the seat and fiddling with her iPod. I stared at her in amazement, seeing this reflection of myself in a way I'd never been able to before.

"It's so strange. I mean, I know that's me when I was

fourteen, but it's so surreal to have her sitting there and me sitting here. And she doesn't even know I'm watching her. Bizarre."

"Aye, it does take a while to get used to it. I remember the first time I cast a memory and saw myself. It was something of a shock." He looked across the seat and a smile played across his face. "Still, I think she's quite bonnie, even if she isn't clothed decent." I rolled my eyes, since we were essentially wearing the same thing.

"What is that white string hanging from her ears?" he asked.

"Oh, that's for listening to music," I began, but then Aiden jerked backward as the car engine suddenly roared to life beneath us. I put my arm out instinctively to steady him like he'd done to me in the horse carriage. We both realized what I'd done at the same time and he smiled.

"I see what ye mean about it being alike." Dad backed out and closed the garage door with the push of a button on the dash. Aiden's eyes grew wide like he'd just seen a magic trick. "That door just shut by itself! Is there someone else inside the house?"

I opened my mouth to answer but was cut off when Mom switched on the radio and loud, thumping music flooded the car. Aiden startled at the unexpected sound and assumed a defensive position, his eyes darting around in confusion, not comprehending where it was coming from.

"It's all right," I said. "I know you're going to have lots of questions and I'll answer every one, I promise. But maybe you should just sit back and enjoy the ride for now." He nodded and made that familiar Scottish harrumph in his throat. We sped through the neighborhood with ease but ground to a halt when we hit the freeway.

"Damn traffic. I swear it gets worse every year," Dad groused.

"And you complain about it every year. We could move closer to town like I told you before, but no, we won't. So instead we just sit in traffic and I listen to you bitch about it." Mom shook her head with an air of resigned irritation, and looked out the window. Dad glowered but didn't say anything, his hands gripping the wheel.

"I thought you were going to take me to a happy memory from your childhood," Aiden said. "They don't seem very happy to me." My counterpart sat cheerily humming away with her earbuds in, oblivious to the tension in the front seat. Realization pressed down on me like a wet, heavy cloak.

"I guess I just never paid attention to it. I didn't know how unhappy they were until later."

Aiden gazed out the window in awed silence and I tried to see the city through his eyes. Nearly everything around us would be completely foreign to him: planes in the sky, enormous cranes littering the cityscape for construction projects, streetlights, neon signs for restaurants, and gigantic photos of people pasted onto billboards. My mind whirled at how I might begin to explain it all. We drove past skyscrapers so tall we couldn't see the top of them and accordion buses that were the length of four cars combined.

The monorail train cruised overhead on mammoth concrete pillars and people of every size, shape and color crossed the street in front of us. Some were taking pictures with digital cameras, others drinking from plastic fountain cups, but all of them new and different to Aiden. I glanced over at him, worried that it might be too much, thinking maybe I shouldn't have brought him here. To my surprise, he seemed to be enjoying himself, his eyes scanning the city with interest as we drove.

Dad parked and we got out. I pointed up at the Space Needle excitedly. "See the windows that wrap around it? We're going to ride up to the top and look out over the city. It's amazing." He shielded his eyes with one hand, squinting up at the top of the building shaped like an enormous pushpin.

"Aye, if you say so."

I took his hand as we crossed the street and made our way inside. Mom immediately got sucked into the gift shop, picking up all the little trinkets and thumbing through merchandise with the Space Needle logo.

"Oh, for God's sake, Elizabeth," Dad barked. "We haven't even been to the top yet and you already want to buy all the crap they sell. Come on." He headed up the ramp with us trailing behind, until we came to the end of the line of customers waiting for their chance to ride to the top. Aiden shook his head in disapproval at two teenage girls wearing cut-off shorts and tight tank tops.

"That's not right. I cannot imagine their fathers know they're strutting about so indecent. Or is that how whores dress now?"

I was shocked at first, but then laughed out loud. He straightened up, offended that I was laughing at him. "They're not whores!" I said. "They're just teenage girls, probably about my age, out enjoying the sunshine. That's just what kids wear now. It's no big deal." It was a losing battle so I just shrugged and dropped it. The line crept slowly forward and I became acutely aware of my parents' bickering as we waited. I gazed with longing at the younger me, wishing I could use the iPod myself to tune them out.

Aiden broke into my thoughts and asked, "I saw a building of some sort when we were standing outside. It was blue and copper and red, and it rolled like waves instead of having walls, but people were going into it through a door. What is that?"

My face lit up and I instantly recognized the EMP from his description. "That's the Experience Music Project building and the Science Fiction Museum. I love the EMP because it's all about music: listening to music, playing music, learning about music. There's a huge tower of guitars in the center, and you can mix and record your own CD if you want. The Science Fiction Museum is pretty much about aliens and robots and make-believe monsters from comic books and movies."

He stared at me blankly. I realized with chagrin that I hadn't really clarified anything at all, but had actually said a bunch of gibberish to him.

"All right, then. Truthfully, I don't have to understand all of it. I'm just happy to be here with you." We finally made it to the elevator and crowded in with a bunch of strangers for the ride to the top. The attendant spoke in a soothing voice, recounting the history of the Space Needle, explaining that the structure is 605 feet tall and that the glass elevator we were standing in travels at a speed of ten miles per hour or 800 feet per minute. The rest of the crowd seemed to be barely listening to her while Aiden hung on every word.

His face turned a little green while he stared out the glass panes of the elevator, but he looked excited, too. I felt a rush of pride in him for his willingness to experience something so radically new. Within seconds, we made it to the top and stepped onto the Observation Deck outside. Aiden's jaw dropped as he gazed out over the expansive water, the snow-capped mountains and the city below. I pointed out areas of interest.

"See that skinny line there with all the tiny cars moving across it like ants? That's the road where we came in, where Dad was complaining about the traffic. And over there are the skyscrapers that were so tall we couldn't see the tops of them. Now they look like children's toys!"

Astonishment shone on his face. "You were right, my love. It is the most incredible view I have ever seen. It reminds me of the Five Sisters of Kintail, a mountain ridge near my home in Scotland." He shook his head in wonder and then grinned at me with a mischievous twinkle in his eye. "I've always wondered how we must look to God as he watches over us from heaven, and now I know the truth. We look like ants." I laughed out loud and hugged him close, breathing in the fresh air and Aiden's warmth.

Dad put his arm around my look-alike. "So what do you think, kitten? Pretty cool, isn't it?"

She gave him a silver smile, her mouth full of braces. "Yeah, it's awesome. I looked through the telescope and you can see everything from here. There's Alki Beach and Gas Works Park and some funky building that's growing grass on the roof. Here, you try." She pulled the telescope over for him to take a look and he bent down to take a peek.

"You're right, that is cool." He stood up and leaned over the telescope with a strange, sad smile on his face. "Lindsey, pumpkin," he said hesitantly. "I love you so much honey, no matter what. I hope you know that."

She stared at him, forehead wrinkled in confusion. "Yeah, I know. I love you, too." Her eyes searched his for the rest of the story, since his declaration seemed really random. He sighed and gave her a bear hug. "Dad! You're squishing me!" she protested, squirming out of his grasp. He tickled her ribs and she giggled, grinning up at him. She held his hand as they walked around the rest of the deck, pointing things out to each other.

I watched them walk away, a new understanding heavy in my chest. "He knew it was over, with my mom, I mean. They didn't get divorced for a few years after that, but he must have known it wasn't going to last." A tear slid down my cheek. Aiden drew me into his arms and his strength buoyed me. He didn't say anything, but simply held me as I processed the emotions. The beautiful view and the sunlight on the water calmed my spirit.

"I really wanted to share this with you," I said, "because I remember it so fondly, this trip to the top of the Space Needle. But I didn't realize how hard it would be to see my parents again."

"I know just what you mean," he agreed. "I saw both of my brothers when I showed you my own death, and I hadn't seen them since that day. It's not easy. We don't have to stay,

71

if you want to go."

"No, there's more I want to share with you from this day."

Mom came around the corner, her face pinched in irritation. "There you are!" she said. "I swear I have been around this thing ten times trying to find you!"

Dad didn't seem at all ruffled by her agitation, but looked boyishly happy holding onto the hand of fourteen-year-old me. We headed back to the car, Dad having somehow miraculously diverted Mom's attention from the gift shop on the way out. He bought a cotton candy from a street vendor, which younger me messily picked apart with her fingers, getting pink threads of sugar everywhere.

"Mmmm... I'll have to cast some cotton candy sometime for you to try. It's nothing but spun sugar, but it's so yummy." We barreled back into the car and drove the short distance along the waterfront to the aquarium. "You are going to love this place!" I was nearly hopping with excitement, pulling Aiden by the hand across the street. My enthusiasm made him laugh but he looked a little nervous, unsure of what to expect.

The large lobby area showcased a floor-to-ceiling glass wall of a fish tank. It was feeding time and a scuba diver floated in the tank, breathing from an oxygen tank and speaking through a microphone to the crowd as she tossed food to the fish. Aiden cocked his head to the side, obviously trying to make sense of the scene but not wanting to ask. The diver asked questions about the fish, and kids in the front row tried to outdo one another with raised hands to be the first to answer. Another employee stood by the side of the glass wall, speaking into a microphone that allowed both the crowd and the diver to hear the children's answers.

"Come on, there's lots more to see," I urged, dragging him by the hand. We entered the jellyfish circle and his eyes widened in wonder. A thick glass tube ran up from the floor over our heads and back down, filled with water and floating jellyfish. A neon light illuminated the tube, making the gelatinous orbs glow in fluorescent hues as they pulsed, moving gracefully through the water.

"I don't know what I'm looking at, but it's very beautiful."

Rather than take the time to explain, I moved on to the octopus tank, craning my neck to see where the creature was hidden. "Look! There he is!" I exclaimed.

He squinted at the glass, unsure of what he was supposed to be looking for. The octopus camouflaged itself to look like a piece of coral and was barely visible. A child in front of us knocked on the tank and the octopus suddenly changed to an angry red and swam away in a swirling mass of suctioned tentacles.

"What the bloody hell?!" Aiden jerked upright and backed away from the tank, nearly knocking me over. I laughed at his unnerved expression and explained how an octopus can change colors, but he just frowned and shook his head, apparently convinced that the creature was freakishly unnatural. "I don't like it," he harrumphed. As we moved on, he warily kept one eye on the octopus like it was going to jump out of the tank at any second.

The next exhibit was an elaborate faux cave with dozens of small tanks set into the rock façade. Aiden peered diligently into each one, noting the variety of crabs, eels, seahorses, and saltwater fish. His features gradually relaxed and he even occasionally pointed to a fish he found particularly fascinating. "Look, this one is called a Pinecone Fish, and I'll be damned. The wee bugger really does look like a pinecone!"

"Look at this Fiddler Crab," I said. "They're called that because one of their claws is great big while the other is really small, like a fiddle and a bow."

"One thing's for sure, lassie," he said with a grin. "Our God in heaven certainly has a sense of humor to make such wee beasties as these."

We moved on to the Underwater Dome, which looked like a glass version of the deck of the Starship Enterprise. But instead of space and starlight, sharks, salmon and sturgeon swam past us and over our heads. Aiden's eyes were wide, trying to take it all in. "Are we underwater, then? How did that happen?"

"Yeah, we went through that little tunnel and now we're in a special room underneath the sea. So the fish are not in a tank anymore. We are!"

He stared at me like that was the craziest thing he'd ever heard. "If you say so, love, I believe you. It's like we're right there swimming in the water with them."

Dad got a dreamy look on his face and absently reached out, taking Mom's hand. She looked surprised at first but then the corners of her mouth pulled up in a smile and she stood quietly watching the hypnotic movement of the fish with him. Seeing them together, knowing that they would eventually split in a bitter divorce was harder than I could have imagined. I sighed deeply, wishing in retrospect that I'd cast the scene without all the people instead of as a memory so I didn't have to relive my parents' struggle so intimately.

Is everything all right, Lindsey?

His thought caressed me and I smiled, thankful for his presence and strength. He didn't have to touch me or even talk and I could feel the force of his love, holding me close.

God, how am I ever going to leave him? Please help me.

I sent up the silent prayer, ever conscious of the tension in my core that grew stronger each day.

We left the dome and came out into the sunlight. A marine biologist flung a dead fish to one of the sea lions. The large, slick black animals waddled back and forth on their flippers, entertaining us in return for their supper.

"Finally a creature I know!" he said. "Selkies have the most lovely, mournful eyes. There's a legend in Scotland about them, that they're actually fairies who can shed their skin and come ashore as beautiful women. 'Tis said that if a man finds and hides the selkie's skin, that she can't return to the sea but will stay married to him. But she won't be happy, always longing to return to the water of her home."

The sea lions barked at me with their sad, glossy eyes. I could see where the legend might have some merit. "It probably makes just as much sense as us being in the tank with the fish outside, huh?" I conceded. "I think if I were going to pick a creature to turn into," I mused, "it would probably be an otter, since they always seem to be having so much fun." We peered into the sea otter pen and watched them playfully twirling and diving, cracking mollusks open on their chests.

"Aye, they are cute. Their spirit is more like yours, playful and sweet." He tucked an unruly curl behind my ear affectionately and put his arm around me.

Mom glanced at her watch and grimaced. "Crap, it's getting late. We have to go or we'll be late for the symphony. Gary, are you ready?" she called, looking around for him.

Dad was watching the otters push a beach ball around with their noses. "Huh? Oh, yeah. We'd better get going," he agreed.

Chapter 11

I pictured the concert hall in my mind and the ripple of change passed over me. I'd cast Aiden in a black suit with a white dress shirt underneath and a sky blue tie that accentuated his eyes. He was so handsome that it literally took my breath away, even though I'd imagined the outfit myself.

"Aiden, you're..." I stammered, trying to put into words how beautiful he was to me, how I could barely breathe when I looked at him.

"Thank you. I was about to say the same to you."

I wore a fitted ice blue dress with spaghetti straps and my hair fell loose over my shoulders. He held his arm out formally to me like he'd done at the king's palace and I took it with a mischievous grin. "I decided it wouldn't be appropriate to have you share in my memory of getting dressed in the bathroom of the restaurant with my mom earlier, so I skipped us over that part," I said.

He laughed out loud and shrugged, looking over at my mom. "Wouldn't have been so bad, I think."

Mom looked fantastic as a matter of fact, in a low-cut flowing black dress, her long blonde hair cascading like a waterfall down her back. Dad cleaned up pretty nice too, though he did seem uncomfortable in his suit and tie. When I turned back to Aiden, his gaze traveled appreciatively over my dress. My heart raced at his unspoken admiration.

We made our way into the expansive auditorium where

oddly shaped walls were acoustically designed to best reverberate the sound throughout the hall. An enormous pipe organ decorated the stage, its tubes extending from floor to ceiling in a majestic display. The musicians tuned their instruments on stage and the lights dimmed as we quickly found our seats. The conductor walked on stage and the audience applauded in anticipation. He turned to the first chair violinist and shook her hand, then struck a pose on the podium with his arms high in the air.

With a sudden downward stroke, he brought the symphony to life. The sound of violins, flutes, trombones, timpani, and French horns filled the air as if they were playing in the seats right beside us. Aiden's eyes widened briefly in surprise at the intensity of the sound. The violinists' bows floated rhythmically over their strings and the trilling notes of the flutes bounced off the uneven walls all around us, drawing us in. The music flowed through the air like the fish we'd seen swimming in the sea and my spirit swayed with the movement. The piece rose in a crescendo then fell away to a tender pianissimo as the melody echoed through each of the instrumental groups, one by one. The symphony hung on one final note, waiting for the conductor's cue, then set down their instruments in synch as he brought his arms down to his sides.

The audience erupted in applause. Enraptured, Aiden and I instantly jumped to our feet, though no one could see us. The musicians stood and bowed, then followed the conductor off the stage. The lights in the auditorium came on and the audience rose as one, moving to the exits for the intermission.

"Is it over already?" he asked, disappointed.

"No, only half. Everyone gets up to stretch and go to the bathroom, then we come back and they play the other half."

My younger self hung out in the hallway, studying the photos of the musicians along the walls and reading their bios. Dad headed off to the restroom and Mom wandered over to the bar for a drink. She struck up a conversation with a man in line, flipping her hair back over her shoulder and laughing at something he'd said. I couldn't quite see him but he was tall with wavy black hair and well dressed in a dark pinstripe suit. He turned toward my mother with a smile and whispered something to her. I gasped in shock, immediately recognizing him. Aiden was at my side in a heartbeat, his arm tightening around my waist protectively.

"What's wrong?"

"It's Nick…" I stammered, struggling to make sense of it. "What the hell is he doing here?"

Nick had a wolfish grin on his face as my mother leaned close. She trailed her hand down his arm and then threw her head back, laughing at what he'd said.

"My mom left my dad for him," I explained between clenched teeth. "She said she hadn't known him very long, that they'd met at the library." I shook my head in disbelief at what my eyes were seeing. "And yet here he is in my memory, years before their divorce and my mom is throwing herself all over him like a whore. Oh my God… She must have been cheating on my dad for years before he found out."

I could hardly breathe as the nauseating scene played out in front of me. Mom toyed with her necklace while running her fingertips over her cleavage, her eyes twinkling up at him. Nick openly noticed her invitation and leaned in, his eyes darkening with interest. Aiden took me by the shoulders and turned me to face him, breaking my trance.

"We should go. It's not good for you to be here."

I shook my head vehemently and pulled myself together. "No. I won't let her spoil this for me." The lights in the lobby dimmed briefly, then came back up. "Come on. That means it's going to start again so we need to go sit down." I could feel his resistance but I was determined to enjoy the rest of the symphony in spite of my mother and Nick.

The second movement of the composition was a tribute to Mars, the Roman god of war, and the percussion instruments on stage had doubled in number. The cymbals crashed over me like waves breaking on the sea as I listened, unable to move. Emotions raged within me as the music pounded and pulsed in a symphonic battle. I closed my eyes and concentrated on the movement of the air, which swirled around and through me as the violins built momentum in a frenzied cadence. The timpani rolled like thunder through my blood, the horns blasting staccato in a defiant march to the finish. I felt battered and bruised with my heart tossed against the rocks when the piece ended, and could hardly muster the energy to stand and clap with the rest of the audience. Aiden frowned down at me, concerned.

"We're going," he said. "I'll make the cast myself if I need to, but we are not staying here any longer. I won't allow anything to cause you pain if it's in my power to stop it."

"Just one more thing," I pleaded. "I want you to see the city lights at night. Then we can go. Just come with me on the drive home. That's all I ask."

He stared at me for a long time without answering, his brow furrowed. "Fine, then. I'll do as you ask, but this is the last time. I haven't much time with you, Lindsey and I don't want to spend it like this." His eyes searched mine for any sign of distress. Finding nothing but a tired peace, he sighed and kissed me lightly on the forehead.

An instant later, we were back in the car with my family. Soft classical music was playing on the radio and Mom sat in the front seat with her eyes closed, swaying slightly to the music. "Mmmm, isn't it heavenly?" she said. "Lindsey, you should marry a man who can play an instrument so he can serenade you." I rolled my eyes, realizing that she was likely recounting her encounter at the bar with Nick.

Dad glowered at her. "What kind of ridiculous criteria is that for a husband?" He craned his neck to see me in the rear-view mirror. "All that matters is that he loves you, respects you, is honest and trustworthy, and wants nothing more than your happiness. And if he is all of those things, you'll know he'll never leave you, no matter what." He glanced over at my mom with a sigh, shaking his head. My heart reached out to him since I could tell he was talking to her as much as to me and she didn't even get it.

"Gary, you're such a romantic. What are the chances she's going to find someone who meets all of your lofty criteria?" She waved her hand at him in dismissal.

To my surprise, Dad and Aiden frowned at her with identical expressions and responded together sternly, "She will." Mom sighed in exasperation and looked out the car window, obviously done with the conversation. Aiden put his arm around me possessively, his face set like stone.

"You guyyyyys!" my younger self whined from the backseat. "It's not like I'm interviewing anyone for a husband right now so you don't need to fight about it. Geez!" She settled back in a huff with her arms crossed.

Hoping to dispel some of the tension, I pointed out the downtown buildings all-aglow.

"Look, Aiden! Isn't it beautiful? I've always loved the city at night, with the twinkling lights and the reflection of the moonlight on the water. It's as if the stars came down from the sky and landed on all the buildings."

"Aye, it is lovely. I can't say I've ever seen anything quite like it."

Suddenly a loud strain of pop music burst out from the front seat and Mom reached into her purse for her phone.

"Hello? Hey, Suzanne. Yep, we just got back from the symphony. It was fabulous. What? Oh yeah, I'll be at the PTA meeting on Wednesday. Is there anything I should bring? Okay, I can pick up some cookies from the store. It's not like I'm gonna be baking them myself! All right, talk to you later."

Aiden watched her, confused, and I tried to explain. "It's called a cell phone," I said. "You can talk with people on it, if they have a phone, too."

"It's not attached to anything. I saw it! How could she

81

have been talking to someone? And where is this Suzanne woman anyway? She's not in the car!"

"Truthfully, I don't know how it really works," I admitted. "It has to do with signals passed between the two phones. And it doesn't really matter where the other person is because the signals travel all over the world. We could call someone in Scotland and it would sound like they were sitting in the car with us."

Dad pulled the car into the drive, pushing the garage door opener on the dash. Aiden made his trademark grunt as he watched the door magically open for us, shaking his head but not saying anything.

"You've had enough for one day, I think," I said. Closing my eyes, I cast the image of my girlhood bedroom. The garage melted away, replaced by a bed with ruffled pillows and a pink comforter covered in white daisies. Lacy curtains hung in the octagonal bay window. Music posters plastered the walls and a whimsical purple lantern hung from the ceiling right above a large beanbag chair of the same color. It was familiar and comfortable and I sighed contentedly, grateful for the change in pace. For the first time all day, we were blissfully alone with no memories to follow, no agenda, just the two of us. He surveyed the room, smiling at the girlish decoration.

"I like it. It looks like you. It has your spirit."

"Best of all," I said, "there's a trundle bed so you don't have to sleep on the floor." I pulled the extra bed out from underneath my own with a triumphant flair. He lifted one eyebrow at the twin size mattress.

"Now if only I were a young maiden and could fit on that wee bed, eh?" He lay down on the bed in demonstration, his feet sticking off the edge by a good twelve inches. I threw one of my ruffled pillows at him, which he caught and tucked behind his head. "Nah, it's not so bad. I can roll over on one side. But I'm going to change back into my kilt, if you don't mind."

The shimmer of his change rolled through me and I did the same, choosing a pink nightgown rather than the grungy t-shirt I usually wore to bed. I crawled onto the higher bed and lay on my stomach, my fingertips trailing over the edge and playing with his hair.

"So what did you think of Seattle? Did you have any fun at all?" I asked. He stared up at the ceiling and chuckled softly.

"Aye, for certain. But truthfully lass, I wouldn't be surprised if you climbed the walls like a spider and hung from the ceiling like a bat, for all I've seen today. I cannot even describe what it's like to go forward three hundred years in the future and to see how things have changed. I don't understand it, but thank you for showing me your home." He kissed my fingertips and I sighed, thankful to have shared my memories with him, but also very glad the day was over.

Chapter 12

A heavy mist shrouded Eilean Donan Castle and the cool evening air pinched my cheeks. Energy bubbled up from my core and I ran with that same effortless strength that I'd had upon first awakening into this mysterious place. I focused my mind on the movement of my muscles under my skin.

"Come on, let's go!" I shouted over my shoulder to Aiden, who had fallen behind. His labored breathing grew faint as I sped away from him. The greenery surrounding me was sparse but welcoming, and I had no fear of tripping or falling. It was as if the ground itself was rising up to meet me with each step. The air rushed around me and through me as I ran. My lungs pulled in the nourishing substance like water to parched lips. My mind emptied of all thoughts and I concentrated on this extraordinary sensation of being one with the elements.

I win!

A thrill ran through me that I'd reached the church before Aiden. The moonlight reflected brightly on the mirrored surface of the water and I marveled at its beauty. The air began to vibrate and swirl around me in an embrace, caressing and holding me where I stood. It moved through me, filling each cell in my body with a wholeness I'd never known before. I closed my eyes and breathed deeply, feeling God's presence and recognizing it like a long-lost friend.

Music emanated from the presence within me, powerful and delicate like an angelic symphony. My soul soared at the

sound. I swayed in place as the song built majestically to a
crescendo, my heart full of unspeakable joy and peace. I
turned to share my happiness with Aiden and found him
standing far-off, one hand held up in a silent farewell.

"No," I whispered. "No, I don't want to leave him.
Please don't make me, God," I said, my chest constricting
with loss. The power slowly seeped out from me, the notes
diminishing and fading into silence. I stood looking out over
the water for a long time, aware of the remnants of His
presence still with me, calling me home.

Chapter 13

I woke to the familiar scent of the rosebush outside my bedroom window, the morning breeze blowing lightly across my face. A stray curl tickled my cheek and I brushed it away with a yawn. I grumbled sleepily, not wanting to wake up, knowing Mom would be down any second to yell at me to get ready for school. I furrowed my brow in protest and clamped my eyes shut, burying my face in the pillow.

"Don't wanna. Lemme alone. Rhf grn strk..." I argued blearily. A hand stroked my cheek and I slowly roused as whispers of fluid French wished me a good morning. Confused, I peeked open one eye and saw Aiden's gentle face smiling down at me. His presence was a balm to my spirit and I sighed contentedly, reaching out to touch him. He took my hand and pressed it to his cheek, then turned and kissed my palm. A tingle ran across my shoulders.

"You're always awake before me," I observed.

"You're a good sleeper. You will not wake until you're ready, and you don't notice the sound of me moving around the room." Embarrassed, I dropped my gaze, feeling like a sloth. "I love to watch you sleep in the morn," he continued. "You look so bonnie and your face is very expressive when you dream. I wish I could see what you're dreaming about, though." I seldom remembered my dreams, and something niggled at the edge of my mind, but I dismissed it. I shrugged and sat up, stretching, and then shot him a sly smile.

"Well, they've got to be all about you, but you probably

wouldn't approve of them anyway because I'm sure they are entirely inappropriate. Well, at least the best ones are." He threw his head back with a full belly laugh. The sound echoed joyfully around the room and I joined in. He knelt on the trundle bed mattress beneath me and pulled me into his arms.

"Ah, my love. I'm certain I've already seen those dreams because I've had them myself. And you're right, those are the best ones." He kissed me full on the lips as if to prove his point, but I didn't need any convincing. I loved the feel of his mouth on mine, his strong arms around me, and my heartbeat skipped erratically in response to his touch. An image sprang to mind and I started to giggle.

"Sorry, it's just that I had this vision of my mom coming down the hall to check on me, and here I am kissing you in my bedroom. I had a sudden compulsion to hide you in the closet so she wouldn't find out." He chuckled and sat down on the bed below me, his hand still holding mine.

"I was going to cast you some breakfast," he said, "but I wasn't sure what you might like. We've already established you're not fond of parritch."

"You noticed, huh? Actually, I'd like to cook breakfast for you," I said.

"Aye, I'd love that. Shall we go to the kitchen, then?"

"No, not here. I want to take you to my favorite place in the whole world, our family cabin on the lake in Idaho. I'll make you eggs and potatoes in a cast iron skillet on the old wood stove."

"Mmmm, a cabin on the lake sounds lovely. I've had eggs before but never potatoes. What are they like?"

"You've never had potatoes? Oh, I'm so glad I didn't live with you in the 1700s. Potatoes are my favorite food! French fries, tater tots, baby reds, mashed potatoes, baked… Oh my gosh…" Just thinking about it made me salivate.

"All right, all right, I'll give them a try if you like them so much. Maybe I'll like them as much as parritch." He gave me a teasing wink.

"Come on, now I'm hungry," I said and made the cast.

The kitchen of our family cabin materialized out of thin air as my girlish bedroom faded away. Aiden was still in his kilt, but I'd changed out of my pink nightgown into a yellow sundress and sandals when I'd cast the change. The fresh country air filled my lungs and I inhaled deeply, closing my eyes in bliss.

An antique wood stove and an old red refrigerator dominated the small kitchen. The fridge had three cooling boxes with latching handles and made a loud humming sound that filled the room. The walls consisted of rounded hand hewn logs, painstakingly fitted together. Gingham curtains framed the windows and the lake sparkled in the sunlight through the trees outside. I reveled in the ability to imagine the cabin and miraculously be there moments later.

"Dang, that's cool. It used to take us seven hours to drive here from Seattle. That's like the distance from Scotland to London, England, I think."

Aiden looked at me like I was crazy.

"No, lassie. You can't go from anywhere in Scotland to London in seven hours. It takes much longer than that." I shrugged and reached under the sink to grab some kindling for the wood stove.

"Actually, I was just talking about driving. I'll bet you can fly there in a couple hours." He made a derisive cough in his throat and rolled his eyes.

"Right, let's just sprout some wings now and go for a wee flight. Aye, two hours seems about right." He licked a finger and stuck it out in front of him as if checking the direction of the wind, his tone dripping with sarcasm and I had to laugh.

"No, smart alec, we don't turn into birds but it's just about as cool. Do you remember seeing the planes in the sky when we were in Seattle? They were really high up and looked like big metal tubes with wings like birds." He nodded with a frown. "I honestly don't know how it works," I said, "but you can fit hundreds of people on a plane and it can fly at like 600 miles per hour."

His eyes narrowed suspiciously. "You don't mean to tell me that there were people in the belly of that metal bird in the sky." He'd seen a lot of crazy things yesterday but I could tell he thought I was pulling his leg.

"Yep, I do. Maybe sometime I'll cast the memory of flying from Seattle to Portland so you can see it for yourself. But for right now, I promised you some potatoes." I opened the cover on the firebox of the stove and layered in the kindling and newspaper like my dad taught me.

"Would you like to use my flint?" he offered, reaching into his sporran.

"No, thanks. I've got a lighter." I pulled out the adjustable butane lighter and pressed the button, a flame instantly leaping to life at the tip.

"That's a right handy wee contraption you have there!" he said, visibly impressed. "Mind if I have a look around?"

"Sure, go ahead. I'm going to be here a while. Breakfast probably won't be ready for another fifteen or twenty minutes. Be sure to go upstairs," I pointed over my shoulder with the peeler in my hand, "to see the loft. There are several beds up there, since the cabin sleeps about eight people. So you won't have to sleep on the floor. Your feet won't even hang off the edge on some of them." I winked at him and he grinned before wandering off to explore.

The centerpiece of the living room was a large rock fireplace built by hand with rocks drug from the lake. A couple of armchairs sat on either side with homemade footstools that looked like mushrooms. I smiled as I remembered making those with my dad when I was about eight, stretching the red naugahyde leather over the foam caps and stapling it to the squatty wood logs with Dad's staple gun. He'd been very careful to show me how to do it so I wouldn't get hurt and I was so proud of myself for having made the little rustic cushions.

"Made from genuine naugha cows," he used to boast and it wasn't until I was much older that I learned there's no such thing as a naugha cow. I shook my head at his goofy sense of humor. Two old mismatched couches faced the center of the room, behind them a heavy pine dining table where we often sat to play games. A painted wooden toilet seat cover attached to the wall held a small table lamp made to look like a woman's leg in a fishnet stocking. The room was corny and welcoming, comfortable and rustic, and I absolutely loved it.

The butter started to sizzle in the skillet and I breathed in the delicious scent. Aiden appeared, his hand on my waist, and peered into the pan. "Mmmm, smells good." He kissed me on the cheek and gave me a squeeze, then headed up the stairs like I'd told him to. The loft was one big bedroom with a pointed ceiling and a picture window looking out over the water. A king sized bed sat under the window, flanked on either side by a double bed and two twin beds tucked under the eaves.

I added sausage and potatoes to the skillet and grated the cheese, humming to myself. I barely heard Aiden come up behind me, his footsteps were so light coming down the stairs. He wrapped his arms around my stomach and pressed his face into my hair.

"Breakfast is not the only thing that smells delicious," he purred softly in my ear. I smiled dreamily and pressed my bottom against him, wiggling it against his sporran. "Hey now, careful. That'll get you into trouble," he warned, his voice a deep rumble.

I grinned up at him, my eyes daring him to prove it. "Don't be making threats you aren't willing to carry out," I countered. I squeaked in surprise as he whipped me around and kissed me hard, his body pressed tight against me. His hand slid down my back and grabbed my butt, and I caught my breath in surprise at his aggressiveness. I wiggled my eyebrows at him suggestively, checking to see if he was really serious this time. His face told me that he might just be. My heart leapt in my chest as I wrapped my arms around his neck and kissed him with everything I had. The smell of the scorching butter reached my nose and I jerked away from him.

"Crap! I don't want to burn your breakfast. You'll never get to love potatoes then!"

He stood smiling at me lustily, still breathing hard, then stretched his shoulders and adjusted his sporran with a cough. "Right. I'll, er... go make a fire, then." He moved into the living room and I smiled, enjoying the rekindled heat between us. He hadn't kissed me like that since our fight back at the château and I was glad to see his feelings hadn't changed.

I moved to the edge of the kitchen and put a CD in the stereo. The sweet sounds of piano music floated through the room. After I mixed together the eggs, potatoes and sausage, I sprinkled them with grated cheddar cheese and some diced green onions, then set the table and called him to join me. The fire was crackling in the living room, and he appeared in the doorway, smiling and content, looking very much at home.

"This looks delightful, my love. Thank you." He sat down next to me, said a quick word of thanks to God and put a forkful in his mouth. A look of rapture crossed his face.

"My family calls this 'taties and eggs,'" I said. "It's a cabin staple and one of my favorite meals of all time. It's not good for you like parritch, but I'd eat it every day if I could."

"Well, I suppose you can, if that's what you'd like. I certainly will not mind if you want to make this for breakfast every morn." I flushed at his praise and we fell silent, listening to the classical music and eating our meal. Violins joined the piano as the next song began to play and it reminded me of the orchestra at Versailles.

"Hey, whatever happened with Marie Hélène de Saint-Simon? Did you ever see her again after that night at the palace?" Aiden choked on his orange juice at my question. I hastened to explain my random thought. "Sorry, it's just that the music reminded me of that night all of a sudden and I realized I'd never asked you."

He shook his head, composed once again. "Don't fret, you just surprised me. Aye, I did see her again once. She and the Duke came to the château to visit Uncle Alex later that summer. The king was planning to give some horses to the ambassador of Spain as a gift and they came to choose which ones would be sent." He took another bite and sat back in his chair, like that was all there was to the story.

"And?" I prompted.

He narrowed his eyes in confusion. "And what?"

"And... what happened?" I sighed in exasperation. "Did she say anything to you? Did you kiss again? Tell me!"

He furrowed his brow like he wasn't sure I was well in the head. "Nothing happened. We were never alone again, praise be. She was even skinnier and more bird-like in the daylight than I'd remembered her. I never found her at all attractive."

"Did she at least recognize you? Did she mention anything about the night at the palace?"

"She did," he conceded, non-plussed. "She kept smiling at me while we looked over the horses, trying to get my attention." He shuddered with the memory and I giggled, watching him. "No, lassie. You've nothing to worry about with that one. Besides, the king died that fall and then the Earl of Mar declared James Stuart King of Scots, and all bloody hell broke loose. I left Versailles and returned to Scotland after the Battle of Sherrifmuir that November and never returned." His face clouded over at the memory and I quickly changed the subject.

"Would you like to go for a boat ride on the lake?" I asked and he agreed. We walked hand in hand down to the beach, where our rowboat floated on the water, gently tapping the dock. He stepped into the boat, then held out a hand to help me in. He untied the boat from the dock and picked up the oars, expertly pushing off. He skimmed them through the water until we were out in the open, his strong chest and arm muscles working with each stroke.

The sun reflected off the surface of the lake, the sounds of his rowing and birds chirping magnified by the total solitude. Normally this place would be humming with speedboats and jet skis, the sounds of people out on their docks, laughing and playing in the water or having a barbeque. But today it was quiet and serene, and I couldn't think of anywhere else I'd rather be. Closing my eyes, I turned my face up to the sun, thankful for the moment and wishing it could last forever.

"You look very happy." Aiden's voice broke the silence and I opened my eyes, blinking as they adjusted to the brightness.

"Aye, that I am," I said in my best Scottish accent and he laughed. The sound of his laughter echoed off the water, joyful and infectious.

"I was just thanking God for this incredible place. And for you," I said. My heart fluttered when he smiled and tipped his head to me in acknowledgment, his bright blue eyes sparkling like the water. "I can't imagine that heaven could be any better than this," I swept my arm out across the water and smiled at him, continuing on softly with a catch in my throat, "since I've never been happier than I am right now."

He dropped one of the oars in its cradle and took my hand. "I know just what you mean." He kissed the pulse at my wrist and I felt that my heart would burst, so full of love and longing. "I don't know what heaven is like, since I've only been to the gate, never inside. But you're right, I can't imagine anything more wonderful than this."

"What was it like, being a transporter all that time? What kinds of people did you meet? Did you see a lot of gruesome death scenes? What happened when you took them to the gate?" I was suddenly full of questions, realizing I didn't know anything about that part of his past. He chuckled softly, waiting for me to finish peppering him with questions, then picked up the oars and resumed rowing.

"Well, where do I start? I have met all sorts of different people, young children, old women, men who died in battle, all colors and ages and sizes."

"What if they spoke a foreign language?" I asked. "Were you still able to communicate with them?"

"Aye, I always spoke to them in English and they responded the same, though I could tell when it was not their native tongue. Sometimes I'd transport someone who spoke French or Gaelic, and I would use those languages, but mostly it was English." I sat back, considering this, and he continued.

"Let's see, what else did you ask? Ah, what it was like at the gate, that's right. Well, every now and then I would spend a wee bit of time with a person but other times, they'd want to get to heaven straight away. So I'd cast the entrance for them like the angel taught me all those years ago and St. Peter would be standing there at the gate, smiling and waiting. I call it a gate, but it isn't really, not like a gate on a fence. It's more like..." he struggled to try and find words to describe the scene, "more like a glow, bright and shining a rich golden yellow color, swirling and moving like a swarm of bees, but soft and welcoming like a mother's arms."

He shook his head, agitated at his inability to put it into words. "I don't know how to explain it, since I've never seen anything like it on earth. It is beautiful and inviting, though I tried not to look at it, since I could not go in. Instead, I watched the people's faces as they saw it for the first time, which was always very lovely. They'd walk towards it in a trance like a force was pulling them forward." He stopped and chuckled to himself, shrugging. "Aye, I guess it was, God's force, eh?"

I smiled at him in encouragement and he rowed absently,

caught up in the memory. "But then they would stop, surprised, and just stare at St. Peter. I always wondered why they did that until finally one day, I was taking a wee child to meet him and I was holding her hand as she walked toward the gate. Then she stopped and looked at him like they always do, her eyes wide with surprise. But then she turned to me and whispered, 'He just said my name and I heard it in my head. His lips didn't even move!' and I laughed, thankful to finally understand the mystery."

He reached out to brush my cheek with his hand. "I'll never forget the look in your eyes when I spoke to you with my mind the first time. You looked at me like I was St. Peter himself and my chest was afire with joy and relief, I was so thankful to have finally found you."

I wanted to fling myself into his arms and hold on tight, but knew that if I did, I'd rock the boat and dump us into the lake. So instead, I wound my fingertips in his and caressed him with my eyes. Worry chewed at my insides, but I didn't want to spoil the moment, so I pushed it away. The warm summer breeze wrapped around us like a blanket and the rustling sound of the wind in the trees filled me with peace. We stayed that way for a long time, swept up in each other's faces, holding hands and floating slowly through the water. The sun was creeping down the horizon when he finally turned the boat back toward the dock.

"You asked if I'd seen grisly death scenes and aye, I have. Though I didn't always meet people at their deaths. Sometimes I would come to them afterward, in a beautiful place that they'd cast right after, like the meadow where I met you."

I shook my head in confusion. "What do you mean? I didn't cast that meadow. I didn't even know what casting was until you took me to the château."

"No, lassie. That meadow came from inside you. I'd never seen it before we met."

I tried to puzzle out how that could be since I'd never

been someplace like that. A photo came to mind, one from a National Geographic I'd been skimming through at the dentist's office two weeks before the accident. "It was a picture from a magazine. I remember now, thinking it looked so peaceful and inviting."

"Aye, it was. I've seen many landscapes over the years as people cast what makes them the happiest. Sometimes it's in the countryside or on a mountain, but there is usually water of some sort." I looked out over the lake and could easily understand why that would be, since the water had such a naturally soothing nature. Still, I felt like he was forgetting something, so I thought back through the questions I'd asked him. The vision of a man dying in battle sprang to mind and I narrowed my eyes at him curiously.

"You said that you sometimes arrive at the scenes where the people have died and take them from there. Do you..." The words caught in my throat as a terrifying thought froze the air in my lungs. He looked at me quizzically, not sure what I was getting at. I coughed, trying to think of the most delicate way to put it, the question burning in my head. I couldn't bring myself to say it out loud, so I asked the question in my mind, unable to look him in the eye.

Did you take people to hell, too?

Chapter 14

He growled as his face registered understanding and didn't say anything more, but picked up the oars and continued to row in silence. I held my breath and searched his eyes, waiting for the answer. Finally, he shook his head and responded quietly, his face unreadable.

"No, I didn't, though I have seen one who does." My eyes grew wide with fear and morbid curiosity, but I sat silently, waiting for him to go on. "It was a long time ago, though I remember it like it was yesterday. There was a terrible accident with a long metal tube that looked like a caterpillar, but with people inside."

"Do you mean a train? Like the one we saw over our heads in Seattle?"

He nodded grimly, "Aye, a train. That's what I heard someone call it. It was longer than the one we saw and on the ground, but this one was broken to pieces, with bodies scattered everywhere and people crying." He shuddered at the memory and seemed to gain strength from the act of rowing, his strokes becoming deeper as he recounted the story.

"I was there to bring a young mother to heaven. I could see other transporters around the train, talking to the dead and disappearing with them as they cast a new scene. The young woman was having a hard time letting go, since her child was not coming with us, so we didn't leave the place right away. A swirling black mass appeared at the opposite side of the train, with a screeching sound like ravens fighting over a carcass. It had the horrific stench of a body that's been rotting in the sun for several days and I nearly retched at the smell of it.

"When it touched the ground, it formed into this..." he struggled to find the words to describe it, his lips pulled down in a sneer, "... thing. I don't even know what to call it. It was small and thin like a woman, but hunched over like a wolf, with sharp claws at the tips of its fingers. It had black snarly hair and dry, crackling skin. Its tongue stuck out over its fangs with a wicked grin of violent, lusty excitement. I met its eyes for just a second and they flashed blood red at me, then I took the girl's hand and cast us out of there immediately."

He gripped the oars with white knuckles and his chest shook with the memory. My flesh crawled at the description of this hell transporter and I immediately regretted having asked. The rowboat bumped against the dock, making me jump, and he reached out a hand to steady me. He leapt onto the dock and tied up the boat, then helped pull me out.

"I'm sorry, love," he said. "I probably shouldn't have told you about it and now I've gotten myself all het up. I think I'll chop some wood to replenish the pile and try to burn that vision out of my mind." I nodded mutely, unable to offer him any comfort and he strode off up the dirt path to the cabin.

The sun dipped into the lake in a liquid orange pool and I stood alone on the dock for a moment, drinking it in and chastising myself for having upset him. I walked up to the cabin, kicking pinecones along the way. The fire had died out in the cabin, so I built it back up, then put a new CD in the stereo. I changed it to some more up-tempo dance music, the kind I liked to listen to whenever I cleaned.

Bobbing my head to the beat of the music, I wandered into the kitchen and loaded the sink with soapy water, scrubbing off our breakfast dishes and setting them to dry on the counter. I could have done a new cast to avoid washing them, but I welcomed the mindless activity. Rinsing out the cast iron skillet, I sang into the long-handled scrub brush like it was a microphone.

I could hear the rhythmic crack of Aiden splitting wood outside over the sound of the music. Drying my hands on a towel, I walked over to the window to watch him. Facing away from me, he bent over to grab a new log from the woodpile, then placed it on the chopping block. He'd taken his shirt off and his back glistened with sweat. He pushed his hair away from his face with the back of one hand, concentrating. He pulled the heavy axe up easily with one hand, but brought it down with both, cleanly splitting the log in two with one stroke. He reached down and gathered the pieces, tossing them onto the pile he'd started. The axe had stuck in the block with the blow and he yanked it free, then began the process again.

He didn't notice me watching him, as he was consumed by the repetitive and physical task, likely blotting out the bad memory and clearing his mind. I licked my lips, enjoying the way the muscles rippled in his back when he swung the axe. Finally, I tore my gaze away and went upstairs to change the linens, dancing and singing as I went.

I heard Aiden come into the cabin and drop off an armload of chopped wood while I was upstairs making the beds. *"Voulez-vous coucher avec moi, ce soir?"* I sang, along with Christina Aguilera, Lil' Kim and Pink. Heat sprang to my cheeks and I wondered if Aiden had heard the song when he'd come in, but the cracking sound of splitting wood quickly resumed outside. Singing to myself and shaking my groove thing, I padded down the stairs and started cutting vegetables for our dinner.

Aiden's voice cut into my thoughts. *I'm going for a dip in the lake. I'll be back in a minute.*

I caught a glimpse of him out the window as he started off toward the water. "Mmm, a swim before dinner. That sounds fabulous," I said to myself, dropping the knife. I grabbed two beach towels off the hook by the back door and followed him down to the lake. A short rock stairway cut into the side of the hill provided easy access to the beach below and I stopped at the top, watching him as he walked down the stretch of the dock. He pulled off his shoes and undid his belt. In one swift motion, his kilt, dirk and sporran pooled at his feet.

I sucked in a breath and bit my lip. My pulse pounded so loud in my ears that I was sure he could hear it. As he stood at the edge of the dock, my eyes devoured his naked body, admiring his strong legs and firm round cheeks. His hair cascaded over his shoulders and his back glistened with sweat. A blissful sigh escaped me as he dove into the lake and swam under the water a good distance, then popped up like a seal and slicked his hair back with his hands. He closed his eyes and floated on his back, treating me to a delicious view of the rest of him.

Without even thinking, I dropped the beach towels on the stairs and tiptoed down to the dock, drawn to him like a magnet. He didn't open his eyes as I came near but lay floating on his back, peacefully soaking up the late afternoon sun. I quickly pulled off my clothes and dove in to join him. He snapped upright at the sound of my splash and his eyes grew wide as he saw me swim near. I stopped just beyond his arm's reach and tread water, my breasts bobbing in the lake, my hair slicked back against my neck.

"That's not very lady-like," he scolded, though his tone was cracked and husky, his eyes drawn to my bare breasts.

"What?" I asked, smirking at him. "You started it! Telling me you're going to go for a dip in the lake and then standing there naked like a glistening Adonis. What did you expect me to do?"

He looked shocked at my teasing accusation. "I did not! What was I supposed to do, swim in my kilt?"

I shrugged, my eyes dancing with fire. "Fine then. You

don't have to swim with me, if you don't want to." I turned away and dipped my head down into the water to swim off, knowing full well that my bare white bottom flashed above the surface of the lake like a tantalizing bobber. I kicked my feet as I swam away, splashing him in the face.

Ah, ye cannot get away that easy, vixen.

I giggled back at him in my mind and swam with all my might to give him a good chase. He quickly caught up with me though, and his arms coiled around me like a snake. He pulled me up out of the water and I barely got in a breath before he possessed me with his mouth, his tongue demanding and pulling against mine.

I wrapped my legs around his waist and he moaned with pleasure, his hands running up and down my naked back. His kiss broke off sharply and he held me close, breathing hard and watching the water play over my breasts, pressed against his chest.

"Wait," he said, and I instantly began to argue until I saw the smile in his eyes. He kissed me once again and then swam away, leaving me quivering and confused. He swam over to the dock and dug something out of his sporran, then returned to me with a triumphant smile, taking me in his arms again. "I wanted to ask you proper and do this right, but you've forced my hand and called me out, as it were, so I cannot wait any longer." His face got serious and he pulled one hand up to stroke my cheek.

"I've wanted to make you my bride since the moment I laid eyes on you in that meadow, but I didn't know how. I could kiss you and touch you, but I could never lie with you because I'd no way to offer you marriage. I've no priest for a ceremony and I couldn't ask for your father's blessing. I prayed to God every night and every morn as I sat watching you sleep." I opened my mouth to protest and he put one finger to my lips.

"And then, last night on the way back from the city, God answered my prayers and gave me an extraordinary gift when your father outlined the criteria of his blessing over your future husband." His eyes were full of emotion as they held mine. "I've naught much else to offer but I do promise you, Lindsey Waters, before God himself and to your father on earth, that I love you more than my own soul, that I respect you, that I will always be honest and tell you the truth, even if it hurts me to say it. There is naught in this life or the next that I want more than your happiness, and I swear to you that I will stay with you as long as it is in my power, if you will be my bride."

Tears streamed down my face as I nodded feebly, overcome with emotion. He took my hand in his, intertwining our fingers and holding it against his heart. "Many years ago in Scotland, couples would have to wait as much as a year for a priest to come through the Highlands before they could be rightly married in the eyes of the church. So we had a tradition called handfasting, where a couple could pledge their love for one another and be married in the eyes of God for a year and one day. And at the end of that time, they'd either be officially married by a priest or they'd go their separate ways."

"But I don't want to be married to you for a year and a day. I want to be married to you for the rest of all time. And we may not even have another week." The flame of hope within me started to dim with worry.

"I don't know how much time we've got, but I love you this moment and I'll love you forever. The angel promised that love would redeem me and I don't know how, but I know that it will. So I will not count the days if you'll promise me the same, my love." I nodded, slowly at first and then more emphatically, the tears beginning again.

"I do. I do! I love you, Aiden MacRae." I flung my arms around his neck and kissed him, my heart straining in my chest. I felt the warmth of God's presence flow throughout my limbs and knew that He approved, however much time we had. Aiden held me close as we kissed, then pulled away, grinning.

"And I love you, Mrs. MacRae."

The title sounded strange and wonderful to my ears and I could tell he felt the same as he said it. He slid a ring on my finger and I realized it was what he'd taken out of his sporran earlier. An intricate looping design was carved into the gold ring, with a large emerald in the center and two brilliantly clear diamonds on each side. I squealed with joy and he laughed, swinging me around in a circle in the water.

He scooped me up in his arms like he was going to carry me across the threshold and walked slowly toward the beach, his eyes full of emotion and passion. I clung to him with my arms around his neck as the water fell away and he lay me down gently on the sand. He stood before me, dripping wet, and my whole body shivered with desire. I reached my arms up to him, and we made love in the sand, our bodies moving together in rhythm with the waves.

"Oh, my love, *ma chérie, mo chridhe.*" The words tumbled out of him as we lay there panting, twitching with aftershocks. I was completely spent, physically and emotionally, lying there in the sand with Aiden in my arms, and yet I'd never felt more alive and in love than at that moment. I kissed his forehead and his breathing slowed to a deep, satisfied rhythm, and he rolled onto his side next to me.

"You are amazing, my bride. I cannot even describe what you do to me." He propped himself up on one elbow and smiled down at me with half-closed eyes. He ran a sandy finger down the length of my body from my neck to my knees and I returned his dreamy smile.

"Oh, I think I know."

He grinned at that, chuckling softly and lay back on the sand. I nuzzled up under his arm with my head on his chest and curled my leg around him, and we lay there talking and touching in the sand until the stars came out.

Chapter 15

Goose bumps rose on my flesh in the cool evening air, though Aiden still felt warm to the touch. "Brrr... how do you stay so warm?" I asked.

He rubbed his hands over my back to try and warm my skin. "I can't say for sure. I've just always been that way. I very rarely get cold and when I do, it doesn't take me long to get warm again. It's no wonder that you're chittering though, since you've skin as thin as paper, my bride."

"Well, it's going to be freezing," I said, "but I've got to rinse off all this sand." I jumped up onto the dock, ran to the edge and dove in. Gasping from the shock of the cold water, I emerged to find him smirking at me. When I dared him to follow suit, he shrugged and slowly walked into the lake, eyes locked onto mine, his face never registering the chill of the water. "How do you d-d-do that?" I asked.

"The lochs in Scotland are colder than this by far and we lads used to jump in when there was snow on the ground," he said as he pulled me into his arms. The warmth from his body wrapped around me, drawing out the chill and heating my blood. Moonlight reflected on the water and in his eyes as he held me. I ran my hands over him, rinsing off the sand. He dipped his head back into the water and sighed contentedly as I worked my fingers through his hair. He did the same for me, then scooped me up into his arms and started walking back toward the beach.

"Again? Already?" I said. His chest shook with laughter

as I held onto his neck.

"I had in mind to carry you to the cabin so you wouldn't get sand on your feet. But aye, I would love to do it again whenever you like." Heat flashed in my cheeks at having mistaken his gallant gesture.

Once he set me on my feet inside the door, he cast himself back into a dry kilt and linen shirt, though he left his feet bare. I didn't exactly have a trousseau but remembered that this was, in fact, my bridal night, so I imagined myself in a floor-length white silk nightgown with spaghetti straps. Aiden set to work rebuilding the fire and I sat on the couch, watching him with my feet tucked under me.

"You know, I'd never seen a man in a kilt before I met you," I said.

Aiden kept working with his head in the fireplace as he arranged the logs and paper. "Aye?" he responded.

I think it's really sexy.

He froze for a second, then dropped the wood into place and turned to me, one eyebrow raised. "Aye?" he repeated. I nodded and giggled. His eyes swept over my nightgown and he smiled appreciatively. He lit the fire and then sat next to me on the couch. I put my legs over his and he stroked them under my nightie.

"You have the softest skin," he said.

I played with his hair, enjoying the warmth that had begun to emanate from the fire. "Well, I haven't had to shave at all since I came here, which is nice."

"You shave your legs? Like a man shaves his face? With a straight edge?"

I chuckled at his perplexed expression. "Sort of. My armpits, too."

"I noticed you've no hair in your oxters. But why would you do that?"

"For the same reason you just said—because it's soft and smooth. And because guys like it."

"Hmph." He frowned and pulled my nightgown up to

my knees, exposing my legs. After running his hands over them, he sighed, his eyes meeting mine in surrender. "You're right. I do like it."

I grinned and he leaned forward to kiss me softly. I held his face as we kissed and the firelight glinted off the gems in my wedding ring. "Where did you get this ring? It's so beautiful," I said.

"I'm glad you like it. It belonged to Uncle Alex's mother, Nanny Fraser. My aunt and uncle didn't have any children, so he gave the ring to me. My brother Duncan had Graunie MacRae's ring to give to his bride, but since the Frasers were very wealthy, my ring was worth a great deal more than what Duncan had. I never showed it to him, though. I didn't want him to punch my face in."

"Come on, he wouldn't really."

"Oh, indeed he would. Mam used to call us wild dogs because we were always bloodying each other over something. We had an unspoken rule that we couldn't use our weapons against each other, but anything else was fair game. Mind you, he was a fair bit older than me but I held my own." He barked out a laugh then, his face breaking into a huge smile. "In fact, once I even..." His face flushed red and he turned away, waving his hand in dismissal. "Never mind."

"What? Tell me!"

"It's fair embarrassing. I cannot tell you."

"Please?" I asked in my sweetest tone.

He laughed and shook his head like I was mad. "I don't know what it is about you but you always surprise me. You seem to get pleasure from the oddest things. First my kissing the bird woman at the palace and now this. I'm not sure you're well."

I smacked him on the arm, my face set and determined. "Quit stalling. Come on, out with it."

"All right, all right. I was going to say that we had such a bad brawl one time that I broke his nose." My eyes grew

wide but I kept quiet, waiting for him to elaborate. "I was...
well... how do I say it?" He coughed, steeling himself, and
the words tumbled out of him in a confession.

"I was thirteen years old, out in the field tending the
horses. Eachann, our brown stallion was mating with the grey
mare Arabella. She had her tail in the air and he was pulled
up behind her, his front legs pressed against her sides as he
took her, and I stood there watching them. And to be quite
honest, I was very excited by it. Duncan saw me watching
the horses and said something that I will not repeat to you."
He frowned at me in warning to not push him on it. "I was so
embarrassed that I went after him in a wild rage and didn't
stop until I'd broken his nose and he apologized."

I stifled a giggle, not wanting to hurt his feelings but he
could see the mirth in my eyes. He shook his head, laughing.
"Uncle William took the strap to me awful fierce for what I'd
done. Twenty lashes and my arse was so blistered that I
couldn't ride a horse for a week!" He winced and
dramatically rubbed his backside. "But it was completely
worth it. I'd do it again in a heartbeat. He so deserved it, the
auld bugger."

My giggles broke loose and he joined in, relieved to
have gotten through his story. "Well, I'm glad your uncle
didn't do any lasting damage to your arse," I said, "since I
happen to be rather fond of it." I reached out and pinched
him in demonstration.

"Are ye now?" he asked, laying on the accent thick.
With a wicked gleam in his eye, he leaned me back against
the couch and I promptly forgot what we were talking about.

Chapter 16

In the morning, I sang along with the stereo while making huckleberry pancakes. Aiden came up behind me as I ladled batter into the skillet and put his arms around my waist. We swayed back and forth to the music.

"You've a beautiful voice, *mo chridhe*. I've been meaning to tell you that."

"Thanks," I said. He spun me around and we danced around the kitchen. "Did you know that you sing in your sleep? I've spent a fair amount of time watching you sleep and you'll often hum a song in your dreams."

"No, no one's ever told me that before." I giggled as he twirled me around, then dipped me dramatically at the end of the song. He gestured to a small, framed picture on the wall, one of me when I was about five years old.

"I like that painting of you as a lassie with the pig tails in your hair, holding up the wee fish that you caught, looking so proud. How did the artist make it so clear?"

"It's not a painting, actually. It's called a picture," I said, setting a plate in front of him as he sat at the card table. "It's made with a little square box called a camera. Come to think of it…" I rustled through the drawers in the kitchen. "Aha!" I exclaimed, digging the digital camera out from under a stack of cloth napkins. I sat down on his lap, my cheek pressed close to his and, holding the camera out in front of us, snapped our picture. I switched it to playback mode and handed it to him. "See?"

111

"That's incredible. How do you get it out of the box, then?" He shook the camera up and down.

"No, you have to have it printed on paper. Would you like to see some more?" He nodded, taking a bite of breakfast, and I fetched the old photo album from the living room. He thumbed through it as we ate, then pointed out a photo of me at age two in a pink polka dotted bikini making a sandcastle, my toddler belly sticking out like a round melon.

"My goodness, you were a cute wee bairn with your curly hair short and tight on your head like a bonnet." He turned the page. "Ah, here's one of your parents back when they were younger," he said. Mom and Dad were gazing into each other's eyes, sharing a private smile, obviously unaware that someone was taking their photograph. "Perhaps they weren't always so unhappy together, eh?" I pulled the album around so I could see it better and studied the picture with a frown.

"You're right. They look like they're in love to me," I said and pushed the album away, not willing to examine the feelings that stirred up in me.

"What about your parents?" I asked. "What were they like? I remember your mother from the painting at the château, but I don't know what your father looked like. Do you remember him much at all?"

"Aye, I have a few memories of him before he died." He smiled in remembrance, his eyes far away as he ate, quietly thinking. I was eager to ask him more but decided to wait until he was ready to continue. He took a sip of coffee and then leaned back in the chair with a deep breath, his hands behind his head. "My Da... he was... how do I describe him? Larger than life, I suppose, though I don't know if he really was, or if that's just how I remember him because I was so young when he died. He was tall and strong, but agile like a man half his size. He loved to joke around and people would cross a room to be near him.

"My mam, she was drawn to him like a moth to a flame.

She was gentle and motherly, but easily overwhelmed by us lads. Da kept us in line, but she had a very hard time with us after he died." He grew silent, swept up in thoughts of his family lost long ago. He shrugged, trying to shake it off. "They loved each other something fierce, though. That I knew fine, even as a wee lad. And though I was only six when he died, I learned what it means to love a woman from my Da." He reached out and took my hand, looking down at my wedding band as he rolled it back and forth with his fingers.

"Do you suppose I could meet them?" I asked, knowing it would be difficult for him to see them again, but really wanting to share in his past. He raised his eyebrows in surprise, as if he'd never thought of casting the memory for me.

"Hmph. Aye, I suppose I could take you there to see them. It's a pity they cannot meet you. I think they'd like you very much."

When I leaned across the table to kiss him, his lips were sweet with maple syrup.

"I would love for you to meet them. Still, I must warn you that I don't have many memories to choose from. They may not be so… delicate." His eyes twinkled and I cocked one eyebrow at him, intrigued. He broke into a full belly laugh and set me on my feet, taking my hand as he cast the memory before us.

The warm kitchen melted away in waves and the cold, damp air of Scotland wrapped its fingers around me, making me shiver in my long skirts and heavy woolen cloak. Our breath created translucent puffs in the wintry air and I huddled close to Aiden. He seemed perfectly comfortable in his linen shirt and kilt even though a light dusting of snow covered the ground. His mother stood next to us outside the front of the castle, trying to contain two fidgeting little boys.

"Shhh, lads, they'll be at the gate soon enough," she said. Her plain skirts and overcoat hung on thin shoulders, though she stood a head taller than me. Curly strands of blonde hair snuck out of her bonnet, trickling down over her shoulders. Anxiety lined her face as she attempted to keep the boys in line. Aiden and Duncan pushed and shoved one another, completely undeterred by their mother's admonitions to be quiet. I smiled at their miniature kilts and wavy blond hair, flowing loose over their shoulders.

The sound of horses reached us and I could just make out a small band of men at the far end of the bridge. Aiden's mother released her hold on the boys' shoulders and they took off running across the bridge. Duncan reached the men first and cried out to the big, red-haired man at the head of the group. His father's face broke into a wide smile. He reached down a calloused hand and pulled the boy onto the horse in front of him in one easy motion. He ruffled Duncan's hair and squeezed him with a large forearm until the boy gasped for air. Aiden finally made it to the horses, wheezing out a "Da!," his face filled with pure joy at the arrival of his father.

"Aiden, my boy!" his father called out in a deep, booming voice. He expertly shifted his weight on the horse to reach low enough to pull him up. Aiden crawled over his brother, purposefully stepping on Duncan's hand, I was pretty sure, and latched himself onto his father's back like a monkey.

"Hugh, them's a couple o' wee devils you've got there," said a dark-haired and heavily bearded man in the party.

"Aye, but if they've horns and a tail, they come by it honestly, as I've never been much of an angel myself," Aiden's father responded. "Come to think of it, neither have you, Rory," he continued. "So 'tis a good thing they look like me or I might have cause to wonder, eh?" Hugh raised an eyebrow and grinned at the man, who responded with a good-natured laugh.

Aiden's dad had passed on his wide forehead and defined cheekbones to his sons, though he had a mass of red-gold hair that reminded me of the sun setting over the loch. A green and red kilt hung loose over his legs, the plaid swung up over his shoulder and pinned with a simple gold brooch.

He was heavily armed, carrying a broadsword, dirk, and two pistols, which made me wonder what his expedition had been about. He looked as though he'd been riding for days without rest, but the joy in his eyes at being home with his family was clear. As they drew nearer the castle, I could see the silhouette of Aiden's mother, waiting anxiously for their arrival.

"Ah, Leah," Hugh said under his breath in tones of adoration and desire, as he stared at her thin frame, backlit by the setting sun. Rory brought his horse up alongside him and gestured to Leah with his chin.

"I'll take the horses to the stable. Go on and give my best to your wife."

Hugh thanked him and slid off the horse, pulling Duncan and Aiden with him. He held the boys' hands as they walked the rest of the way to the castle entrance. Leah stood, quivering as she waited, then broke into a run as they drew near. He let go of the boys and scooped her up in a bear hug, kissing her and spinning her around. When he set her down, he pulled the bonnet off and combed his hands through her long blonde curls. "Gracious, I missed you, my bride. I told you not to get more beautiful while I was away, but you didn't listen."

She beamed up at him in delight. "I'm glad you're home, Hugh." He put his arm around her and they walked slowly back to the castle, the two boys running circles around them. When they reached the entrance, she started to open the door, but Hugh shook his head.

"No, love, I think I'll take the wee rascals and go for a dip to wash up before supper."

She protested with a hand on his arm. "I'd be happy to draw you a hot bath. I'll even wash and brush your hair for you, if you like. Shave you, too." She ran her fingertips over the wiry red whiskers on his cheeks. He made a low humming noise in his throat as he pulled her towards him.

"If that's not the most tempting offer I've ever heard, I don't know what is. But I fear I will not stay awake long enough to eat my supper, let alone be any use to you later tonight if I don't take a wee dip now." He waggled his eyebrows and she looked away with a shy smile.

Then, to my surprise, she peeked up at him through her lashes and said, "Aye, then. I've plans for you later, so you'd best keep up your strength." Laughter bubbled up from him, loud and infectious, and he swatted her playfully on the rump as she headed into the castle.

"I've never let you down before, lassie. I don't think I'll start now," he called to her retreating form, then turned his attention to the two young boys at his heels. "All right, lads, let's have a bit of a swim, shall we?"

Duncan and Aiden shrieked with excitement and took off running down the hill to the loch, stripping their clothes off as they went. Hugh laughed heartily as he walked behind them, watching the boys' shirts, kilts and shoes sail through the air. He certainly was larger than life and built like a brick wall: thick barrel chest, timber-like legs and massive arms, with not an ounce of fat anywhere on him.

The two pink, naked boys ran the length of the dock and flew off the end in a joyous splash, though the water must have been freezing. I turned my eyes away while Hugh undressed. Aiden tucked me close against him, his chest shaking with quiet laughter. Hugh's footsteps were barely audible as he ran down the dock, and I looked up just in time to see him cannonball into the lake, sending the boys careening with a giant splash.

"Da! Toss me like a caber!" Duncan shouted.

"Aye, lad, but I'd best start with wee Aiden here, since he's more of a tree branch than a caber. I need to work up to tossing you, since you've grown to be such a man." His eyes crinkled with amusement at Duncan, who swelled with pride at the compliment.

"That's a good idea. Go ahead and toss Aiden first, then."

Little Aiden—apparently not put out by being called the Scottish equivalent of scrawny—eagerly swam over to his father who held out his hands, fingers locked. Aiden scrambled up his body to stand on them, his face aglow with anticipation. He stiffened, arms pinned to his sides and Hugh flung him into the air with a quick thrust, sending Aiden flipping end over end across the lake.

"Good one, Da! Now me!" Duncan called. Hugh swam over to the dock and pulled himself up with ease. Averting my eyes, I faced Aiden who grinned down at me and shrugged.

"Well, I warned ye, did I not?"

When I turned back, Duncan had stepped into Hugh's locked grip, his face serious. He nodded to his father, who squatted briefly and sent Duncan flying with a powerful thrust of his arms. After a 360-degree flip, he landed feet first, his face flushed with pride right before he plunged into the water. Little Aiden let out a whoop of congratulations and Hugh laughed, turning to look at his youngest son, whose lips were turning blue, his skinny shoulders shaking with the chill. Hugh jumped down from the dock and announced that they were finished. Both boys protested loudly but he ignored them as he gathered his clothes and weapons from the shore. Duncan ran past Aiden and gave him a solid thwack on the back of the head when their father wasn't looking. Aiden took off after him, hollering as they collected their clothing from all over the bank.

"What was that for, ye sot?" Aiden asked, rubbing the back of his head as he pulled on his shirt.

"If ye weren't such a wee bairn, we wouldn't have to go back in. I think I'll tell Da that only us men should go next time, since weans such as yourself can't handle the cold." He stuck out his lip in a rude, pouty gesture and Aiden leaped on him with all fours, snarling and swearing like no little kid I'd ever heard before.

Hugh strode up behind them and made that Scottish grunt in his throat, rolling his eyes. He grabbed each of them by the ear, lifting them slightly off the ground so they had to walk on their tiptoes. They immediately stopped struggling, their faces pinched with pain.

"That'll do, lads. 'Tis no wonder your mam can't handle ye wee beasties half the time. You'll find fit to treat each other right or I'll take the strap to your bare arse, understood?" His tone held no malice at all, but it was clearly no idle threat. When the boys whimpered consent, he let go, then pat them on the back as they rubbed their ears.

"Good. Now let's go have some supper, aye? I'm so hungry I could eat my boots," he said, heading into the castle.

As we entered, a blast of warmth enveloped us, the air rich with the scent of freshly baked bread, beer, and roasted meat. The hall teemed with people arranging themselves along the long dining table. A great cheer and raised glasses welcomed Hugh, who responded in Gaelic, obviously comfortable being the center of attention. Leah came up beside him and he kissed her on the cheek.

"Leah, ye should have come out to watch us swim. We were three cocks a bobbin' in the loch. 'Twas like a cock-a-leekie soup made of MacRaes!" A chorus of laughter echoed around the table and she grinned, handing him a stein of ale. He pinched her on the behind when she turned to herd the boys into the kitchen.

At the table, he clapped his neighbor jovially on the shoulder, making some comment that caused the man to roar with laughter. People all around crossed the room in order to be near him and hear the tales of his most recent adventure. I longed to stay and listen myself, but Aiden's memory took us along with his mother into the kitchen.

"Go help your Aunt Margaret dish up the plates, lads," Leah instructed, pushing them towards an older heavy-set woman.

"These two walking sticks the best you could rustle up for me, eh, Leah?" Margaret asked, then drew the boys in for a hug. She held them out at arm's length then, frowning as she inspected them.

"You're not much more than a sack of bones, you wee lads. We'll have to fatten you up if you're ever going to grow up nice and thick like your Da."

"They will at that, Maggie. I don't think my sons will reach the age of twenty before the lassies come clamoring for them, trying to get a ring." Pride rang out in her voice and Margaret nodded, her critical gaze sweeping over the boys.

"They certainly have grown a pinch since my last visit over from France. Next time Hugh goes to one of the clan councils, I want you and the lads to come stay with me and Alex for a spell. I think it would do you good. You're thinner than I've ever seen you," she frowned at her sister, "and I cannot think it does you well to be sitting around wringing your hands and fretting about what might happen to him."

Leah put the boys to work filling plates and handing them to an assortment of teenage girls, who disappeared one after the other into the dining hall. She sidled up to her sister and whispered, "You know very well that there's war brewing with the English. I don't know how long it will be before it affects my family, but I cannot be in France when Hugh goes to battle. My place is here with him and he needs me to stand beside him, no matter what happens."

Margaret sighed and Leah went on, her tone lighter. "Though we did enjoy the visit last year when Alex was so kind as to have my portrait painted with the boys. They looked so bonnie in their wee outfits, no?" She smiled in remembrance and I longed to reach out and touch her. A quiet joy emanated from her, and my heart ached at what the future held for her.

She's beautiful.

Aiden looked down at me upon hearing my thought, his

face solemn. "Aye, that she is. That she is."

Aunt Margaret cut into our moment of reverence, barking orders at a young girl who was moving slowly and not doing her share of the work. "Morag! Are you on holiday, then, lass? Or shall I grab a torch from the wall and light your skirts aflame to make you move your arse?"

Morag's cheeks flamed red as the rest of the kitchen turned to stare at her. "Yes, mistress, I mean no, mistress... I, uh... sorry." She ducked her head and bolted out of the kitchen with a plate in each hand. Margaret surveyed the rest of the workers, her face indicating that she was ready to choose another victim if needed.

"I promised Mrs. Menzies that I'd oversee the meal tonight since she was not feeling well, and I'll not have her dishonored by anyone giving less than their best." A girl came in carrying a heavy tray of dirty dishes and Margaret moved quickly to take it from her. "Thank you, Marion. Well done, lass." She smiled at the girl, who beamed back at her, obviously thrilled at the hard-won praise.

The room swam out of focus briefly and I blinked my eyes as Aiden's memory skipped forward. The dinner over, Leah wiped her brow with the back of her sleeve and gave her sister a tired smile. "I think I'll take the lads up to bed now, Maggie. 'Tis been a long day."

"Just a wee bit longer if you will. They haven't had their French lesson today." She winked at Duncan, who turned to his mother with big, sad eyes.

"Mam, can we, please?" he pleaded.

Leah sighed, unconvinced, and little Aiden piped up, his face identical to his older brother's. "Aye, we need to practice, Mam. Please, can we?"

Outnumbered, she shrugged and ruffled Aiden's hair. "All right, but just for one hour and then straight to bed. No complaining, aye?" The two boys' heads bobbed up and down as they promised to be good and I caught little Aiden's very obvious wink at his aunt when his mother turned away.

"I thought you said you couldn't speak a word of French before you went to Versailles when you were fourteen," I said.

"Aye, that's true. She wasn't a very good French teacher. I never remembered a thing she said by the next day."

Margaret led both boys out of the kitchen, down the hall and up to her room. She pulled a small table away from the wall and into the center of the room, then placed three chairs around it. The boys took their seats as she rifled through a box on the mantle above the fireplace. She gave them a conspiratorial smile as she set a flask of whisky, a pile of buttons and a deck of cards on the table.

"All right, lads, before we start, you'd best learn a bit of French for your mam. Repeat after me: *'Je t'aime.'*" The boys gave it their best shot, imitating her until she was satisfied. "That means 'I love you.' Tell her that when you go to bed tonight, aye?"

She dealt the cards and divided the buttons into three small piles. "You know the rules. A dram of whisky to the winner!"

They played in silence, brows furrowed in concentration. Aiden tossed a handful of buttons into the center of the table. Margaret raised her eyebrows but he didn't blink, his small face stoic. Duncan glared at him, then threw in his own buttons with a challenging smirk. Margaret shook her head and laid her cards down. Hands on her hips, she turned a bemused eye to Aiden.

"Well, lad, you've got stones, I'll give you that. Why, you've bet nearly half your pile! Out with it, then. What have you got?" Aiden fanned out his cards and Duncan cursed, slamming his fist on the table and making the buttons jump. Margaret smacked him upside the head and hissed, "Whisht, lad! You don't want your mam to hear. You'll get us all in trouble."

Duncan rubbed his head and begrudgingly apologized as

Aiden pulled his winnings from the center pile to his side with a wicked grin of satisfaction. He grabbed the flask of whisky and took a slug of it, his face contorting as he tried to hide the effect of the alcohol. Margaret chuckled and patted him on the back.

"You'll grow up to be just like your Da, I can see that right now. Some lassie is going to be very lucky to have you, my wee nephew." Duncan made a grunt of dissent as he gathered the cards up and dealt a fresh hand.

The wave of Aiden's new cast flowed over me and the boys' bedroom materialized out of thin air. Leah sat between the two small beds, reading a book in Gaelic. Duncan and Aiden's eyes drooped in sleep as the sing-song melody of her voice filled the small room. She closed the book and stroked Aiden's hair lovingly, then pulled his covers up and bent to kiss him on the forehead.

"*Je t'aime*, Mam. That means I love you in French," he said dreamily.

"I love you, too, my precious son. Sweet dreams, angel." Her gaze lingered for a moment on his face, then she turned to tuck Duncan in.

The door cracked open and Hugh entered quietly, his tall frame filling the room. He dropped to one knee at Aiden's bedside. "*Oidhche mhath*, my son. Tomorrow, you can help me with the horses, if you like." Aiden grinned at his father, the adoration clear in his eyes. Hugh chuckled, a deep rumbling noise that filled the room, and my heart welled up in my chest.

I turned my face up to Aiden and saw his eyes moist with tears, his expression caught between joy and sorrow. He gave me a crooked smile as a tear spilled onto his cheek. I swept it away with my thumb and he drew me into his arms, his cheek pressed against the top of my head.

Thank you, Lord for the chance to share my memories with Lindsey. I know very well that I don't deserve her, but please don't take her away from me now. She's all I have left.

His desperate prayer filled my head and my chest constricted with longing.

"Aiden, the angel told you that my love would redeem you. So what more do I have to do? I can't possibly love you more than I do right now."

"And I love you, lass," he said with a heavy sigh. "But I cannot go with you. Not yet. I don't understand it either. All we can do is pray." His grip tightened around me and this time when he prayed, I joined in.

Chapter 17

When I opened my eyes, we were back in the kitchen of the
family cabin in Idaho, dressed in normal clothes again. I
kissed Aiden lightly and he released me with a sad smile.
While I cleared the breakfast dishes, I marveled at the ability
to relive memories in such extraordinary detail, like how a
video captures so much more depth than just a picture alone.
Still, we couldn't change the past, so it was a bittersweet
experience.

There was a melancholy tension in the air between us as
Aiden wandered into the living room, muttering to himself
softly in Gaelic. He needed some space, so I occupied myself
with washing the dishes while he built up the fire. I heard
him rustling around in the living room, then the chair at the
dining table made a loud scraping noise on the hardwoods.
As I came around the corner wiping my hands on a
dishtowel, he was shuffling a deck of playing cards.

"Fancy a game, lass? I promise I'll take it easy on you."

He winked at me and I laughed, dropping the towel on
the table and accepting his challenge.

"Don't bother. You aren't the only one who learned to
play cards as a kid, you know," I teased.

"Just when I think I know how you'll respond, you
surprise me. All right then, we'll see how you do." I sat down
across from him as he laid out the rules of the game. "First
things first." He blinked and a flask appeared on the table
along with two small piles of gold buttons. He dealt the

cards, explaining the rules for a game he called "Poque-deux" which turned out to be a version of an old French card game that his aunt had modified to make it easier to play with him and his brother.

Like poker, it involved betting and bluffing to try and intimidate your opponent into giving up before your hand was revealed, as well as an opportunity to draw and discard. The combinations of what constituted high-scoring hands were different than what I was used to, but I caught on quickly. We went through a practice round so I could learn the rules. He patiently explained which cards should be played when. Satisfied that I was sufficiently up to speed, he dealt a fresh hand and I frowned down at my cards, moving them back and forth in my hands as I sorted them.

"Hmmm… let's see," I mumbled to myself as I considered which cards to discard, finally choosing two that I wanted to replace. His face was stoic as he regarded his own hand and made his discard selection. I chewed on my fingernail and sighed, then pushed a good-sized handful of buttons into the center of the table between us for my wager.

"You understand that you only have to bet one button to stay in the game, aye?" he said.

I shrugged and gave him my best devil-may-care smile and he regarded me suspiciously, but matched my wager with his own.

"Well then, let me see what you've got."

I gingerly spread my cards out on the table and asked with wide-eyed innocence, "Three red, two black, ace high. That's something isn't it?" Seeing I'd played him with my air of uncertainty while holding a very high-scoring hand, he let out a full belly laugh and splayed his cards out, shaking his head. He smirked and crossed his arms on his chest as I gleefully drew the pot to my side, giggling.

"That's how it's going to be, is it? Fine, we can play your way. No mercy, aye?"

I grinned wickedly at him and relished the spoils of

victory, taking a deep swig from the flask on the table. The whisky seared my throat, making my eyes water. Warmth spread throughout my chest.

He dealt another hand and said, "You don't have to drink it if you don't want to." Even with just the one gulp, I could already feel the effects of the whisky moving through my system.

"No, it's good. Really. It's just stronger than I was expecting. Besides, I haven't been drinking it since I was four, you know."

"Fair enough. And it's no matter"—he shot me a challenging look—"since that's the only one you'll get tonight. I hope you enjoyed it."

I gaped open-mouthed at his jibe and laughed, loving the smack talk. "Oh, bring it on. We'll just see who gets drunk under the table tonight."

He made his Scottish harrumph but a smile played across his lips before he picked up his cards and his face became completely unreadable. True to his word, all bets were off and he cleaned my clock several hands in a row after that. He took each winning swig with a satisfied grin as I playfully glared at him, enjoying the fuzzy sensation in my head as well as the competitive tension between us.

The alcohol didn't seem to affect him at all, though he'd had quite a bit of it. The room was getting quite warm from the fire and I was getting very warm myself for different reasons. Firelight danced off the streaks in his wavy blond hair and I licked my lips, thinking about how gorgeous he was. He dealt the next round and watched me while I picked up my cards. Surprisingly, I'd been dealt a most excellent hand but had only one button left in my pile.

Inspiration struck and I whispered to him in a sultry tone, "How about we go all or nothing this hand?"

"That's not a very convincing proposition coming from a woman with just one wee button left to wager. Why would I want to do that?" He cocked an eyebrow at me in challenge and I locked him with my gaze.

"I have some more buttons to throw in." My hands went to the front of my blouse and I slowly undid the top three buttons of my white eyelet lace shirt, my eyes never moving from his. He made a low, rumbling sound in his throat as he watched, obviously accepting my challenge.

"If I win, I get the rest of the whisky," I said firmly. I felt a shimmer pass over me and he gestured to the flask with his chin.

"There, now it's full again. And if you lose?"

I could feel the blush of desire creeping down my neck and across my chest. "You get the rest of the buttons." The heat from his stare was stronger than the fire as he pushed the entire pile of buttons into the center of the table.

"Ah, you make me an offer I cannot refuse, no matter what the stakes."

I grinned at him triumphantly, thrilled at the power to rouse him and feeling quite excited myself, not sure whether I wanted to win or lose. A log from the fire shifted, sending sparks onto the hardwood floor and making a hissing, popping noise but otherwise the room was completely silent. Tension crackled between us.

"I'm ready whenever you are," he said.

He quirked his mouth and glanced down at my cards by way of explanation but the double entendre was not lost on me. I fanned my cards out on the table and he let out a sigh of surrender as he revealed his losing hand. After feeling his penetrating gaze, I was a little sorry to have won, thinking about his hands on my skin as he collected his payment. Still, I smiled victoriously and took a long drink from the flask, this time enjoying the peppery taste as the whisky flowed down my throat.

I'd watched him take shot after shot from the flask as he won each prior hand, and not to be outdone, I tossed back another hefty swig myself. The effect of the alcohol in my blood was building quickly and my vision begun to blur. His face showed concern mixed with amusement, the corner of his mouth twitching in a secret smile.

"Whoa, lassie. You don't want to drink it all at once or you may not be able to stand up."

Just to prove a point, I took another swallow and walked around the table, my head swimming and my heart hammering in my chest. "Hey, I'm the winner here and I'll do as I please," I said belligerently.

He raised his eyebrows at me but said nothing, one arm coming around my waist to steady me in case I needed it. I brushed it away haughtily and threw one leg over his lap, grabbing his linen shirt in my fist. I pulled him to me fiercely, my mouth insistent and demanding, and his arms closed tight around me. I held onto his hair with my free hand and jerked his head to the side as we kissed madly. He ran his hands up my bare legs to the hem of my shorts, then over my hips, his fingers digging into my flesh. A drunken lust pulsed through me. Pulling away from his kiss, I gasped for air in the stifling heat of the room.

"I need to cool off. I feel like I'm on fire," I said. My legs were a little shaky as I stood up and he reached out to help me.

"Lindsey, we really—" he started to say but I cut him off.

"Ooh, I have an idea. Let's take a shower together!" I ran my fingers down his chest and proceeded to tell him in explicit terms exactly what I intended to do to him once we got there. He stiffened at hearing my suggestive words, a war of excitement versus propriety taking place in his eyes. He grabbed my wrist and pulled me over to the couch.

"That sounds delicious, don't get me wrong, but I think maybe you'd best sit down instead." He lifted me onto his lap and encircled me in his arms. His chest shook with silent amusement beneath me.

What's so funny?

He broke into a wide grin but then looked down

sheepishly. "I probably should have told you before, but I was enjoying it too much to want to stop you." His eyes danced with mirth and I shook my head in confusion, suddenly impatient with whatever secret he was keeping.

"Told me what, Aiden MacRae?"

"It's nothing, really. I just… well, you don't feel the effects of the whisky here unless you want to. You're not really drunk; you just think that you are. It's all in your head."

Now I was really irritated and I scrambled off his lap, frowning with indignation. He reached out and grabbed my hand, not letting go though it was clear I wanted him to.

"That's not true! It's just that you've been drinking since you were practically a baby, for crying out loud. I'm not even twenty-one yet so it's no big surprise that your crazy strong Scotch would make me loopy! Don't make fun of me!"

I yanked my hand out of his grasp and folded my arms across my chest. Defensive anger bubbled up in me. His voice was quiet but clear, though I wouldn't look at him.

"I'm sorry, Lindsey. I didn't mean to make fun of you. And you're right, I should have told you instead of letting you go on. I was just enjoying seeing you so relaxed and confident that I didn't want it to stop. Of course, I let it go a little far when you started talking like a French whore…"

My head snapped around.

"What?! Oh no you didn't just…" I leapt off the couch in a rage. "I can't believe you just called me a whore!" I spat.

"Sit down, Lindsey."

"I am not a whore! You of all people should know that."

He made a big production of sighing and shaking his head like I was a child throwing a tantrum. And at that moment, I felt like throwing a tantrum, childish or not.

"I didn't say you were a whore, just that you were talking like one. There's a difference."

"You're damn right there's a difference," I responded with a huff. I wanted to say something sarcastic and biting, but I couldn't think of anything, so I just stood there, seething.

"Please, I didn't mean it the way it sounded. Sit down," he said.

I fought with myself about giving in, but finally plopped down next to him, my arms locked in defiance. Finally, I narrowed my eyes at him in a deathly challenge, my voice steely. "Fine. But what about you, huh? You say that I'm talking trash, but you can't tell me you didn't enjoy it. I saw the look on your face before you got all high and mighty. You wanted me."

His face softened and his eyes held mine, though no words passed between us. Reaching out, he brushed his finger down my cheek. I jerked a bit but held firm. He bent his head forward slowly and lightly touched his lips to mine. I sat stiffly next to him, though my traitor heart thumped loudly in my chest at his soft mouth's gentle caress. Still, my mother used to call me as stubborn as a mule and I did not give in, my back stick straight, feeling that I had let my guard down with him and that he'd hurt me for it.

He suddenly shifted away from me, his hands dropping into his lap. For as much as I'd struggled to maintain my angry distance, I felt very cold and empty when he broke contact.

"I'm sorry," he said to the fire, which popped and hissed in response. We sat there in silence for a time as I tried to calm down and think of the right thing to say. When I did finally speak, it came out in a hoarse croak.

"I trusted you, Aiden. I only said those things because I knew that I was safe with you. Was I wrong?" His eyes met mine, his face etched with regret.

"No. I was wrong." He gingerly reached out his hand between us and I took it, feeling torn between pride and reconciliation. "You will always be safe with me, *mo chridhe*, and I should not have teased you." His sincerity broke through my thin veneer of bravado and I nodded. He gathered me into his arms once more and spoke softly in French as I melted into him.

"And yes, to be honest, I did enjoy it. You're a sexy wench." His eyes lit with a hint of a smile and I couldn't help it, a giggle escaped me. I smacked him on the arm and his smile blossomed into a full-blown grin, then we both began to laugh. He brushed a stray curl away from my face and pulled me higher on his lap so he could easily look at me.

"Truth be told, I love the way that you surprise me, the way you respond like no other woman I've ever met. You are sweet and tender and caring, but at the same time, you're feisty and daring and wild, and God help me, a wee bit nasty too. You make my blood boil in my veins when I hold you in my arms, and I cannot touch you enough to make the wanting go away. You are everything I could ever want in a woman and I love you with all my heart, Lindsey MacRae."

Hearing him say my new name sobered me and my heart skipped a beat in response. "I love you, too." This time I moved forward for the kiss, sealing tight the gap that had threatened to begin between us. He kissed me back, holding me close like he'd almost lost something precious.

We sat together on the couch, kissing and holding one another for a while. I leaned my head against his shoulder with a sigh and we watched the flames in the fireplace, their orange tongues flickering over the logs and thin wisps of smoke disappearing up the chimney. It was hypnotic and soothing, the peacefulness of the room settling over me like a soft blanket. We sat in silence for so long that Aiden's voice seemed loud in the room when he spoke.

"I've been meaning to ask you. What's that forked metal rod for?"

I followed his eyes to the woodpile next to the fireplace and the object in question propped up against the wall behind the pile.

"Oh, it's for roasting weenies and marshmallows in the fire." He stared at me blankly. "Weenies, wieners, you know, hot dogs?" He shook his head and I thought for a moment. "Sausages?"

Understanding lit up his face and he nodded with a smile. "Aye, but what was the other thing you said? Marsh something?"

"Marshmallows. I'll grab some and you can try them. You use them to make s'mores with graham crackers and chocolate." I collected the supplies out of the kitchen and handed him the bag of marshmallows. He pulled one out and squished it curiously between his fingers.

"You mean to tell me you eat this?"

"Yeah, they're yummy, especially when you cook them over the fire. But first you have to get your s'more ready so you can drop the hot marshmallow on the chocolate as soon as it comes out of the fire." I pulled out a graham cracker and broke it in half, then placed a square of chocolate on top. He stared at the chocolate, picking up the rest of the candy bar in fascination. "Didn't you have chocolate in your day?" I asked, horrified at the thought of living in a time without chocolate. He nodded, holding the candy like it was a bar of gold.

"We did, but it was very expensive, so I've only tasted it once before."

"Well, no wonder you guys were always trying to kill each other. Life is hardly worth living without chocolate," I said. He broke off a little piece and placed it in his mouth.

"Mmmm... maybe you have a point there."

I laughed and stuck two marshmallows on the roasting fork, then handed it to him, explaining how to hold it over the flames just right so that the outside turned a golden brown. He pulled a footstool over to the fire and gave it a try, but got the fork too close to the flames. In the blink of an eye, the soft white mounds turned into miniature fireballs. He jerked back reflexively, causing one marshmallow to slide off into the fire and the other to go flying like a meteor across the living room.

"It's all right, I've done that many times. Don't worry about it. We have lots more."

Frowning, he pulled two new marshmallows out of the bag and poked them onto the fork. I could hardly keep from grinning but I didn't want to hurt his feelings, so I worked on preparing another s'more. He made that familiar harrumph in his throat and stuck the fork over the fire, determination written on his face. He kept the marshmallows high over the flames this time, patiently turning them until they started to bubble.

"Those look beautiful," I said. "Here, I'll show you how to take them off. They're sticky and hot on the inside, so you don't want to touch them or you'll burn yourself."

He held the fork out to me and I encased one of the marshmallows with the graham crackers and chocolate, squeezing it between the crackers and sliding it off the rod. With pride, I held up the oozing finished product and he followed my example, extracting the other marshmallow onto the s'more with ease.

"Give it a second to melt the chocolate and then you can bite into it. Careful though, it'll be hot." He nodded seriously, like this was some sort of initiation rite, and I giggled, thinking of how I'd been eating s'mores since I was old enough to walk. After a pause, he gingerly bit into the treat, the gooey marshmallow sticking to his lips as he chewed it. He broke into a wide smile as he finished and my heart leapt in my chest, thrilled to get to share in his first taste.

"It's thick though," I said, "so we need something to wash it down with. I'll get some milk." I leaned forward and planted a sticky kiss on his lips, enjoying the way we stuck together slightly as I pulled away.

He reached up and stroked my cheek before I headed into the kitchen, wiping the crumbs from my hands and humming happily to myself. I could hear him digging into the marshmallow bag to reload the fork as I reached for the metal refrigerator handle.

An electric shock passed through my arm when I touched the handle and I jerked back, staring at the refrigerator in confusion. Cautiously, I reached out to touch it again and nothing happened, so I opened the door and pulled out the milk, frowning.

That's weird. I didn't realize we'd have static buildup here. I thought to myself, but shook it off as I poured two glasses of milk and put the jug back in the fridge. I turned back toward the living room to see Aiden setting up two sets of graham crackers with chocolate for our next round.

"Aiden, the strangest thing just happ—"

I broke off mid-sentence as a fresh wave of electricity ripped across my chest like a lightning bolt. My whole body spasmed with the shock and the glasses I'd been holding dropped to the floor and shattered, spraying milk everywhere.

Aiden's head jerked up and his eyes widened in horror. He leapt up off the couch and ran to me with his arms outstretched, yelling, "No!" But he was so far away. The distance between us seemed to stretch out like saltwater taffy as I reached for him, confused and afraid.

"Help!" I cried, but the words did not leave my lips.

Lindsey, no!

His panicked voice filled my head as my vision blurred and he melted away. Another jolt wracked my body and I clamped my eyes shut in pain. Blackness swirled around me and an icy chill engulfed my body as I fell, flinging my arms and legs wildly in an attempt to grab onto something. Mind-bending fear consumed me and I felt as if I were being pulled inside out and torn limb from limb all at the same time. I slammed down into something hard, like hitting the pavement after a fall from a tall building, and went limp, my body racked with excruciating pain and my mind unable to contain it.

"She's alive!" an unfamiliar voice said and I struggled to breathe, a heavy weight pushing down on my chest, then releasing as a flood of fire filled my lungs.

Aiden, where are you?

I reached out to him in my mind with my last coherent thought before I succumbed to the icy blackness.

Chapter 18

"She's waking up! Honey, can you hear me?"

My mother's worried voice called to me through the fog. I cracked open one eye, the brightness in the room making me immediately shut it again. A wave of nausea hit me, rolling and heaving. A hand gently pressed on my shoulder until the dizziness passed. I lay there trying to steady my breathing and get a grasp of what was happening. My throat burned as I tried to call out to my mom.

"Shhh, don't try to speak, honey. The doctor said you would have a really sore throat from the tube, but now that it's out, you should feel better soon."

Did she say a tube? Doctor? What is going on?

Confused and anxious, I peeked out of the one eye again, the other one not functional for some reason. My mother's anxious face swam in and out of focus. Slowly, the blurred edges of her face became clear and she smiled at me, stroking my forehead like she used to do when I was a little girl.

"Mommy's here, Lindsey-belle. Don't you worry, sweetheart."

Soothed by her voice, I breathed a deep sigh and closed my eye, settling into the mattress. The fog was a powerful force drawing me back down and I tried to shake my head to clear it, which was a terrible mistake. Another crashing wave of nausea rolled over me and I jerked to one side as my stomach wrenched and my throat constricted with a dry heave. Pain racked my chest and I lay back, panting, tears rolling down my cheeks.

"Where the hell is that nurse?" Mom said. A woman's unfamiliar voice piped up, bright and cheery.

"Ah, you're awake sweetheart! That's wonderful. Lindsey, I'm Sharon, your nurse. Be a good girl and give me a squeeze if you can hear me, okay?" A warm, soft hand gripped mine and I did my best to respond as instructed. "Good, good. I understand you're feeling a little nauseous which is completely normal, so I'm going to add some anti-nausea medicine to your drip. You'll be feeling better in no time, so just hang tight, kiddo."

My drip? What is she talking about?

My mind couldn't take it all in and the insistent fog closed around me, cutting me off from any cohesive thought.

"Lindsey, are you there, baby?" My mother called to me from far away before the blackness descended completely.

~

Faint twinkling notes of music grew stronger as I woke and I followed along with the familiar melody in my mind. My father mumbled, his words incoherent but insistent, repeating something I couldn't quite hear.

Why is he here? Dad never wakes me up.

"Lindsey, pumpkin, can you hear me? I'm so sorry I wasn't here before when you woke up. I love you, baby." His deep voice was stricken and my heart reached out to him, not knowing what was wrong but wanting to comfort him.

"Dad..." My voice was little more than a hoarse whisper but I heard his sharp intake of breath.

"Lindsey! Oh honey, you're awake!"

Knives raked my throat as I tried to swallow and I croaked out "water." His chair squeaked on the floor next to me.

"Right, I'll go find the nurse and get you some water. Stay right here," he said, his voice giddy and frantic.

Stay right here? I don't even know where 'here' is.

I blinked with one eye and stared up at the ceiling, absently tracing the little dots on the sterile, white tile while my mind grappled with the limited information I had.

He said 'nurse.' Mom said 'doctor.' Am I in the hospital?

With great effort, I slowly turned my head, taking in the plastic sea foam green couch under the window. Light from the lamp in the corner reflected on the glass in the dimly lit room so that I got a view of myself in the hospital bed, brown curls splayed against a stark white pillow, IV bag on a silver stand, tubes running everywhere.

Shaking, I propped myself up to get a better view. I wanted to see. I needed to see. My reflection stared back at me in horror, one eye completely swollen shut, my lip swollen twice the normal size on one side. I looked as though I had been beaten with a baseball bat, my face covered with bruises. A tube ran from my right breast into a container on the floor and gauze encircled my right arm. My fat lip began to quiver and my eyes swam with tears.

Did someone assault me?

I struggled to remember what had happened, but I was at a complete loss. I couldn't tear my gaze away from the sight of my battered face, like driving past the scene of a terrible accident.

Accident?

Something bubbled up as that word came to mind and I tried desperately to figure out why. My scattered thoughts were interrupted though, as the nurse entered the room, followed close behind by my father. She was short and round with a curly bob of burgundy red hair and bright lipstick to match.

"Oh, honey, you need to lie down," she said. "You can't be getting up now. That's it, that's better." I didn't have the strength to argue with her as she swiftly settled me back onto the mattress. My muscles relaxed into the bed and I had to admit she was right.

"Your dad said you asked for water. I brought you some ice chips, sweetie. You can't have water because we don't want you throwing up, but the ice chips will make your throat feel better. Open up now. That's a good girl." She tugged lightly at my swollen lip and I winced in pain. "Oh, sorry, honey. I know that's still tender. Just need to open up a little bit." I dropped my jaw slightly and she placed the cool sliver of ice on my tongue. It was heavenly and gone far too quickly. "Here you go, Dad," she said. "You can keep feeding them to her while I take her vitals."

She proceeded to putz around me, pulling on things and talking to herself while Dad placed one ice chip after another on my tongue, his face piqued with worry.

"What happened?" I asked, my voice hardly recognizable. His eyes darted frantically to the nurse for help. She encouraged him with a nod.

"Do you remember anything, pumpkin?" he asked.

I closed my eyes and shook my head, just enough so he could see. He let out a long sigh and took my hand in his own. Fear started to build in my chest.

"Well, sweetie, you were in a really bad car accident. The doctors didn't know if you would live. You fractured several ribs and had a collapsed lung—" he broke off, his voice wavering, "—and you almost bled to death because of the gash in your arm." Anxiety spiked in the pit of my stomach at his description of the damage. He squeezed my hand for reassurance. "You were really lucky, honey. We thought we were going to lose you. I don't know what I would have done if..."

A tear rolled down his cheek and he looked away, unable to contain the emotion. He rubbed his face with his other hand and took a deep breath, then turned back to me with a forced smile. "But the surgeon was amazing, baby, and you're going to be fine. You're going to be just fine." His smile became more genuine as he talked himself into this diagnosis, and I wondered how much of it was true.

A car accident.

I lie there silently, trying to remember. A mental image came to me: rain and streaks of light shining through droplets of water with dark trees beyond. I felt strangely detached though, like I was looking from the outside in. None of it made any sense and I closed my one eye, relaxing into the pillow.

"I don't remember." I sighed, frustrated at this gap in time but Dad squeezed my hand and his voice took on a more cheerful tone.

"That's okay, pumpkin. It's probably better that way anyway. Just try to get some rest. Do you want some more ice?" I declined and Nurse Sharon touched me on the shoulder.

"Lindsey, I need you to tell me how much pain you're feeling," she said. "What would you rate it on a scale of one to ten—one being a little cut and ten being you slammed your fingers in the car door?" My dad made a horrified gasp and she realized her faux pas at the same time. "I'm sorry, that's the example I always use and I just didn't think about it. I'm really sorry." My dad muttered something unflattering under his breath and Sharon turned back to me, determined to get her answer. "Sorry, honey. One to ten? How much pain are you in?"

I took stock of my body for the first time and while everything was stiff and I did have shooting pains when I tried to move, nothing really hurt too much at that moment.

I must be pretty heavily drugged, then.

"I don't know. Two, maybe three. It really only hurts when I move."

She nodded like she'd expected as much and tucked my blankets around me. "Sure, sure. We'll keep you at the same level then. Just try not to move around, but you do need to take deep breaths as often as you can to help heal that lung. If you need anything, you just push the red button on the side of the bed." She pointed out the button with a big, toothy smile and padded off quickly, not meeting my dad's eyes.

"Stupid nurse," Dad muttered. "Did she upset you, sweetheart?"

"No, I'm all right, Dad. Just a little tired." In fact, I was exhausted and could barely stay focused, the pull of oblivion beckoning once again.

"That's fine, Linds. Go back to sleep. I'll be here if you wake up and need anything. I love you, baby." He kissed my fingertips, then tucked my hand next to my side. I closed my good eye and blissfully sank into nothingness.

~

When morning came, I woke with stiff muscles from lying flat for so long. I tried to sit up and got no more than a few inches off the mattress before the pain in my chest forced me to lie back again, breathing hard. My stomach rumbled and I reached out to press the call button on the side of the bed, but stopped when I heard voices in the hall.

"The doctor said it was all right for me to see her. Please?" a lilting Indian voice whispered on the other side of the door.

Nurse Sharon responded begrudgingly, "Well, I guess it will be fine. Just don't upset her. She needs to lay still or she could do more damage."

The door opened and my visitor hobbled over to me on crutches, one leg wrapped in a cast from thigh to ankle. Our eyes met and he stared at me, relief and shock etched on his face.

Ravi.

My hand flew to my mouth at his battered appearance. His face didn't look much better than mine, bruised and swollen with several stitches along his forehead, the black ends of the suture poking out either end of what looked like a deep gash. Seeing him brought back shards of memories from that night, the feel of his kiss and hearing him say, "I love you." Then somehow the next thing I remember was seeing him in the crumpled car saying, "No, leave me. Help Lindsey."

Again, the vision was from the outside of the car and I couldn't understand how that could be, but I had a very clear image of his bloodied face and I shuddered with the memory. He attempted a smile that ended up looking completely pathetic and I laughed, my voice soft and hoarse.

"You look like hell," I teased and he returned my laughter, his face breaking into a real smile.

"I was just thinking the same thing about you," he replied. He stood next to my bed and we smiled at one another for a moment, not sure what to say next. Finally, my curiosity got the best of me.

"Do you remember anything?" I asked. He shook his head and I recognized that same sense of frustration that I'd felt earlier. He took my hand, shifting so he could stay upright on his crutches.

"They told me you almost died. It's all my fault, Lindsey. I'm so sorry." The guilt and pain in his eyes broke my heart.

"It's not your fault. It was an accident."

His face creased in a frown and he shook his head, unable to accept my forgiveness. I didn't know what to say to help him so I just lie there, holding his hand.

"I had to see you. They didn't want me to because they thought it might upset you, but I had to see with my own eyes that you were okay."

"I'll be all right. I'm glad you came." I tried to smile and was rewarded with a small sigh of acceptance. He pressed my fingers to his lips and hesitated, then smiled with decision.

"I have good news. My mother flew here from India when she got the call about the accident."

My good eye flew open wide. "Your mother is here?"

"Yes, she got here last night," he said with a mischievous grin. "And I told her about us." Startled, I instinctively jerked forward. Agonizing jolts of pain shot across my chest. Ravi panicked and nearly fell, unable to bend his leg at all.

"Lindsey, don't do that! You have to lie still!" He struggled to pull himself up straight with one hand on my bed rails. I lay motionless for a moment, panting and concentrating on the ceiling tiles until the pain subsided.

"Yes, I told her about you, that I love you and I don't care that you're not Indian."

"What did she say?" I asked, unease twisting in my gut.

"Well, what could she say, really? Here I am lying in hospital, bandaged and bruised. It's not like she could say no." My mind rebelled at this open declaration of his feelings, but I wasn't really sure why it bothered me so much. "Do you want me to introduce you to her?" he asked hopefully and I shook my head as vehemently as I dared, desperately trying to think of some excuse to avoid meeting his mother.

"No, I... I don't want her to see me this way. Please?"

"Okay, then. Maybe not just now." He hopped up closer to my head and leaned awkwardly over the bed rails to kiss me. Something in me was very uncomfortable with this intimacy and I stiffened a little at his touch.

Maybe I do blame him for the accident after all.

It was the only logical explanation I could come up with, but it made me feel very cold and shallow, so I pushed away the thought.

"Before you came in, I was going to ask the nurse to bring me some food. I don't think I've eaten anything at all since before the accident." He studied me for a moment and then apparently decided against what he was going to say. He nodded and picked up his other crutch, hopping a little toward the end of the bed as he did.

"Sure, I'll let her know you're hungry. I should probably

go anyway and let you get some rest." He smiled and clumsily rounded the corner of the bed, trying to move sideways on his crutches. He stopped at my feet and turned back to me, his face asking a question I was not willing to answer.

"I'm sorry," he said. "I swear I'll make it up to you. I don't know how, but I will." He didn't look at me again, but limped his way out of the room on his crutches. My heart ached, watching him go. I pushed the call button and the nurse came bustling in.

"Hey there, sweetie. Your boyfriend told me you're ready to eat something." Sharon smiled her toothy grin at me, picking up my chart. I irrationally bristled inside at the use of the term 'boyfriend' and shook my head.

"No, I just want to rest. The pain is getting worse. Can you give me something to help me sleep?" Sharon looked at me critically but nodded.

"Sure, sure, honey. I'll crank it up a bit and you should be feeling better in no time. Remember what I said before about taking deep breaths now."

After I promised to carry out the torturous exercise as often as possible, she patted my foot and left me alone with my thoughts. I dreamt of a beautiful meadow with wildflowers waving in the breeze and a sparkling blue stream of water. I knelt down beside the cool water and scooped up a handful. The soothing effects ran through my body, filling me and strengthening me. I smiled and stirred in my sleep then grimaced as a pain in my side jarred me awake.

My dad slept curled up on that tiny, uncomfortable couch under the window and I watched him sleep for a while. His light snoring joined in with the ticking mechanical noises from my monitors and the steady drip from my IV, comprising an oddly comforting cacophony of loving care that warmed me. Here he was sleeping on that God-awful excuse for a couch just so I wouldn't wake up alone in the middle of the night.

Dad.

The memory of our trip to the Space Needle years ago filled my mind and I smiled, remembering that sweet moment walking hand in hand, more vivid now for some reason. He grunted in his sleep and tried to shift into a more comfortable position, but eventually gave up and sank back into a gentle snore. I decided to do my breathing exercises and winced at the pain, but reminded myself of the sacrifice Dad was making for me and suffered through it. Exhausted, I settled into my pillow and joined him in sleep. When I woke in the morning, he was sitting at my bedside.

"Good morning, pumpkin. I'm glad you got some good rest last night." He obviously had not. Disheveled and unshaven with dark circles under his eyes, he gave me a tired smile.

"Thanks, Dad. I'm sorry you have to sleep on that miserable couch. Couldn't you get a hotel or something? You don't have to stay here."

"No, no, it's fine. I'd rather be with you than anywhere else." He patted my hand. "Hey, would you like some breakfast? The nurse told me you can eat a little something now. You must be starving." My stomach growled just then, answering for me and he jumped up, thankful to have a purpose. "I'll take that as a yes."

A warm feeling settled over me as I watched him go. Ever since the divorce, things had been strained between us and it felt good to have that melt away, to be close to him again. He returned shortly, carrying a tray of jello, ice cream and chicken broth.

"I know it isn't 'taties and eggs' but it's all they'd let me give you since you haven't eaten anything for a while. They don't want you throwing up."

I had a brief flash of the family cabin when he said that, but my thought was interrupted as he swung over a mobile cart and proceeded to open all the little containers of food. As much as I hated to admit it, even this pitiful breakfast looked appetizing and I downed the small bowl of chicken broth. It didn't take much before my stomach revolted and I grimaced, wishing I'd taken it a little slower.

"I shouldn't have let you eat that so fast," he said. He swung the mobile cart away from me as if to prevent me from gorging myself on the rest of the items.

"Sorry, it just felt so good to eat again. You know how I love to eat." I attempted a wink, which was more like a blink since I only had one good eye. He tried to maintain a serious face, but couldn't do it and we both started to laugh.

"Knock, knock. Is Lindsey in here?" came a loud whisper from the door. Dad beckoned the visitor to enter and I grinned as Stephanie pulled away the curtain. Her eyes shone with concern behind her round, white-rimmed glasses. My other roommate Jennifer came in close behind her, her cheeks rosy from the cold outside. They carried a bouquet of balloons and a teddy bear that held a plush red heart reading "Get Well Soon."

"Oh good, you're awake! We came by once before but you were sleeping," Stephanie said.

"Yeah, I've been doing that a lot. I guess I need all the beauty rest I can get."

Jen murmured "definitely" but Stephanie frowned, shaking her head as she looked me over critically. "Actually, you look much better than you did before. Your bruises are fading and the swelling has gone down quite a bit on that one eye."

"Well, I guess it's working then, huh?" I answered a barrage of questions about how I felt, what hurt, and what I remembered from the accident. The girls shed their coats and Dad excused himself, leaving them room to sit on the sea foam green couch across from me.

"I'm going to take a shower in your bathroom, Linds, if you don't mind." He left, pulling the room's privacy curtain closed behind him.

"Did your dad tell you the college has decided to give

you and Ravi all A's on your finals, since you couldn't take them?" Jennifer asked.

"Wow, finals, I had totally forgotten about that. Well, I guess there's always a silver lining, huh?"

She laughed and I thought to myself how beautiful she was, but for the first time, I didn't feel that familiar pang of jealousy. She was beautiful, sure, but somehow it didn't bother me now like it did before.

Stephanie broke into my thoughts. "What are you going to do about Christmas? Will you still be in the hospital or will they let you out before then?"

Oh, that's right. If finals are over now, then Christmas break would be...

"What day is it today?" I asked her. "What day was the accident? I don't even know."

"Today is December 20th. The accident was on the 15th." My eyes widened in disbelief that I had basically lost five days, give or take, in my drug-induced state.

Jen piped in, "Yeah, actually we're headed home tomorrow. We were going to leave today but we wanted to try and see you again before we left. We'll be back for January term, though, so we'll see you again soon."

"Oh crap, I was going to take French history during Jan term. Well, at least this won't screw up spring semester. I should be better by then." Jennifer and Stephanie nodded actively, trying to cheer me up, but an awkward lull crept into the conversation. Steph arranged the balloon bouquet, then turned to me as if just remembering something.

"Oh, I meant to tell you, the orchestra concert went really well. My violin solo was perfect and the whole audience applauded when I was done." She beamed at me, not bragging but simply sharing in the joy of her accomplishment. I pouted at her and told her how much I'd really been looking forward to hearing her play. "Well, there's always the concert in the spring. You can come to that one, provided you don't go getting yourself killed again," she said.

Jen gasped and at the same time, Stephanie realized what she'd said. Jen smacked her on the arm and Stephanie winced, her eyes instantly filled with remorse. "I'm sorry, that's not what I meant. I just meant… never mind, I'm being stupid. I'll shut up now." I chuckled, amused that they were so worried about my mental state.

"It's no big deal. Still, I really did want to hear you play. I don't suppose you'd be willing to bring your violin to the hospital and play it for me, would you?"

"You'd really want me to do that? You're so sweet!" I could see the wheels start turning in her head as she worked out how to get to her violin and back to the hospital before having to leave tomorrow. "We'd better go then, if I'm going to have enough time to get back here to play for you later tonight."

The hugs goodbye were awkward, as they were unsure of where to touch me without hurting me. They left just as Dad came out of the bathroom, drying his hair with a towel. "They seemed nice. Are they your roommates?" he asked, freshly shaven and smelling of soap.

I nodded and settled back against my pillow, doing my breathing exercises and scrunching my face with the effort. "I think I'm going to take a nap. Can you close the shades?" He did, and I closed my eyes with a smile, grateful to have good friends.

Chapter 19

Fragmented images taunted me as I moaned and shifted in my bed: beautiful misty landscapes transformed into flaming, smoking battle scenes, a beggar reaching out to me, his eyes sunk deep in their sockets.

A warm hand smoothed my creased brow.

"Hey, sweetie, are you having a bad dream?" My mother's voice sounded worried and I wriggled against my stiff bed, trying to shake off the disturbing images. She chuckled at my scowl and tucked a strand of hair behind my ear. "I can't count the number of times I've come to wake you up for school and you've worn that same grouchy expression. I don't know if it's because you have bad dreams, or if you have really good dreams that you don't want to wake up from." With her long blonde hair pulled back in a ponytail, she looked younger than I remembered. I heard a soft chuckle from behind her and craned my neck to see whose it was.

Nick.

Dressed in a dark blue suit like he'd just come from a board meeting, he smoothed back his black wavy hair with one hand. My mother shot a glance over her shoulder at him, her eyes smiling in a flirty, playful way. The sight of her in a black evening gown talking with Nick, tossing her hair over her shoulder and stroking her cleavage suddenly filled my mind. I clenched my teeth, irrationally upset.

"What is he doing here?" I hissed at her, and she

whipped around to gawk at me.

"He came to see you, honey." Her voice was even but her eyes held a warning, telling me in no uncertain terms that I was to play nice. I glared at her and Nick shifted uncomfortably, looking out the window.

"Elizabeth, I have a couple of errands to run in town. I think I'll leave you two alone for a while. I'll pick you up at eight, all right?" She started to protest but he gave her a look that cut her off. "Goodbye, Lindsey. I am glad to see you are feeling better." He nodded to me and then left.

"What the hell was that all about? I can't believe how rude you were to him just now, Lindsey Marie!" Her eyes demanded an answer and pinned to the bed, I had nowhere to hide.

"I don't know. I'm sorry. I just…" I struggled to think of how to put it without making matters worse, that awful image of my mother's bedroom eyes burning in my brain. "I guess I just didn't expect to see him here, so I wasn't prepared for it. Look, I said I'm sorry."

She studied me with narrowed eyes and pursed lips, apparently trying to decide whether or not to let me off the hook. She sighed and shook her head. "It's all right. You're not really yourself right now. I probably should've warned you before just springing him on you like that, so I'm sorry, too." I was relieved, thinking the issue closed, but she continued on. "Still, you're going to have to learn to get used to him, since you're going to have to come stay with us for a while."

I jerked upright and winced. "What? No! Why?"

"Well, you'll be out of the hospital in another week or so but the doctor told us you'll need care around the clock until you're healed. He said it would take about six weeks altogether, so you'll have to come live with us until spring semester starts."

"But I don't want to live with you and Nick in Bellevue. I want to stay here with my friends. That's part of why I decided to go to college in Oregon, to have some space." I sounded like a whiny child, but I honestly couldn't bear the thought of being around the two of them, seeing his arm around her, watching him kiss her.

"Honey, I know you want to stay here with your friends and I wish you could, but there's no one else to take care of you. Your dad can't do it because he's working full-time and you know your friends have better things to do than help you bathe and get dressed." Tears welled up in my eyes and I racked my brain for some alternative, something, anything to keep from having to go to stay at Nick's.

"What if... what if you came here instead?" I pleaded.

"Well, maybe," she said. "I'll have to talk to Nick about it. I still think it would be easier if you..." She stopped mid-sentence as a tear ran down my cheek. "Okay, okay. I'll see what I can do." She reached up and swept away the tear, a tender smile on her lips. "He's not a bad guy, Lindsey. You really should give him a chance, you know." I was saved from having to respond when Sharon came bustling in with a dinner tray.

"Who's hungry?" Her overly cheerful voice wedged itself between us, disregarding the tension of our conversation. She put the tray of food down and looked me over with a bright smile. "So, I see you're sitting up now. How does that feel, hon?"

"It's getting easier, but my ribs still hurt when I breathe."

"Mmmhmm, yep, it's going to be that way for a while, sweetie, I'm sorry to say. Still, if you're going to be up, we need to get those ribs taped. That will give them some support so they don't move around too much when you breathe. It helps with the discomfort, too." She patted me on the leg and glanced at my mom. "You can help hold her up while I tape her ribs, if you're all right with that." Sharon deftly pulled a roll of thick white tape from her pocket, told Mom to close the door, then pulled off my hospital gown, leaving me bare-chested on the bed. Mortified, I rushed to cover my breasts with my arms. Pain shot across my ribs.

"There, there. It's just us girls. No need to be shy," the nurse cooed as she gently pulled my arms to my sides. I glanced down at my chest and saw the mottled bruising there for the first time. A thin red scar ran down the side of my right breast where the surgeon had inserted the tube that saved my life.

Mom made a soft whimpering sound when she saw my bruised torso. She turned away to hide her tears and Sharon gave her a moment, but was business-like, apparently having been through this before.

"Mom, are you gonna be all right?" Sharon asked. "I can get another nurse to give me a hand if you would prefer."

Mom took a deep breath and shook her head, her jaw set. "No, I'm fine," she said brusquely, moving to my side. "What do you need me to do?" The nurse showed her how to assist while she applied the tape to my damaged ribs.

"There, sweetie," Sharon said. "Now I want to see you take a deep breath and tell me how it feels." I closed my eyes and steeled myself for the now-familiar pain, but surprisingly, the tape actually did help. Sharon smiled and thanked my mother for her help, slipping my hospital gown back up over my shoulders. The experience had erased the tension between us, and we settled into an easy conversation as I picked away at the bland dinner on the tray.

"Lindsey?" Stephanie peeked her head around the curtain. A skinny guy with glasses followed her into the room, looking uncomfortable and lugging a heavy black instrument case.

"This is Brandon. He's in the orchestra with me and I ran into him at dinner tonight. When I told him I was coming here to play for you, he offered to accompany me, which I thought was really sweet." She smiled at him and he blushed, muttering a shy hello and bending to open his viola case. The small hospital room was filled to bursting with my three visitors and I felt like royalty, having drawn musicians to play at my bedside.

Stephanie and Brandon set up quickly and to my surprise, didn't even need sheet music. She placed the violin under her chin, struck a pose and nodded to him as she set the tempo. She closed her eyes and began, her bow gliding over the strings. Her fingers unerringly slid up and down the neck of her violin and her wrist moved back and forth for a smooth vibrato. Their music flowed over me, reminding me of the night at Benaroya Hall when I had heard the Seattle Symphony play. Nurse Sharon stood next to the curtain, enjoying the concert with the rest of us. When they played the final note, we broke into applause.

"That was incredible, you guys! Wow, thank you so much. You are amazing, Steph!"

"It wouldn't have sounded half as good without Brandon. He's our best viola player." I thought I caught a glimpse of something pass between them, but it was gone so quickly I couldn't be quite sure. Stephanie already had a boyfriend, so I was dying to ask her what was up with Brandon, but I didn't get the chance. Instead, I thanked them profusely for sharing their talents with me before they had to pack up and take off.

Nick just missed the concert and came around the curtain, looking a little nervous. "Um, Elizabeth, are you ready?" he asked.

Mom gave me a quick glance, but it was unnecessary. Brightly, I called to Nick and asked him to come in.

"I'm sorry I was so rude to you earlier. Thank you for coming to see me. That was very kind of you."

"It's okay, I understand. I'm just glad to see that you're healing. Your mom has been really worried about you." I could tell he meant it, which made me feel even worse for having been so mean. He turned his dazzling smile to my mother, who seemed to light up in his presence. She gave me a quick kiss on the cheek and stroked my head, promising to be back tomorrow. Alone at last, I turned on the television and settled back against my pillow, humming the orchestra music until I drifted off to sleep.

Chapter 20

"Did you know that you sing in your sleep?"

A strangely familiar voice with a thick Scottish accent came to me in my dream and my heart raced at the sound. I desperately wanted to hold on, but the words slipped away from me. Rolling over in my sleep, my ribs still aching, I was overcome with an inexplicable sense of sadness.

A dark figure snored in the small chair next to the couch. Ravi had his leg propped up on another chair and his head flopped to one side, his crutches leaning against the wall next to him as he slept.

Wow, he didn't have to do that.

I was so touched that he'd come to stay with me, but I felt bad at the same time, my heart torn between a genuine affection for him and an irrational fear of letting him get too close. Dozing off and on, I was tormented by that beautiful voice that I couldn't place, and by images of Ravi being pulled from the car, his face covered in blood. Moaning, I tossed and turned in the torrent of emotion.

A soft hand stroked my forehead.

"Are the ribs hurting you, sweetheart?" Sharon whispered. She leaned over me and tucked a couple of pillows on one side to give me some support. Her hospital name badge swung in front of my face. "Sharon Whitehead" it read and I thought to myself that she must have really loved the man to take a last name like 'Whitehead' when they got married.

As my mind settled on the word 'married,' a popping sound like a champagne bottle being uncorked went off in my head. An excruciating flood of memories came at me like water from a fire hose.

Aiden—in the water, slipping the golden ring on my finger, his voice full of emotion as he asked me to marry him.

Aiden—in Paris with his dirk against the rapist's throat, his eyes filled with steel and venom.

Aiden—dancing with me in front of the Hall of Mirrors in that ridiculous white powdered wig.

Aiden—at the castle, dead on the battlefield, his body broken and covered in blood.

Aiden—making love to me in the sand, his hot, wet skin under my hands.

Aiden—as a child leaping naked off the dock into the ice-cold loch.

Aiden—running toward me with arms outstretched as he faded away before my eyes, his face frozen in fear.

"NO!!"

I clamped my eyes shut and screamed, arching my back and flopping like a fish out of water as the pain cascaded over me, searing my mind with images of Aiden. Gasping for breath, I jerked uncontrollably, the relentless procession of memories overloading my senses.

"No, oh God, no," I repeated between sobs, reaching blindly toward heaven, longing desperately to touch him again. I distantly heard the sounds of shuffling and a number of concerned voices. Strong hands pinned my arms to my side.

"She must be remembering the accident," someone said. Ravi stood at the foot of my bed, mouth agape and eyes wide in horror, watching me scream and thrash wildly. I grabbed the bed rails and vomited over the side.

"You need to leave. Now," Sharon told Ravi, her voice cold and firm. He nodded, limping out of the room on his crutches. The nurse gripped me tightly to keep me from yanking out my IV as I writhed in agony, tears streaming down my face. "Lindsey! Lindsey! You have to stop moving. You're going to injure yourself."

I want to die. I want to go back.

"AIDEN!"

The tormented screech echoed in the small hospital room and Sharon barked at an orderly to bring a sedative. The memory of his beautiful face was crushing my heart and I couldn't breathe.

Aiden, where are you? Oh please Aiden, don't leave me!

I cried out to him hysterically in my mind, my chest on fire and my soul pierced with unbearable anguish. The image of my wedding ring flashed in my thoughts and I jerked my left hand free of the nurse's grasp, staring in disbelief at my bare finger where the band should have been.

"No. No! It can't be. Oh God, why would you do this? Why?" I choked, the agony consuming me like dry kindling in flames and then suddenly everything went black.

Chapter 21

When I finally regained consciousness, my head throbbed and my eyes felt like sandpaper, but I didn't care. My mother was there—I could hear her voice—but I didn't care. I didn't care about anything anymore. My chest ached like my heart had been carved out with a jagged blade, and tears flowed over my cheeks in an endless stream. I didn't try to stop it. I knew I couldn't stop it.

I was completely bound by an overwhelming despair. As I sobbed, I found I was physically bound as well, my arms and legs strapped down to keep me from flailing, which just added to the feeling of being trapped. I refused to talk or even acknowledge anyone. Mom eventually gave up and left me alone, mercifully closing the shades so the room was as dark as my mood. I remembered his arms around me as he cradled me against his chest, stroking my hair.

"I promise I'll be here when you wake, lass."

Latching on to the memory like a raft in an open sea, I played it over and over in my mind.

Aiden, can you hear me? Are you there?

Reaching out to him with my mind, I held my breath, waiting to hear his sweet voice in my head. The clicks and whirring of the machines echoed in the room as I strained, listening for the tiniest indication that he was there, that he'd heard.

Nothing came.

I was completely alone, mercilessly cut off from him, the

love of my life, the man of my dreams, my protector, my lover, my friend, my husband. Gone. Heaving dry sobs tore at my lungs.

Aiden, I love you. I will always love you.

The words sounded hollow in my head, knowing he couldn't hear them, but I had to say them anyway. It was the only comfort I had, to talk to him in my mind, almost like a prayer. And I did pray he would hear, that he'd know somehow I would not let go.

"God, how could you do this to me? I was supposed to redeem him!" I screamed, my eyes scanning the empty room as if expecting God to appear and answer me. I waited and listened, then let out my breath in a dejected sigh. The silence pressed down like a weight on my chest. Dozing off and on, I woke in a sweat, my hair plastered to my face and the sheets damp. Shaking all over, I retched repeatedly but nothing came out.

Sharon came in and muttered something about an infection in a reproachful tone, but my eyes glassed over. Sinking deeper into my pit of misery, I hoped the end would come soon.

I'm coming, Aiden. Wait for me.

Sharon covered my forehead with a cool washcloth and a shiver passed through me. She took my temperature, then forced me to drink a sip of water through a straw and tucked the blankets in around me. Sleep, when it finally came, was mercifully empty of dreams and at last I rested deeply, the pain and the emotional desolation eased in the void of consciousness.

Chapter 22

The warm glow of the lamp cast shadows across the quiet room. Blinking my eyes, I stretched my shoulders, feeling more human than I had in days. An unfamiliar man sat on the couch, watching me silently. He wore a cleric's collar and a black suit, and had short, silvery hair and a kind smile. I frowned at him in confusion, thinking maybe he had the wrong room or something.

"Welcome back, Lindsey. I am Father O'Malley, the hospital chaplain," he said, his voice was calm and metered.

"Back? What do you mean?" I croaked, wondering how he knew I'd been brought back to life.

"You've been out for a couple of days now. I've been coming by to see you often, checking on you and praying for your recovery."

"Oh," I said, unable to hide my disappointment. I didn't have the strength to be polite, so I just stared at him, feeling empty and lost.

"Do you want to talk about it?"

Absolute silence followed his question and I knew that he had no idea what "it" really was, but that it didn't matter. Whatever I wanted to say, he was listening.

Do I want to talk about it?

I couldn't tell my parents or my friends. They would say I'd hallucinated because of shock or something. After all, I had nothing to prove it had really happened. I looked again at my empty left hand where Nanny Fraser's ring had been, my heart aching with loss.

"No... I, maybe... I don't know."

He didn't change expression but waited patiently, listening. I groaned in frustration, torn between needing to talk about Aiden, to tell someone what I was going through, and not wanting to hash it out in words.

"Take your time," he said. "There's no rush." He sat with his legs crossed, hands folded on his lap and though he never looked away from me, his gaze didn't make me uncomfortable. Memories crowded my mind and I couldn't think of where to start. My head told me he wouldn't believe me anyway, so why bother? Still, there was something so serene and open about him, and I instinctively felt I could trust him.

Well, here goes.

"Father, I need you to... I mean, can you keep a secret?" He straightened in his seat and unfolded his hands, turning them palms up on his knees.

"I have a duty to report anything that has to do with abuse." His eyes searched mine as if trying to divine the nature of my secret.

"No, it's nothing like that."

"Then yes, anything you say will be between you, me and our heavenly father. I will not repeat your confession to anyone, my child."

I reared back, frowning and shaking my head. "Confession? No, I haven't done anything wrong. That's not what I mean."

Unruffled, he tipped his head to me. "I apologize, then for assuming. In our broken human state, it is usually our own sin that we seek to keep hidden. What I should have said is that your secret is safe with me."

I lay silent for a long time, trying to get up the courage to talk about Aiden and my experience. He just waited, like he had nowhere else to be and nothing better to do.

"Father, I... I died in that accident."

His eyebrows rose slightly in interest but he said

nothing, waiting for me to continue. I took a deep breath, wincing a little at the pain in my chest, and told him everything. I started out slow, awkwardly trying to describe the beauty of the meadow and the sensation of the air moving with me and through me, but gained momentum as I walked through my memories with Aiden. Tears flowed freely down my face and neck.

"And now he's gone and I'm trapped here in this shell. I want to die again." My eyes sought his for forgiveness, pleading for understanding. "I want to go back." He took my hand in his own as I cried, a fresh wave of sorrow spilling out of me. Finally, the tears ran out and I turned to him, stricken. "Do you believe me?" I whispered, afraid of his answer, yet desperate for that connection and validation.

"Yes, I do." His voice was unwavering.

Relief washed over me like cool water on parched soil. The quiet presence of this stranger had brought the only real solace I'd had in days. I felt compelled to tell him more and realized that I did have a confession after all.

"I'm really angry at God. I don't understand why he would do this to me, to give me love and then tear it away like that. Is it because I didn't go to heaven, because I wanted to stay with Aiden instead? Is he punishing me for that choice? I thought that God loved me. His presence was the most amazing feeling and now... Now, I don't know. I just feel so alone."

"Lindsey, you needn't be afraid of being angry at God. We cannot pretend to understand His ways, but He knows us, our every thought and deed. He already knows you are angry and hurt, whether you tell him so or not. He sees each tear you cry and holds them all in his hands, my child." His eyes were direct and clear as he looked at me. "I don't know why God has chosen you to endure this hardship, but you are not alone. God has promised to never leave you or forsake you, and He won't."

The bonds of anger and depression began to loosen as he

spoke. He didn't push, but sat holding my hand, the kindness on his face an unspeakable comfort. I'd never known such pain in my life and blaming God was the only way I could cope. Yet here was this gentle, unassuming man reminding me of God's love—a love I had experienced first-hand. I began to break free of the misery, floating up to the surface for a much-needed breath of fresh air.

"Can I pray for you?" His caring words washed over me as he lifted me in prayer. As he spoke, the stirring of God's presence warmed my chest as it had done before, the subtle energy radiating throughout my limbs to my fingertips and toes.

Thank you, God. Please help me.

I whispered the heartfelt prayer in my mind, knowing He was there. I didn't know why He'd sent me back, but I knew He was with me. Completely spent and yet feeling more whole than I had since my return, I slumped back onto the pillow.

"Godspeed, Lindsey MacRae," Father O'Malley whispered before he quietly left my room.

Chapter 23

The next day was Christmas Eve and the hospital was doing its best to celebrate the holiday season, giving stockings to all the patients. Volunteers wandered through the sterile hallways singing Christmas carols and I joined in, singing from my bed. I settled against the pillows and switched on the television. "It's a Wonderful Life" was on and I smiled, remembering the many times I had snuggled close to my dad to watch the movie at Christmastime, a paper bag of greasy popcorn on my lap. George Bailey was going on his tirade about how he should never have been born. I felt a kinship with George Bailey, thinking about how my family would have fared had I not been brought back.

I thought about my mother's worried face when I first woke up, and how emotional my dad had been when he described my injuries to me. Ravi obviously felt guilty about the accident; I could only imagine what it would have done to him had I been killed.

You were killed. The ache of loss was ever present, but I made a concerted effort to push it out of my mind.

I miss you. Tu me manques, mon amour. I stroked the soft fabric of my stocking as I spoke to him in my mind, my heart heavy.

"I will not count the days if you'll promise me the same, my love," I remembered him saying when he asked me to marry him, his eyes full of emotion. Apart from him, I felt like a prisoner, scratching the number of days gone by on the cell wall, waiting for the end.

I'll come back to you, Aiden. I don't know when, but I will.

Soft strains of Christmas carols rang through the halls again, but I didn't sing along this time. Instead, I buried my head in my pillow and cried myself to sleep.

~

Christmas morning was unlike any I'd ever had before. As a child, I would wake up early and rush into the living room to see what Santa had brought. My stocking would be sitting on the couch, stuffed with goodies that spilled out over the cushions. Mom and Dad would take their infuriatingly sweet time getting up, making coffee, and getting breakfast started.

We always had the same casserole on Christmas morning. It was the one thing my mom actually enjoyed cooking. By the time breakfast was over, I'd hardly be able contain my excitement, jumping up and down like a jitterbug and pulling on my dad's sleeve. He'd laugh good-naturedly and tousle my hair, then crawl under the tree, distributing the presents into piles, "playing Santa." As an only child, my pile was always three times larger than both my parents' combined, but they loved to watch me open presents. It was my favorite day of the year and they always seemed to get along on Christmas Day, even right up to the end.

This morning though, I woke up to an empty hospital room with no presents, no tree and no casserole. A new nurse came in with a tray of cereal and fruit and wished me a Merry Christmas. She told me Sharon had the day off and I was glad that she did, but the nurse's unfamiliar face just reinforced my feelings of isolation. My parents hadn't called or told me when they'd be coming by, and though I knew they would eventually come, waking up alone and staring out the window from my hospital bed was not my idea of

Christmas morning. I ate my cereal and cheered myself up by talking to Aiden in my mind.

Joyeux Noël, mon cher. Merry Christmas, my love. I wish you were here.

I knew it was foolish, but I found great comfort in talking to him like he could hear me. With a sigh, I switched on the television. *A Charlie Brown Christmas* was on and I settled back in bed to watch it, trying not to feel sorry for myself. Around noon, Mom and Nick showed up with a brightly wrapped present.

"Merry Christmas, sweetie! Santa's here!" Mom beamed at me, her voice overly cheerful as she lay the present on my lap. She was obviously trying too hard, which in truth, just made it worse. I gave her a quick hug and tried not to let her see how I really felt.

"Thanks, Mom. Hi, Nick." I gave him a fake smile that didn't reach my eyes. Still, he seemed surprised I'd acknowledged him at all.

"Hi, Lindsey. Sorry you have to be in the hospital on Christmas Day. That really sucks." He caught me off-guard with his frank assessment and I laughed.

"Yeah, you can say that again." This time I actually did smile at him and he returned it, his eyes warm and friendly.

Mom sat on the bed at my feet, her hand on my leg. "We went over to the dorm this morning to get some clothes for you. The doctor said you're doing really well so they're going to let you check out tomorrow."

"I get to leave tomorrow? Oh my gosh, that's awesome!" She handed me the suitcase and I stroked it lovingly, looking forward to getting out of the horrible hospital gown and feeling like a human being again. She grinned at me, obviously not done with the good news.

"Nick and I talked about it," she said with a sly smile, "and we decided that I'm going to come stay with you until you're ready to go back to school. We rented a furnished apartment here in town, close to the college so you can still see your friends."

"Really? Oh, Mom!" I flung my arms around her neck and she laughed, kissing me on the temple.

"Merry Christmas, sweetheart. Are you going to open your present now?" She gestured to the gift with an expectant smile. I tore off the wrapping paper to reveal a shiny new laptop computer.

"Wow, thanks Mom. This will be really helpful at school."

"It's from both of us." She was quick to correct me. "Your old computer is really outdated so Nick picked out the top of the line laptop and had it pre-loaded with all the bells and whistles. It even comes with a wireless card so you can get the Internet anywhere you get a cell signal. Cool, huh?"

My mom was about the least computer-literate person I knew, so it was clear that Nick did all the work putting the gift together for me. I felt a little awkward accepting such an expensive present from him after hating him for so long, but I had to admit it was a really nice gift. I took a deep breath and smiled up at him.

"Thanks, Nick. It's great." He looked so sincerely pleased that I started to feel bad for harboring such resentment toward him. We all smiled at one another, not sure what to say next.

"Lindsey, pumpkin? Merry Chr—" Dad's voice echoed in the small room as he pushed the curtain aside and stopped mid-sentence. His smile faded as his eyes locked onto Nick's.

"What the hell are you doing here?" Dad said, his voice filled with ice.

"Gary…" Mom started, but Nick put a hand on her shoulder.

"It's okay, Elizabeth," he said.

Dad flinched when Nick touched my mom and he narrowed his eyes, seething hatred. "It's not enough that you're sleeping with my wife, now you have to move in on my daughter as well? On Christmas Day no less?"

Mom leapt to her feet, hissing furiously at him. "Where do you get off calling me your wife, you possessive bastard?"

"Well, that's what I've called you for the last twenty-one years," Dad spat back.

"Well you can stop now, for God's sake. Or have you forgotten that we're divorced? Maybe it's the drinking that's fogged your memory." Nick tried to calm her down, but she shrugged off his hand angrily. "I'm not your wife anymore, Gary. I'll sleep with whomever I damn well please, and I don't want to hear one word about it from you."

Dad didn't back down and they stood nose to nose in front of my bed, snarling at each other. "And how is that different than before, Elizabeth, since you saw fit to sleep with this asshole while we were still married? Or have you forgotten that little detail?" Nick started to jump into the fray but Dad just raised his voice, ignoring him. "And if I drink," he snarled, "it's only because you drove me to it!"

"STOP IT!" I screamed.

All three of them shut up instantly, dropping their eyes to the floor. "I can't believe it's Christmas Day and the three of you are standing at the foot of my *hospital bed* screaming at each other." I shook my head in absolute bewilderment. "If you can't get along for this one day, then you can all just leave right now." Crossing my arms, I gave them my most pointed glare, daring anyone to try and contradict me. Dad mumbled an apology and Nick took Mom by the shoulders.

"Come on, Elizabeth," he said. "Let's leave them alone. I'm sorry, Lindsey." Mom quickly kissed me on the cheek and glared at my dad as she left the room. Dad sat across from me on the green sofa with a heavy sigh and put his head in his hands.

"I'm so sorry, baby. You're right. It's just... Oh God..." He stopped, fighting for control over his emotions, and I watched him in silence, unsure of what to say. "It's just that nothing's been the same since she left, and I thought that

Christmas might be the one sacred day that she wouldn't be flaunting him in front of me, that maybe she still cared enough to spare me that. But I was wrong. And I'm sorry." Tears strained his voice and my own eyes welled up with compassion.

"It's all right, Dad." I felt an inane urge to say 'Merry Christmas' but it seemed weak and pathetic after the spectacle with Mom and Nick. So instead, we just sat there in silence as he struggled to pull himself together. Finally, he took a deep breath and looked up at me, wiping his face and forcing a smile.

"I brought you a present." He glanced at the computer on my lap and nodded in acknowledgment. "It's not as fancy as that, but I hope you like it." It was a hard cover journal, its stiff pressed pages dotted with tiny flecks of color. The paisley pink cover had a swirling capital *L* in the center.

"It's beautiful, Dad. I love it." I beamed up at him and his face relaxed, his pained expression melting away into a genuine smile.

"I saw it and thought of you. I know you've been through a lot lately with the accident and the divorce, and I thought you might like to... you know, write stuff, to help you through it." He reached out and tucked a stray curl behind my ear. "We've got each other. That's all that matters now," he said, almost talking to himself, then gestured to the journal with his chin. "There's something else in there for you." I flipped through the journal, and a cash card fell out from between the pages.

"I thought you might like to go on a shopping spree with your girlfriends once you're feeling better, maybe buy a new outfit or something. There's some extra money on there to help you make it through the school year in case you need to buy some... um, toiletries or feminine-type stuff." I giggled at his discomfort and he grinned sheepishly at me with a shrug of his shoulders. I hugged him close and kissed his cheek.

"Thanks, Dad. I mean it. That was really sweet."

"Merry Christmas, Lindsey. I love you, baby."

"I love you, too." He clicked on the television and *A Muppet Christmas Carol* was showing. I scooted over and he climbed onto the bed next to me where we sat together, watching the show and pretending like it was old times.

After Dad left, I took a nap and woke to find a small package on the cart next to my bed. I stared at it in a sleepy haze and looked around the room as if expecting someone to appear and claim it. When I saw the handwriting on the note inside, I knew instantly whom it was from.

"Lindsey, I wanted to give you this myself, but I thought you might not want to see me. I bought it for you before the accident. I'm really sorry and I hope you can forgive me. Merry Christmas. Love, Ravi."

Seeing his name pierced my heart with guilt since I hadn't thought about Ravi at all since my memory came back. I realized with a start that he'd been in the room when that had happened.

He probably thinks I freaked out because I remembered the accident. No wonder he thinks I don't want to see him.

And in a way, I didn't, but not because of that. I couldn't tell him about Aiden but I also couldn't date him anymore. Still, he was probably my closest friend and I didn't want to lose that. I was so torn between wanting to push him away and wanting to keep him close, and I knew it would hurt him no matter what I did because I couldn't give him what he really wanted. Defeated, I unwrapped the gift. The shining silver necklace had a music note dangling from it, a tiny diamond set into the bottom of the note.

I just stared at the necklace, wondering what on earth I was going to do. Finally, I put it on and fingered the little silver charm, running it back and forth along the chain. What could I tell him? I had no good explanation for how my feelings had changed, but they certainly had.

Father O'Malley's face appeared at the curtain of the

room.

"Merry Christmas, Lindsey."

"Thanks. You, too," I said, surprised to see him. "But you didn't have to come here on Christmas Day. Why aren't you home with your family?"

"All of God's children are my family. And that includes you." He pulled out a wrapped package and placed it in my lap. I grinned up at him, tickled that he'd brought me a gift. It was a beautiful new Bible with 'Lindsey M' engraved in gold letters on the front. He grinned mischievously, which surprised me since it was not a look I would have expected from him.

"I saw on your chart that your middle name is Marie," he explained. "I wanted to get you a Bible with your new name on it, but I knew it wasn't something you'd shared with other people. So I had them just put 'M.' Others will think it's for your middle name, but you and I know the truth." Tears stung the back of my eyes at his words. The tan cover was part fabric and part leather, and I ran my hands over the top.

"I chose a two-tone Bible," he said, "as a symbol of the dual life you have—one here and one there. Both of the materials are lovely in their own way, but very different from one another." I shook my head in awe at the thoughtfulness of this gift, contrasting the fuzzy fabric with the smooth texture of the leather. I smiled up at him through my wet lashes.

"I don't know what to say. It's perfect. Thank you."

His mouth broke into a full smile but he shook his head. "No, thank you for sharing your story with me. Our Heavenly Father works in awesome and mysterious ways, and I am anxious to see what he has in store for you." We smiled at each other in silence for a while.

"Oh, I almost forgot," he said. "I saw you're being discharged tomorrow, so I wanted to give you my number in case you need anything. Or someone to talk to." He scribbled his phone number on a piece of paper and handed it to me,

174

his hand closing around mine as he did. "Call anytime, day or night. I'm usually here at the hospital in the evenings, so you can come by if you need to." He squeezed my hand, wished me a Merry Christmas with a warm smile and left. I clutched the small Bible to my chest and said a prayer of thanks.

Chapter 24

The next morning, the doctor came in to sign my release.

"You're free to go, Lindsey," he said as he handed me a prescription for painkillers. "Keep working on your breathing exercises like I told you and take care of yourself. Nothing personal, but I don't want to see you back in here, okay?"

I promised to be good while Mom gathered up our bags. True to her word, she had rented a furnished, two-bedroom, one-bathroom apartment within walking distance of the college. When we arrived, Mom handed me a bag of stuff and I headed off to check out my new room. The cheerful yellow walls brought an automatic smile to my face. The early afternoon sun streamed through white lace curtains, bathing the space in a soft, soothing light. The double bed with its country quilt and ruffled pillows looked heavenly after two weeks on a stiff hospital bed. I lay down on it experimentally and rolled onto my side like the doctor had instructed. A stab of pain made me wince. He'd said I should try to lie on the side with the broken ribs as often as I could stand it, to promote healing.

"It's not going to be fun, but the only way to get better is to work with the pain instead of trying to avoid it," he'd said. I sighed in resignation, thinking that was the stupidest thing I'd ever heard.

Yeah, embrace the pain. Great.

Rolling onto my back, I breathed a sigh of relief as the tension in my chest eased. The opaque edge of a plastic grocery sack caught my eye, peeking out from Mom's pink canvas bag on the edge of the bed. Curious, I scooted over to see what it was. My favorite green sweater and jeans were crumpled into a ball in the bag. Covered in dried blood, both had been carelessly sliced open from top to bottom. My white tank top and lace bra were in a similar state, and I swallowed hard as the bile rose in my throat. My shoes were in the bottom of the bag and I thought they, at least, might be salvageable with a little industrious cleaning. Something small and round landed on the bed as I dumped out the shoes.

"What the—"

My heart instantly stopped.

Nanny Fraser's golden ring lie on the bedspread, the large center emerald glinting in the sunlight.

All the blood drained from my head and I let out a strangled cry before falling back against the pillow with the ring clutched in my fist.

The next thing I knew, Mom was slapping me lightly on the cheek, her voice frantic.

"Lindsey, honey, wake up. Oh God, oh God!"

I shook my head, staring at her in shock. My breath came in quick, ragged gasps. Instantly, I clenched my fist tight and was soothed by the feel of the cool metal against my palm.

"Oh, honey, I'm so sorry! I meant to get rid of that bag but I couldn't find anyplace to throw it away. I never meant for you to see that. The nurse pulled it out from under your bed right before we left and handed it to me, so I just stuffed it in with the rest of your stuff. I don't know why they even kept it."

"It was under my bed the whole time?"

She nodded, her face contorted with guilt and worry. Images of Aiden sliding the ring on my finger poured over me and I clamped my eyes shut, struggling to breathe. My whole body shook with the torment and exultation of knowing that everything was true, that it had really happened and now he was gone.

She gathered up the bloody clothes and stuffed them back into the bag. "I'm going to get rid of these right now. I'm so sorry."

When she left, I slowly opened my fist, staring in awe at my wedding ring. I slipped it on my finger. It fit perfectly, just as it had when Aiden gave it to me. Tears streamed down my cheeks.

Aiden, it's real. All of it was real. I still have your ring, Nanny Fraser's ring.

Mom came back and I quickly hid my left hand between my knees. She was a nervous wreck, strain etched on her face, and I took a deep breath, trying to pull myself together.

"It's all right, Mom. I was just surprised. Really, I'm fine."

She looked at me warily and then let out a heavy sigh. "That's really not how I wanted to start this off. I'm supposed to be taking care of you and as soon as I get you home, you faint."

"It's not your fault. It's no big deal." I put my right hand over hers and squeezed.

"Let's get out of here and go get some dinner. Do you know of any good places?" she asked. I smiled and mentioned a little Italian place downtown.

"Would you give me a minute, Mom? I want to, uh, freshen up a bit."

She patted my leg and shut the door behind her, leaving me alone to admire my ring. I splayed my fingers out and turned my hand from side to side, watching the sun beams dance off the clear gems, making little streaks of light on the wall. Reluctantly, I took it off and held it to my lips for a moment, then undid my necklace and slipped it onto the chain. The solid weight of it rested on my chest under my shirt, close to my heart.

Thank you, God. I prayed silently and pulled a comb through my unruly hair. I put on some lip-gloss and looked at my reflection in the mirror. My face had healed completely, a thin white line through my right eyebrow the only visible scar, but I was not the same girl I'd been before the accident. And I never would be the same.

"Hello, Mrs. MacRae," I whispered to the girl in the mirror and she smiled back at me, cherishing the secret we shared.

Chapter 25

The final week of the year was mercifully uneventful as Mom and I adjusted to living together again. Because we spent so much time together, I started to notice little things about her. She'd always been particular about her looks, but I'd never realized how much time it took her to get ready in the morning. She took forever to do her hair and make-up, and would often completely change outfits between getting up and leaving the house. In truth, I preferred the way she looked at the end of the day when she'd wash her face and sit with me in front of the TV in her pajamas. It wasn't glamorous, but it was more real somehow than the face she showed the rest of the world.

Dad called me every other day to check in and see how I was doing, which was sweet but awkward. Mom never left the room while I talked to him, but would pretend she wasn't listening, becoming suddenly engrossed in the television or a crossword puzzle. Of course, I could tell she was hanging on every word, so I tried to be as vague and nonchalant as possible. I disliked being in the middle of their bitterness toward one another, so my conversations with Dad were always brief. After one of his calls, she asked me in a disinterested tone how he was doing and I just stared at her, confused. She waved it off and shrugged.

"You're right. It doesn't matter. Never mind." She never asked again, but the subject of my father was always there between us.

Sick and tired of being sore all the time, I missed my friends and Aiden most of all. The constant rain only added to my overall crankiness and boredom, trapping me inside. As it was, I had no one to go see anyway. Even though I knew he was staying in town over the winter break, Ravi hadn't called me once, which relieved and irritated me at the same time. On New Year's Eve, Mom apparently decided that she'd had enough of my moping around.

"Lindsey, we need to do something fun tonight. Nick has to work so he can't come down, so it's just you and me in this God-forsaken little town. Still, it's New Year's Eve for crying out loud and we need to celebrate." She grinned at me expectantly, waiting for my suggestion of a lively evening's entertainment. I just shrugged.

"What about a game?" she suggested. "Do we have any around here?" She got up from the couch and pawed through the drawers in the entertainment center. "There's a deck of cards," she said, holding them up. "We could play cards like we used to at the cabin, remember?" I dropped my gaze as I remembered little Aiden playing cards with his brother and aunt, the satisfied grin on his face when he won.

"Come on, it'll be fun," she coaxed. "Do you know any good games or should we just play gin rummy?" I nodded, smiling reluctantly at Mom's excited face.

Work with the pain. That's the only way to get through it.

"Yeah, I learned a new one not that long ago. He called it... I mean, it's called 'Poque-Deux' and it's kinda like poker. It's actually pretty fun, only..." I tried to think of how to explain the game without the spoils of victory. "I guess we could just keep score on a notepad."

"How do you usually keep score? Lindsey...?" she asked with a suspicious smile.

I squirmed under her penetrating gaze.

"Um... the winner of each hand takes a shot of whisky," I said finally, not looking at her. To my surprise, she clapped her hands and threw her head back with a raucous laugh. I raised my eyebrows at her in surprise and she grinned at me mischievously.

"Oh, come on. Do you think your mom's such an old fuddy-dud that she thinks college kids don't drink? I was young once too, you know. And I'll bet I did plenty worse than you've ever done. You've always been a goody two shoes, to be honest." I opened my mouth to protest and she waved a hand in dismissal. "Really, it doesn't bother me in the least. It'll be fun. Let's go to the liquor store and I'll let you pick out the bottle."

My jaw hit the floor and she laughed with girlish glee, dragging me off the couch and shoving my coat into my hands. Fortunately, I hadn't taken any painkillers in a while or alcohol would have been out of the question. As it was, we had the kitchen table decked out with dessert, the bottle of whisky and two shot glasses within an hour. We didn't have buttons, so settled for a couple rolls of pennies to wager with.

Once the shock wore off, I really enjoyed teaching Mom how to play. She was fun to be with when she let herself relax. It had been a long time since I'd seen her really smile like that, and I felt closer to her than I had in years. It took her a bit to get the hang of the game and I squirmed in my seat as I poured my first shot of whisky.

"Oh, don't be a pansy," she said. "Bottoms up, Linds." I threw back the shot, coughing a little as the fiery liquid ran down my throat. She slapped one hand on the table, making the pennies jump. "That's my girl!"

"You're crazy, you know that?" I laughed and shook my head. She grinned back at me and dealt another hand. We talked and laughed all night, playing cards and occasionally stopping to watch fireworks or some New Year's Eve display on television. After about three shots, I started to feel a little queasy. The last thing I needed was to get sick.

Yeah, crack another rib puking up whisky. No, thanks.

I decided to switch to brownie bites for my reward, but

Mom kept downing the whisky, her features softening as the alcohol affected her. She shuffled the cards and regarded me with a far-off look.

"You're lucky, Lindsey."

"Because I made it through the accident, you mean?"

"No, not that, but that's true." She shook her head and dealt the cards. "No, what I mean is, you're lucky because you have your whole life ahead of you. You could do anything, go anywhere, be whatever you want to be. In a lot of ways, I wish I could go back to those days, to be where you are again." I didn't know what to say. The silence stretched between us.

"Have I ever told you how your dad and I met?" she asked, her voice wistful. I shook my head, intrigued but a little apprehensive, since the subject of my dad never seemed to end well. Still, she had a soft smile at the corner of her mouth like it was a pleasant memory, so I encouraged her to go on.

"I was taking dance classes at the University of Washington," she said, "and he was a sales and marketing major. We met in the cafeteria at school. He was behind me in line and made some inane comment about something on my tray." She chuckled, her eyes lighting up in remembrance.

"I don't even remember now what he said, but it was pretty obvious he was trying to start a conversation. I thought he was cute though, so I let him sit with me. He made me laugh and he adored me. Followed me around like a lovesick puppy dog." A shadow passed over her features and my chest tightened with worry.

"I wanted to be a dancer. It was my passion. Did you know that?" She looked up suddenly, as if she'd just remembered I was there.

"No. I'm surprised you never mentioned it before."

"Yeah, I loved jazz dance in particular: the flow, the movement, the energy. When I danced, I just… melted into the music like it was part of me, like air that lifted me and moved me. I don't even know how to explain it." She shook her head in frustration.

"I got a scholarship to Juilliard in New York and I was going to transfer, but I got pregnant. I was going to dance and travel, see the world, make something of myself, but I became a mom instead and stayed home with you." She tried to smile, but regret was written all over her face. Speechless, I just stared at her. She sighed and took a bite of chocolate chip cookie from the dessert tray.

"Don't get me wrong. I love you and I love being a mom, but I always wondered what could have been, how my life might have turned out if I'd gone. And you..." her eyes were tender as she gazed at me across the table, "you have that chance now, to choose what you want to do and follow your dreams. I have to admit, it makes me a little jealous."

Cards be damned, she grabbed the whisky bottle and took a swig, foregoing the shot glass altogether. The announcer on the television started counting down as the ball dropped in Times Square. We both turned, watching it in silence.

"Three, two, one. Happy New Year!" the television chimed. Mom's eyes misted with tears. I got up and hugged her from behind, and she put her hand on my arm.

"Happy New Year, Mom. Thanks for being here with me."

She turned to look at me, a real smile on her face. "There's nowhere else I'd rather be, sweetheart. I love you." I kissed the top of her head and yawned, then turned in for the night, leaving her to her memories and the rest of the whisky.

Chapter 26

Stephanie called on Saturday night and asked if I wanted to go to a movie, which lifted my spirits considerably. When I got to the dorm, she and Jen gave me awkward hugs, afraid to hurt me by squeezing too hard. It was weird being in my dorm room again, seeing the empty bottom bunk where I normally slept. It was home and I missed it.

"So what movie are we going to see?" I asked, not caring, just thankful to be with my friends again. Jen rolled her eyes dramatically.

"Well, the guys wanted to see Death Raiders and Steph wanted to see Sarah's Promise." She poked her finger in her mouth and made a gagging sound, then laughed when Steph smacked her on the shoulder. "But I convinced them it would be more fun to see a comedy, so we're going to go to Vacation at Woody's."

"The guys are coming, huh?" It made sense that Jen and Steph would want to hang out with their boyfriends, but since Ravi lived in the same dorm, I knew he'd be coming, too. My pulse quickened at the thought of seeing him again and I told myself I was being ridiculous. A knock sounded at the door.

Paul, Micah and Ravi waited while we grabbed our coats and followed them into the hall. The January drizzle stuck to my eyelashes as we walked to the movie theater. Paul and Jen walked in front, followed by Micah and Steph, with me and Ravi bringing up the rear by default. He fidgeted nervously and I tried to break the tension.

"Hey, the cut on your forehead healed up really well," I said. "I can barely even see where the stitches were."

He rubbed the spot absently and nodded with a shy smile. "You're looking really good, too. I'm glad you're feeling better. I've been kinda worried about you, to be honest." He spoke the last words to the sidewalk, and I remembered the last time he saw me, I'd been completely freaking out. Guilt flooded through me.

"Yeah, I know. Sorry about that."

"*You're* sorry? You don't have anything to be sorry about. I'm the one who was driving."

I touched him on the arm and stopped walking. "Let's make a deal. No more saying 'I'm sorry,' okay? Let's just have fun tonight and try to forget about it." He took my hand as we continued to walk and I stiffened, thinking maybe I shouldn't have made that first contact. When we got to the theater and he let go to pay for his ticket, I stuffed my hands in my coat pocket and kept them there.

The movie was pretty lame and the other two couples quickly lost interest, choosing to entertain themselves with hands and lips instead. Ravi sat next to me in the darkened theater and his thigh pressed against mine in the tightly packed seats. His hand rested within easy reach on his leg, obviously available should I choose to hold it. Instead, I hugged myself close, pretending to be engrossed in the movie. I caught glimpses of him watching me out of the corner of my eye and occasionally turned to smile at him.

For crying out loud, Lindsey! This is misery. You have to do something.

Finally, the credits rolled and our friends disentangled themselves. Back in the cool night air, we decided to head to our favorite 24-hour restaurant for some coffee and dessert. All six of us crammed into a semi-circle booth, which left me pressed up against Ravi again. Paul started talking about taking Calculus for Jan term, which we all agreed was an awful choice, and Ravi offered to help him out if he needed it, having already taken a slew of math classes in preparation for his engineering degree. Stephanie was taking an Art History class, Jen was working on political science and Micah was retaking an English composition course that he'd failed last year.

I asked Ravi what class he was taking and he replied, "Piano. I've been working on writing some songs for the band anyway, so I thought I might as well get credit for it. Besides, this way I can spend more time working on my music and not feel guilty about it. Are you still interested in singing for our band?" He'd asked me to be the singer for their band before the accident. Before everything. It seemed like a million years ago now, but I still wanted to do it.

"Yeah, it sounds fun. When do we practice?"

Micah piped up, "We're gonna start on Tuesday night at the music hall. Todd said he'll bring his drum set. You reserved the room, right, Ravi?"

He nodded, then turned back to stare at me, purposefully taking my hand under the table. He stroked my palm with his thumb and I tried to concentrate on the conversation, which had moved on to which concerts were coming to Portland. I fidgeted and played with my hair as the heat from Ravi's gaze burned the side of my face. I didn't look at him—I couldn't—and I breathed a sigh of relief when the others finally stood up to leave.

We paid our respective tabs and headed back out into the cold, drizzly night. Ravi intentionally held back from the rest of the group as we walked, taking the first opportunity to hold my hand again. When I hesitated, he stopped abruptly and stared at me.

"You don't want to touch me, do you? Is it really that bad?"

"It's not you, Ravi. I just… I can't explain it."

Instead of dropping my hand, he took my other one and drew me toward him, his voice barely more than a whisper. "I never meant to hurt you and I'd do anything to take it back, to make it go away. What can I do? Tell me, and it's yours." I just stood there, blinking at him, inhaling his warm breath.

"It makes me crazy to be so close to you and to not touch you, to not kiss you, to see the pain in your eyes and know that you're hurting because of me." Guilt poured over me, biting the back of my neck, and I tried to pull free but he held me close and continued, determined. "I don't know what I can do to make it up to you, but I promise I will. I'll find a way."

"You don't have to make it up to me. I just can't... it's not the same between us anymore and I don't think it ever will be. I love you and I don't want to hurt you, but I can't be with you anymore. Not like that. I'm sorry."

His body registered my words like bad news he'd been expecting, but did not accept. "Fine. Friends—for now. But I want you to know I'll be here waiting when you're ready. I'm not giving up. You mean too much to me."

I couldn't meet his gaze. He released me and the cold fingers of the night wrapped around me, emphasizing how alone I felt.

God, why did you bring me back? This is killing me.

"Come on, I'll take you home." I was dreading an awkward goodnight and my steps grew heavy as we approached my front door. We stood there a moment until he said, "I guess I'll see you tomorrow." He gave me a half-hearted smile, then turned and walked away. I stared after him, the fine drops of rain collecting on my eyelashes and the light from the porch lamp throwing liquid rainbows on his retreating figure.

Chapter 27

Light from a table lamp pooled in the corner of the dark living room, and the green glow from the digital clock told me midnight had come and gone. I crept upstairs, careful not to wake up my mom, and crawled into bed, my head swimming with emotion. The sound of Mom's mumbled voice through the wall interrupted my thoughts and I felt a pang of guilt that I'd been too noisy. A deep rumbling voice responded to her and I froze. She giggled and began to make low, humming noises. He responded with moans of pleasure and the bedsprings began a predictable rhythm.

My stomach clenched in knots as I tried to block out the sound of Mom and Nick having sex on the other side of the thin wall. I lay stock still on the bed with my fingers in my ears and the pillow over my face, anger and revulsion churning within me. As their voices grew louder, so did the screaming in my head. Finally, I threw back the covers and pulled on some clothes.

I stomped down the stairs, grabbed my coat and slammed the door on my way out of the apartment, then strode off into the dark until I was out of earshot and let out a scream of frustration. Rain lashed my face and dripped down the nape of my neck but I didn't care. My mind conjured images of my mother and Nick in the bedroom, her eyes flirting like that night at the symphony, and I wanted to throw up. I pounded my temples with my palms to try and dislodge the images but that just drove them further in.

My feet sloshed through puddles as I ran, the chill wicking up my socks. My lungs burned with the effort and I swore out loud, remembering how easy it had been to run in the meadow where I'd met Aiden. I slipped on a wet patch of grass and landed on my butt, scraping my hands. My palms stung with dirt and blood while I sat on the soggy ground and cried, wishing with all my heart that I could be back with Aiden again.

"God, help me!" I shouted to the milky night sky as my body shook with cold and anger. I searched the heavens for some answer, wishing they would open up and take me home again. Car lights blinded me momentarily and the driver pulled up next to me, rolling down his window.

"Miss, are you okay?"

I nodded irritably and waved him on. Soaked clear through and shivering, I stood up and tried to brush off the mud, wincing at the sting in my palms. The driver muttered something and drove off, his tires sending an arc of dirty water across my legs. I turned and trudged back to the apartment, defeated and depressed.

The apartment was mercifully quiet when I returned and I stripped off my clothes, leaving them in a sopping heap on the floor. I crawled into bed and lay there numb, physically and mentally, until exhaustion finally brought sleep.

My dreams were filled with images of my mom and Nick, my parents fighting, and the memory of Aiden running after me with his arms outstretched. After a fitful night, I woke with swollen, stinging eyes and a pounding headache, so I took a couple of ibuprofen and went downstairs to make coffee, hoping the caffeine would help improve my mood. A gurgle in the pipes told me that Mom and Nick were showering. I blared the television to try and block out the sound.

Coffee in hand, I tucked myself into a ball at the end of the couch and glared at the television as if it had somehow wronged me. A blonde woman with fake boobs and a matching smile was hawking jewelry on the shopping network and I tried to channel my irritation toward her. Nick came down the stairs, the picture of cheer, my mother right behind him.

"Good morning, Lindsey!" he practically sang, giving me his best 1000-watt smile. He stopped at the bottom of the steps and kissed my mother goodbye.

"I wish you could stay," she pouted.

"I wish I could too, but I have to go. I've got to drop off that contract at Major & Sons or I won't be able to write off my mileage as a business expense. You are my favorite customer to visit, you know," he said with a wink. "I'll try and come back next weekend, all right?" He kissed her on the nose and she swatted him playfully.

"Have a great day, Lindsey!" he chimed to me as he left and I gave him my most menacing glare. Mom saw it and descended on me as soon as he closed the front door.

"What the hell was that for?"

"Don't even start with me. You know exactly what that was about."

"What on earth are you talking about?"

I rolled my eyes and gripped my coffee cup until my knuckles were white. "Don't play innocent, Mom. Next time, warn me before he comes to stay so I don't have to spend all night wandering the streets to try and get away from the sound of you two having sex right next to me." If I thought she was going to be apologetic, I was wrong. She shook her head and curled up her lip in disdain.

"Oh, grow up, Lindsey."

Livid, I jumped off the couch, my eyes narrowed into slits. "Me, grow up? Me, really? Aren't you always the one who told me I should wait to have sex until I was married? And here you are, doing it with your *boyfriend,* and you don't even care that I'm trying to sleep in the very next room? Yeah, that's real mature, Mother." I spat out the words in disgust, anger boiling in my guts.

"Listen, young lady. I'm a grown woman and I can do what I like. I don't have to answer to you. Besides, he's really a good guy, which you would find out if you ever gave him half a chance."

"Yeah, I'm sure he is," I said, my voice filled with venom. "I mean, what's not to love? He's tall, dark and handsome. Oh yeah, and he just happens to cheat on his taxes and destroyed my family by fucking a married woman!"

She drew back and slapped me hard across the face, the sound echoing in the small room. My hand flew to my stinging cheek and I stared at her, shaking with resentment. Her eyes were hard and her voice came out in a hiss.

"Don't you dare speak to me like that. I am your mother, Lindsey Marie, and I don't care if you disagree with the choices I've made, you will not disrespect me. Do you understand?"

I clenched my jaw and met her gaze, not backing down. Silence stretched between us, the clock ticking loudly on the wall. To my surprise, she barked out a disdainful laugh and shook her head.

"I swear, you are just as stubborn as I am. It used to drive my mother crazy. She always said I'd be cursed with a daughter just like me. I guess she was right." Her face was bitter and distant as she sat down on the couch and clicked off the television.

"You don't understand, Lindsey. You think you do, but you don't. Hell, I thought I knew everything when I was your age too, but I didn't. Why should you be any different?" She spoke the words to the blank screen on the television. I sat down in the chair across from her, wary and confused by her response.

"Try me." The words hung there, unanswered. After a long pause, she sighed and looked up at me dejectedly.

"Do you understand what it's like to have your dreams stripped away from you in one fell swoop, to give up a life you always wanted, to wake up one day and find yourself an empty shell of a person and not even want to live? Do you know what it's like to be caught between two men, one who is steady and faithful, who says that he loves you and yet doesn't really understand the ache inside of you," she clutched her fist to her chest with a hollow look in her eyes, "and another who is wild and dangerous, who fills your senses and makes you feel alive, but that you can't be with, that you have to hide? Do you understand that?" Her words pierced my soul and I could hardly breathe, my eyes misting with tears. She gave me a sad shake of her head.

"No, I didn't think so. And honest to God, I hope you never do." She went back up the stairs, leaving me staring at the wall.

Mom and I came to an unspoken truce after that and I didn't bring up the subject again. When Nick stayed over the following weekend, I informed her that I was going to be out late with my friends, so I'd just sleep at the dorm. She nodded silently as understanding passed between us.

~

"Everything is looking great, Lindsey," the doctor said during my final check-up in late January. "The cut on your arm didn't heal up quite as well as I would have liked. I was hoping you wouldn't have much of a scar on your arm, but you did lose some of the surrounding skin, so I'm afraid it's here to stay."

"I'm all right with a battle scar here and there." After all I'd been through, a thin pink mark on my arm was nothing. With a clean bill of health, I could go back to living in the dorm, could get back to some semblance of a normal life.

Mom and I packed up our things from the apartment, a melancholy tension between us. "I know it's been a rough month and I'm not the easiest person to live with. Just ask your father," she said as she sat on the bed. "But I've really enjoyed getting to know you better, as a young woman instead of just a little girl. I'm really proud of you honey, and I'm going to miss you." I stopped packing and sat next to her, patting her on the leg.

"Thanks, Mom. Truthfully, I feel like I never really knew you before, not really. I mean, you were always just my mom and it hadn't occurred to me that there was more to you than that. I know that sounds stupid, but I guess I just never thought about it."

She laughed and put her hand over mine. "It's not stupid. You never needed to know me as more than just your mom. Now that you're a woman... well, maybe we can be friends, too." She smiled hopefully and I gave her a tight squeeze.

"Definitely. I love you, Mom."

She bit her lip a little as a rush of emotion flashed across her features, but quickly regained her usual strength and control. "I love you, too, sweetheart."

Chapter 28

Since I'd only audited a French history class during the January term, I had to take a pretty heavy load of courses during the spring semester to catch up. I spent almost all my free time studying, which forced me to focus on something productive instead of wallowing in the ever-present ache of missing Aiden.

The first band practice with Ravi, Micah and Todd was a welcome distraction. We rehearsed every other day, which made it hard to get all my studying done, but I really looked forward to it. I arrived at practice early one night to find Ravi at the school's baby grand piano, his eyes closed, his fingers running effortlessly over the keys. The hauntingly beautiful melody echoed in the empty room. He must have sensed my presence because he abruptly stopped playing.

"Don't stop," I said. "That was amazing. You're really talented, you know that?" He shrugged off the compliment and moved to set up his electronic keyboard. "What song was that? I've never heard it before."

"It's something I wrote, but I don't have lyrics for it yet."

He showed me a techno dance riff he'd recorded on his keyboard and I bobbed my head to the rhythm, contributing vocal trills and singing scales around the base notes as his fingers tickled the keys. The guys came in and quickly set up, adding their own expertise to our makeshift jam session. Dancing in place to the infectious beat, I felt lighter and more alive than I had in weeks. I grinned at Ravi and his eyes twinkled as he returned my smile. A moment of pure, unapologetic joy passed between us with the vibration of the music, and a void deep inside began to heal. At the end, we all laughed and congratulated ourselves on our awesome jam, then got down to business in perfecting a couple of songs we'd been working on.

"Hey, I heard there's going to be a talent show in May," Micah said, brushing his sandy brown hair away from his face. "I think first prize is like five hundred bucks or something. Do you guys want to enter?"

"Totally!" Todd chimed in. "I think we should do new material, though, instead of cover tunes, if we want to win," he said with a pointed gaze at Ravi.

"Well, maybe we could nail down the jam we did tonight and put some words to it. Lindsey, do you want to try and write something?" Ravi asked.

"Uh, sure. Why not? I'll give it a shot, but no guarantees it will be any good," I said. The rest of the band promised to try their hand at creative writing as well. I gathered my things at the end of practice, feeling slightly giddy. Ravi walked to the door with me and switched off the light.

"You sounded awesome tonight, Linds. I had no idea you could improvise like that. It was really cool."

"I didn't know I could either," I said, beaming at him. "I guess I just never really tried it before. It was fun. Thanks for asking me to be part of the band." I touched him affectionately on the arm but then pulled away, fearing he might take it wrong. The easygoing connection between us had been hard won and I didn't want to lose that. He looked down at my hand and then at my expression and rolled his eyes.

"You don't have to be afraid to touch me, you know. It's not like I'm going to freak out and jump on you or anything. I know we're just friends." Tension began to seep back into the room. I started to apologize and he sighed, irritated.

"Forget it. It's not a big deal. Goodnight, Lindsey." I watched him walk away, feeling stupid and wondering how the rift between us could ever be healed.

Chapter 29

For spring break, I went home to stay with my dad in Seattle. When he picked me up at the airport, we walked through the parking garage and he stopped at a car I didn't recognize: an older white Saturn 4-door sedan with a sunroof and a stick shift. I asked him where the Blazer was and he replied, "I sold it. I figured that I didn't need that much room anymore now that I'm not carting you and your mom around."

"So you bought this?"

"Well, actually I bought a black Lexus for me." He grinned mischievously. "This one's for you." He tossed me the keys and laughed as my jaw fell open.

"For me?"

"Yep. I was thinking it's about time you had a car of your own. I love you and all, but it'd be a heck of a lot more convenient if you could just drive home from school next time instead of me having to pick you up from the airport." I squealed and gave him a huge hug. He chuckled and squeezed me back, then kissed me on the forehead. "Welcome home, pumpkin."

During the week, we went out to dinner just about every night, though I was able to talk him into letting me cook a couple of times. I enjoyed making 'taties and eggs' for breakfast, though I had to push the image of Aiden out of my head when I did so. Mom called while he was out to tell me that she'd accidentally packed one of my sweaters in her bag. I offered to drive over to her place to retrieve it, but she said she had some errands to do in town and would drop it off. I forgot to mention it to Dad when he returned, so he was completely caught off guard when she showed up on the doorstep. His breath caught when he opened the door to see her standing there.

"Elizabeth. What are you doing here?" His brow creased with worry, but I caught a murmur of hope in his voice.

"I came to return Lindsey's sweater to her. Didn't she tell you? I did call." Dad shook his head blankly, still staring at her. She pursed her lips at me, looking over his shoulder. "You were supposed to tell him. I'm sorry, Gary, I didn't mean to barge in on you." He recovered his composure and invited her in. She hesitated, but then put on her brightest smile, the one that said 'I'm uncomfortable but making the best of this.' She gave me a quick hug and handed me the sweater, then glanced around the living room. "You changed the decoration," she said, taking in the new framed prints and tapestry on the wall.

"Yeah, I needed a change of scenery, you could say," Dad stammered.

"No, I like it. It's nice." She picked up a photograph of me from the fireplace mantle and her features relaxed into a real smile. "I remember that day. You were eight years old and got sent home from school for fighting. You were defending another girl from a bully and got punched in the face. We took you out to ice cream and your dad told you that the dessert would feel good on your swollen eye because it was cold. So you plopped the cone on your face before I could tell you he was kidding. You said it helped and he took the picture of you with that crazy ice cream cone stuck on your face. We didn't know whether to laugh or cry, and we both just about wet our pants when you pulled it off and kept eating it like nothing had happened."

Dad moved beside her to look at the photograph.

"Yeah, I remember that, too. She tried to lick the drips off with her tongue before you hauled her into the bathroom to get cleaned up." I giggled and they smiled at me, lost in remembering better times.

"Mom, do you want to come to dinner with us? We were going to go to P.F. Chang's. We could get your favorite lettuce wraps."

She set down the photograph and shook her head. "No, I really shouldn't. I... I should probably go."

I took hold of her arm, giving her my best puppy dog eyes. "No, stay. Please? I never get to see you. I miss you. Come to dinner. For me?"

She sucked in a breath and fidgeted with the hem of her blouse, a painful expression clouding her face. She turned to Dad, uncertain. "Are you sure you don't mind?"

"We'd love for you to join us," he replied.

She rubbed her hands together and frowned at me, then straightened with decision. "All right, I'll come. I wouldn't, but it's just that I've missed you so much." She hugged me, and I beamed back at her, deliriously happy to have the two of them together again.

Dinner started out quiet as we searched for neutral territory. Mostly, I talked about school and my friends, which classes I liked and those I didn't. I told Mom about the car Dad got me and she raised her eyebrows in surprise. He shrugged, his cheeks tinged pink.

"I finally closed on that premier property on Mercer Island. Blew the sales figures out of the water, so it was a really good month." She congratulated him and the table fell silent again.

We shared the family style meals like we'd done so many times before, with Dad automatically saving the pineapple chunks in the sweet and sour pork dish for Mom because she liked that part best. The corner of her mouth twitched with the hint of a smile. I told Dad about my recovery and how the doctor had given me a clean bill of health.

"That's great, honey. Thank you, Elizabeth, for taking

care of her." Their eyes met and something passed between them as I watched. Mom broke the eye contact and coughed, abruptly excusing herself to use the restroom. "Damn," Dad muttered under his breath and pushed his chair back, running a hand through his hair. When Mom returned, she'd freshened up her lipstick and reapplied the forced smile. We wrapped things up in a hurry.

When we got home, Mom gave me a squeeze and bid a courteous good evening to my dad, thanking him for the meal. He simply nodded, his shoulders slumped and his hands in his pockets. When she left, Dad breathed a heavy sigh and went into the kitchen to pour himself a drink. He threw it back in one gulp and refilled his glass before heading down to the family room and switching on the television. I could tell he wanted to be alone with his thoughts, so I went to my bedroom to read.

After a couple hours, I glanced at the clock, my eyes tired and scratchy. I yawned and padded down the hall to the bathroom. Blue light from the television glowed in the dark hallway and I crept downstairs to see if Dad had fallen asleep in his chair. The TV was muted but he sat silently staring at it, wet tracks on his cheeks and a half-empty bottle of whisky on the end table next to him.

"Dad, are you all right?" I whispered, afraid to startle him. Dazed, he turned to look at me, his eyes blurry and red.

"No," was his quiet reply. I sat in the chair next to him and put my hand on his arm.

"Did your mom ever tell you she wanted to be a dancer?" he asked.

"Uh, yeah she mentioned it," I replied, uneasy.

"She was studying dance when I met her in college, and she was incredible—so strong and yet so small. The way she moved, I can't even describe it. It was like gravity didn't have a hold on her." He paused to take a drink from his glass. "She was the most beautiful woman I'd ever seen. Still is, really. And she laughed at my jokes. I couldn't believe she wanted to be with me, but by some grace of God, she did. I wanted to marry her from the moment I laid eyes on her, but she had big dreams, your mom.

"She was going to go to New York—to Julliard—and I was so happy for her. I would have followed her, you know. I would have gone to the ends of the earth for her. But then she got pregnant with you." He stopped and gave me a sad smile, patting my hand.

"She was devastated, but I couldn't have been happier. We got married and when you came along, she was happy… for a while. She was a great mom but I left her alone too much. I got a corporate sales job and traveled a lot when you were little. I made plenty of money, but I hated being away from the two of you. So I quit and went into real estate so I could pick my own hours. That's when it was the best. We had the days together because I would show houses to people in the evenings after they got off work, and I took a whole month off in the summer so we could spend it at the cabin."

He grew quiet and I wondered if he was going to continue. He sniffed and wiped his cheeks with the back of his hand, then finished his drink. "But when you were gone at school, she was restless. She used to tell me how much she wanted to travel, to see the world, to make something of herself. And I didn't listen. I had everything I wanted—my wife, my daughter, a flexible job—and I couldn't understand why she wasn't happy. I thought if it was enough for me, it should be enough for her. Eventually, she stopped asking and just became bitter and resentful toward me. I tried to make it up to her toward the end, even offered to take her on a cruise, but it was too little, too late."

My heart ached for him and I tried to make it better. "It wasn't your fault, Dad. She's the one who had an affair."

He flinched but shook his head. "No, it was my fault. I drove her to it. She couldn't get what she needed from me, so she went somewhere else to find excitement and fulfillment. I was a fool and I lost her because of it." A tear rolled down his cheek. He didn't even try to wipe it away.

"Nothing's been the same since she left. She was—well, the two of you were—my whole world. When you went away to college, I was all alone in this empty house every night and the only solace I found was in this damn bottle, trying to forget everything I'd lost. I wanted to die because I had no reason for living once she left. You were the only thing that kept me from killing myself and believe it or not, I actually resented you for it because it meant I had to endure the pain." He chest shook with a sob and I held on tight to his hand.

"You're all I have left, pumpkin, because I was stupid and let her go. When she called to tell me you were in that accident, I felt like my heart had been carved out of my chest. If you had died... oh God..." His words became incomprehensible as the grief and pain poured out of him. I got up and sat on his lap with my arms around his neck and he clung to me like a life preserver, his face buried in my shoulder as he cried. Finally, he straightened up and wiped his face with his sleeve.

I felt an overwhelming compulsion to tell him the truth about that night.

"I did die in that accident, Dad. I went to this beautiful place where the ground moved underneath me and the air was a part of me, and where time stopped. It was amazing and wonderful. But God sent me back, back to my body, back to you." A lump built in my throat and I swallowed hard, but the ache of loss was more than I could bear and I started to cry as well. Dad held me close and whispered words of love and comfort to me as he'd done when I was a child. I dissolved in his arms, releasing the pent up pain and emotion until we were both exhausted.

"Thank you, God, for bringing my baby girl home to me," Dad whispered to the dark room, the first prayer I'd ever heard him utter, and I repeated it in my head.

Chapter 30

Even with the new car, I was in a melancholy mood when I returned to school after the break. While I appreciated my father's confiding in me, his sullen state wore me down and I found myself spending long periods of time thinking about Aiden. I couldn't get him out of my head and as much as I tried to focus on the present, a dense fog had taken up residence in my brain. The long drive back to school by myself hadn't helped.

Unable to concentrate, I felt as though I were just going through the motions in class. My friends kept asking me if I was all right and I assured them I was fine, but I wasn't. I spoke to Aiden in my mind constantly, describing to him what I saw, what I felt, what I was thinking. A part of me wanted to believe that if I sunk deep enough into my thoughts that I would somehow hear his voice again. It wasn't rational, but I wasn't firing on all cylinders anyway, so logical thought was not a prerequisite. I sank farther into depression day after day and not only was I powerless to stop it, I didn't really want to.

I dreamt of Aiden that night, his easy smile and his thick Scottish accent as he teased me.

"Sit still!" I said as I tried to paint his portrait. He sat on the stool for a while, his sky blue eyes twinkling at me, but invariably got bored and came to see what I'd painted so far.

"Why, ye haven't painted a stroke yet, lassie!" he complained and I scolded him for peeking. I frowned at the canvas, which seemed to clear away all my work like an Etch-a-Sketch every time he moved. He took his place again and I started over, outlining the curve of his face, his brow and strong jaw. Just when I'd started to make some progress, he'd jump up and the image would be washed away.

"Don't! You have to stay put until I'm finished. I keep losing you when you move!" I tried again, but the colors all mixed together as I painted, swimming together in pools of gold and blue. Aiden frowned and I finally gave up, standing to go over to him. But I couldn't move past the ruined painting. Tears streamed down his smeared face on the canvas. I reached for him and he for me, but the easel stood firmly between us, keeping us apart, mocking me with the barely recognizable image of my love.

"Lindsey, are you okay?" Stephanie's voice woke me as her hand lightly pressed on my shoulder. My wet pillow stuck to my face as I groggily turned to look at her.

"You were crying in your sleep. Were you having a bad dream?" She whispered in the dark room, seated next to me on my bed. I sat up and nodded feebly to her. She opened her arms and I leaned against her, letting the tears flow freely while she held me.

"Thanks. You're a good friend, Steph," I snuffled, wiping my face with the sleeve of my nightgown.

"My mom always told me the way to combat a nightmare is to think of something that makes you happy. Like Christmas morning, or your birthday, or a trip to the beach." She smiled in encouragement and I assured her I would try it as I lay back down, but every happy thought I could come up with centered around Aiden, which didn't help to dispel the emptiness in my chest at all.

I remembered Christmas in the hospital when my dad gave me that journal to help me "write stuff" and promised myself I'd dig it out and give it a try in the morning.

Chapter 31

It turned out I didn't get a chance to write anything until later the next day. I wanted to go sit in the oak grove but since it was April in the Pacific Northwest, everything was sopping wet. So I slogged through the marshy grass to the library and sat in an isolated corner where the lamp cast a warm pool of light around me. I began to write, to empty out some of the pain and brokenness in hopes of finding peace.

Students moved about the library in hushed tones, ignoring me as I sniffled and wiped my nose with a tissue, my head bent over the journal. The words spilled out of me in a flow of ink, the pen moving across the page almost by itself. Exhausted and emptied at the end, I closed my eyes in a silent prayer of thanks, my hand clutched tightly to the ring I wore around my neck, hidden under my blouse.

"What are you writing?" Ravi's lilting Indian accent startled me and I squeaked in surprise, dropping my journal on the floor. The noise echoed throughout the library and several heads turned in my direction.

"Sorry," I whispered, and the students quickly lost interest. Ravi picked up the journal and sat in the chair across from me, murmuring "Can I see?" as the book naturally flipped open to where I'd been writing. I lurched forward to retrieve it, but he started reading aloud, his voice soft yet sure in the still room.

My God, my God
My heart is pierced, my foundation shaken
I'm pressing hard against the dam but it's not   enough
I can't keep the pain at bay
The leaks are killing me, memories of joy stripped
*   away*
Flashes of love, a smile, a touch and the ache starts
*   again*

You're there, God, I can feel you near
But you don't save me from despair
Your love keeps me breathing, keeps me moving
But I don't understand your ways

Bring peace again, my God
Give me strength to bear the pain
Make me whole again, Lord
And hold me through the flood

I am not God, I am barely even me
My heart is battered in this storm
Make me whole again, Lord
And hold me through the flood

Ravi finished reading and sat staring at the journal in his hands. "Wow," he said and finally looked up at me, his face stricken and awed at the same time. "That's beautiful. I had no idea you felt that way." I couldn't meet his gaze but when he set the journal on my knees, I clutched it tight. "I know I'm not supposed to say 'I'm sorry' anymore, but..." his voice trailed off as he grappled for words. "Actually, everything I want to say is off limits." He sighed in frustration.

"Screw it," he muttered under his breath and put his arms around me in a firm embrace. His breath was hot against my cheek and he whispered "I love you" before he kissed my temple and released me, then left the room without another word. I stared helplessly after him, tears dropping unchecked onto the swirling pink *L* of the journal in my lap.

Chapter 32

Tension built steadily during the last few weeks of the school year. Stephanie decided things were moving too fast with Micah and suggested they take things slow. He didn't respond well and she came back to the room in tears after they had a big fight. The emotional undercurrent made our band rehearsals uncomfortable, but I was so excited about the talent show that I tried to push it aside. Still, I looked forward to each practice session with a mixture of anticipation and dread.

Before the talent show began, my stomach churned with nerves and I kept an eye on the nearest restroom, just in case I had to make a run for it. Micah's face had gone a pasty white color and Ravi fidgeted, rocking back and forth on his heels and twisting his hands. Todd practiced his part by drumming on anything that would sit still: the wall, his knees, the chair. When he tried to add Micah to that list of drummable objects, I thought things might come to blows.

When the emcee finally announced us, we strolled out onto the stage, pretending we weren't one breath away from hysteria. The stage lights shone pink and blue in my eyes as Todd counted the time with his sticks. The familiar rhythm of our opening song enveloped me with its thumping beat and the bonds of anxiety fell away.

The crowd of students in the auditorium jumped and danced along with us like a swirling mass of pure adrenaline. A cheer broke out from the audience when we finished and I beamed as bright as one of the hot stage lights, waving to the sea of unfamiliar faces like a rock star. In the end, we took second place and won $250, but you'd have thought we were Grammy award winners, we were so stoked.

Todd lived in an apartment off-campus and invited us over for an after-show party, along with twenty or so of his closest friends. Jen, Paul and Steph joined us and the energy was high. It was right before finals week and we'd studied as much as humanly possible, so we were all in the mood to celebrate the end of the school year, not to mention our second-place win. Alcohol flowed freely and since the party was within walking distance of the college, no one had to hold back as a designated driver, so we enjoyed ourselves more than we should have.

I'm not sure if it was the alcohol, but Stephanie and Micah had apparently made up and were joined at the hip. Though I wasn't very fond of Micah, it was good to see her happy again and I smiled when I caught sight of them kissing in the hallway. The pressing fog I'd been living under had receded and I felt happier than I had in a long time, laughing with my friends and fondly recounting the story of our success like it hadn't just happened hours ago.

Ravi touched my arm as he added his own perspective to the story and it felt completely natural. In fact, he found multiple opportunities to touch me: as he brushed past me in the narrow hallway to the restroom, moving behind me in the kitchen to get another drink and conducting me across the living room to introduce me to someone from his Physics class. I didn't care—in fact, I enjoyed it—and when he offered to walk me home at two in the morning when the party finally broke up, I happily accepted, thankful for his company and the renewed ease of our friendship. Deliriously buzzed and light-headed, I hooked my hand over Ravi's arm as we walked back to the dorm.

"Do you mind if we stop at the music hall on the way?" he asked. "I've been working on something I want to play for you."

The hall was unlocked, I was surprised to find, and he explained that he often comes to play in the evening, so had worked out a system with the janitor. The familiar room stood quiet and still, and Ravi flipped on only one bank of lights, which gave the space a warm, intimate glow. He led me to the piano and we sat on the bench next to one another, our thighs touching. He rested his fingers on the keys for a moment, then began playing the haunting melody I remembered from earlier in the spring. The minor key wrapped around me in a sad embrace as the beautiful music echoed in the empty room.

I closed my eyes and let the sound wash over me, its melancholy tendrils weaving through my mind. His voice was soft but clear as he began to sing, *"My God, my God, my heart is pierced, my foundation shaken..."*

My hand flew to my mouth as I recognized the lyrics to the poem I'd written in my journal. He didn't turn to look at me but continued on, singing the words from my soul. My chest constricted and I trembled with emotion, the music wringing my heart, his voice breaking through my defenses.

"Bring peace again, my God, give me strength to bear the pain," he sang as I struggled unsuccessfully to hold back the tears. I mouthed the words along with him, the song building in intensity to the finish. *"Make me whole again, Lord and hold me through the flood."* His fingers flowed across the keys, his face drawn in concentration.

His voice wavered slightly at the end, the final notes lingering in the air. My head swam with alcohol and I couldn't think straight. The pain and tenderness in his eyes made my heart swell in compassion. Silently, he wiped away my tears, then took my face in his hands and brought his lips to mine. My body responded before my mind could object, the warmth of his mouth a powerful aphrodisiac. I kissed him back and his arms came around me, pulling me close. The blood pounded in my veins as we kissed and I completely lost myself in the moment. The sound of the music still echoed in my head, surging like waves on the shore and his embrace was like a life preserver in the flood of emotions that threatened to overwhelm me. At last we broke apart and he smiled down at me.

"I'm glad you liked it," he said. "I've been working on it ever since that day in the library." My mind flashed to that moment and my hand went automatically to the ring I wore hanging from Ravi's chain.

Misunderstanding, he grinned at me. "I never did ask you if you liked the necklace with the music note. Can I see it?" He reached to pull the chain so the charm would be exposed and I jerked backward, fumbling as I stood up.

"No, Ravi, I… oh God, I shouldn't have… I'm sorry." I turned to go and he reached out, grabbing my hand.

"What is it? What's wrong?" I shook my head, pulling my hand free and clenching my fists, trying to gain control of myself.

"Ravi, you are magnificent and I don't deserve you." He tried to protest but I cut him off, my voice shaking. "No, it's true. You're my best friend and I can't stand to hurt you, but I can't do this anymore." The words echoed in the stillness of the room. "I never told you because I didn't want to hurt you. But I've already hurt you so much more than I…" I took a deep breath and closed my eyes, unable to look at him. "I died in that accident and I gave my heart away. It's not mine to give you anymore, as much as you deserve it. I can't be with you, Ravi. I can't. I'm sorry. I'm so sorry."

A sob tore at my lungs and I ran out of the room, my hand over my mouth. I fled to the dorm, trying to outrun the frustration and pain, and collapsed on my bed. Stephanie murmured acknowledgment when I came in but rolled over and quickly fell back to sleep. Staring up at the base of Jen's top bunk, I prayed that God would release me from this anguish. At long last, the solace of sleep arrived.

Chapter 33

Curled up in Aiden's lap, I ran one hand over his bare chest, brushing the light blond hairs with my fingers. He stroked my back, his fingers gliding up my silk nightgown until they wove in my hair at the base of my neck. His warm, musky scent enveloped me as we kissed, and a sound of pure pleasure emanated from deep in my throat. He slowly fell backward on the couch, pulling me on top of him. He breathed short phrases of love to me in French, sending a wave of tingles down my spine. I leaned forward and kissed him fiercely, the passion burning like fire in my chest. Our bodies molded together perfectly as I pressed against him.

But his kisses grew slack and I tasted the metallic flavor of blood on my lips. My hands slipped over his chest, suddenly wet and sticky. Hot iron burned my nostrils and I opened my eyes to see Aiden splayed out beneath me, his body limp and covered in blood, his sightless eyes staring right through me.

"NO!"

I screamed and bolted upright. Both Jen and Steph rushed to my side, but I was already on my feet, pulling on my clothes. "I have to go. I have to get out of here," I stammered, grabbing my coat. I ran down the stairs of the dormitory and out into the black night air. I threw up in the bushes right outside the door; the alcohol from the party scoured my throat as I retched.

The late spring rain chilled my skin as I crossed the

commons area. Stumbling on the slippery grass, I ran with a desperate need to get away from the school, away from everything. Light from the streetlamps scattered in the pouring rain, reflecting dimly on the slick puddles under my feet. As I made my way into town, my lungs burned with fire and an ache stabbed me in the side, forcing me to slow down. The streetlights blinked red at the intersection, and I wandered across the deserted road, taking gasping breaths of the moist night air. Without conscious thought, I found myself headed toward the hospital. Father O'Malley's request that I come see him if ever I needed to talk replayed in my mind and I picked up the pace again, eager now that I had a purpose. The nurse at the receiving desk of the emergency room took in my drenched appearance with mild concern.

"I need to see Father O'Malley. Is he in tonight? It's an emergency."

Surprise flickered in her eyes but her professional expression of calm never wavered. She consulted a schedule on the computer and gave me a reassuring smile.

"He's here this evening. I'll call him to let him know you need to see him. He may be with another patient though, so I'll need to ask you to sit and wait until he is able to meet with you." She gestured to the bank of chairs in the lobby and I anxiously ran my fingers through my sopping wet hair.

"Tell him to hurry, okay? I really need to talk to him." She nodded and handed me some paperwork on a clipboard. I stared at it blankly, then took it over to a hard plastic chair and sat down.

Visions of Aiden and Ravi whirred through my mind, and I squeezed my eyes shut to try and block them out. My hand shook as I tried to fill in the simple form that required my name and address. I returned the clipboard to the nurse, trembling with cold and desperation. She mumbled something into the phone and then turned to me as she hung up, her tone pleasant and unconcerned. "He will be with you soon."

Pacing around the small waiting room, I picked up a magazine and thumbed through it, not seeing it at all. The wall clock's ticking pounded on my temples; the space between each second grew longer and longer. I dropped the magazine and wrung my hands, trying to take deep breaths as tears threatened to overtake me.

Oh God, I am losing it. Help me!

"Lindsey?" Father O'Malley's kind voice broke through my despair and my heart leaped at seeing him again. I wanted to fling myself into his arms and tell him everything, since he was the only one who knew my secret. "My goodness, you are soaked clear through. Did you walk here? No matter, come to the chapel. I will get you a warm blanket and some tea. Thank you, Gladys." He smiled at the nurse and led me by the arm down the hall.

Once inside the sanctuary, I started to calm down, the twisted knot in my gut slowly unraveling. Six rows of wooden pews faced an altar and a cross, with a place for kneeling at the front. Dozens of votive candles adorned the altar, their light casting a warm glow on the stained glass windows on either side of the cross.

I huddled in the pew closest to the altar and Father O'Malley wrapped a heavy blanket around my shoulders, then sat down beside me. The surprise at seeing me had worn off and he was as calm and composed as I remembered him, his face giving away nothing except a faint curiosity. I stared at the cross, which flickered with shadows from the candles.

"Father, you have to forgive me. I... I'm married to Aiden and I kissed someone else tonight." Guilt and shame pressed down on me as the vision of Aiden's glassy, lifeless eyes seared my mind. I told the priest everything that had happened since I'd seen him last: confronting my mother about her affair, my father's near suicide, Ravi and the song he wrote. He listened, as I knew he would, as the words spilled out of me. The relief of being able to talk about my pain—and to someone so kind and caring—was like a salve on a burn. When I'd emptied myself, I took a deep breath, still shaken but somehow comforted by the soft glow of the candles on the altar and the chaplain's presence.

"I hesitate to suggest this, Lindsey, since I know that your feelings are certainly real. But is there a chance that what you experienced was—"

"Oh! I completely forgot!" I cut him off, knowing what he was going to say.

I reached into the neck of my wet blouse and pulled out my wedding ring, which hung there as tangible evidence of Aiden's love. When I told him what it was, his eyes grew wide and he tentatively reached out to touch it. I unclasped the necklace and dropped it into his hands.

"I was wearing it when they pulled me from the car, but the paramedics took it off. I didn't find it until after I left the hospital."

He crossed himself and murmured something I didn't understand as he held the ring in his open palm, the chain dangling through his fingers.

"It was real, Father. And I miss him so much I can hardly breathe. God brought me back here and I think I understand why. I mean, at least, for my father... but I can't be free here when my heart belongs to Aiden. I've wanted to die—thought about it often, in fact. But I know that's not the solution. I just don't know what to do. It hurts so bad." I stared at the candles with an empty, throbbing ache in my chest. He placed the ring in my hand and closed his fingers around my fist.

"You're right; suicide is not the answer. God brought you back to this earth for a reason, of that we are sure. But He also provided you with this extraordinary ring as proof of your marriage to Aiden, so we can only assume He wants you to remember that as well." He shook his head slowly, deep in thought.

"Let us pray, Lindsey, and seek His will." He moved to

the altar and knelt down, and I followed him, unsure of what to do. We bowed our heads and he prayed aloud for guidance, for God's will to be shown to us, for peace that passed all understanding. My heart joined in with him fervently. When he finished, we returned to the pew. Physically and emotionally exhausted, I gazed up at him with raw, aching eyes.

"When I perform a marriage ceremony," he said, "I use the phrase 'Til death do you part,' but in your case, life is what has parted you and Aiden. I think it's the same. On earth, when you are separated from your spouse by death, you are no longer bound to the marriage covenant that you made. In your case, since your return to earth has separated you in a likewise fashion from your husband, I do not believe that you are bound to him while you remain here." His words made sense, but they were like a knife in my heart. I shook my head vehemently. He touched my hand, his skin soft and warm against mine.

"You need to grieve, my child. You have lost the man that you love, whether through life or death. He is gone and you must go through the grieving process in order to heal. Holding on to him will only hurt you further and draw out your pain. Grief is different for every person, so I can't say how long it will take before you feel whole again. But you must begin. Find a place where you can be alone. Cry and pray and let out the painful emotions inside of you. Write a letter to him, say goodbye, whatever it takes. Read your Bible and ask God to comfort you. He says 'Blessed are those who mourn, for they will be comforted.' Let Him comfort you in your mourning, Lindsey."

I remembered with shame the beautiful two-tone Bible that he'd given me that lay untouched on my dresser. I hadn't the strength to disagree and reluctantly admitted to myself that he might be right, as painful as it was to contemplate letting go. The longing for Aiden was tearing me apart and the prospect of healing was like a pinpoint of light in the darkness. He prayed for me again and then kindly drove me home.

I didn't get out of bed all day Sunday and when finals began on Monday, I was at least rested if not focused. At the end of each day of testing, I crawled back in bed and stayed there. My roommates were worried about me, but I told them I was just tired. It was true; I was tired. Tired of hurting, tired of crying, tired of feeling like half my soul was missing. So I slept.

At the end of finals week, Jen and Steph were packed up for the summer and hugged me goodbye, their concern evident. "I'll be fine," I assured them. "Next year is gonna be better, just wait." I gave them a brave smile and promised to email them over the summer. Sitting on the bed after they left, I knew what I needed to do. I picked up my cell phone and called my dad.

"Hi, Dad. Yeah, finals went okay. I won't know how I did for a few weeks though, since they still have to be graded. Yeah thanks, I hope I did well. Um, listen, Dad? I... I'm not coming home right now. I need some time away, some time to myself so I can just think. It's been a really rough year. No, it's not your fault. I just need to be alone for a while, so I'm gonna to go to the cabin. I'm not sure how long I'll be there. Maybe I'll get a job in town or something, but I need to go."

Thankfully, he understood and even insisted on adding to the cash card he'd given me so I could buy supplies. "Thanks, Dad. I love you."

"I love you, too, pumpkin. Call me if you need anything, all right? Be safe." I promised him I would and hung up, then just stared at the phone.

Chapter 34

I busied myself with packing up and going into town to buy the necessary supplies for a couple of weeks at the cabin. In truth, I had no idea how long I'd be there. I just knew I had to go. The doctor's words echoed in my head as I pulled onto the freeway heading north.

It's not going to be fun, but the only way to get better is to work with the pain instead of trying to avoid it.

So I drove headlong into the pain and the closer I got to the cabin, the more excited and anxious I became. I told myself he wouldn't be there, that it would be empty, but just the idea of standing in the place where I'd seen him last made my pulse quicken in anticipation. Moonlight struggled to illuminate the hazy midnight sky as I finally pulled onto the dirt road. Driving slowly, careful not to kick up dust, I held my breath until the dark shape of the cabin was visible in my headlights. I shut off the car and stared at it, unable to go in.

Give me strength, Lord.

I left the headlights on so I could see the path to the front door and felt around underneath the eave for the spare key. A sliver pierced my finger and I jerked my hand away, irritated, then grabbed the key and unlocked the door. The floorboards had swollen over the winter so I had to shove hard to get it open.

Well, fixing that will give me something to occupy myself at least.

I flipped the power switch on the electrical panel and a

low, steady hum filled the room as the antique refrigerator sprang to life. When I turned on the light in the kitchen, my eyes immediately went to the little card table where he'd sat watching me cook breakfast. My chest constricted and I couldn't breathe.

Empty.

I swallowed hard and turned away, flipping on the porch light and heading out into the cool night air to retrieve my bags. The familiar scent of the pine trees welcomed me back and I gave myself a mental shake.

Hold it together, Lindsey. You can do this.

After hauling in the supplies and loading the fridge, I took my bags upstairs and shivered with the cold as I turned on the lamp next to the bed. The memory of sleeping with Aiden on that king-sized bed taunted me and I squeezed my eyes shut to try and block it out of my mind. Thinking it was more neutral ground, I set up my blankets on one of the twin beds under the eave instead.

After turning off the lights, I changed into a flannel nightgown and burrowed under the covers. Tired as I was, sleep was not likely to come anytime soon. The special scent of the cabin, musty pine and wood smoke, curled around me in a comforting embrace. This was my favorite place in the whole world, now even more so because I'd shared it with Aiden. And though the loss of him consumed my every thought as I lay there in the dark, I knew I was where I needed to be. And that was enough.

The next morning, I woke to the sound of birds chirping as the sun streamed through the window. I smiled and stretched, remembering many other days from my childhood when I'd awakened the same way, in this very bed. I changed clothes and padded down the stairs, humming softly. I realized it had been a long time since I'd sung to myself. The thought made me sad and I frowned, more convinced than ever that Father O'Malley was right, that I needed this in order to heal.

I set to work building a fire in the antique wood stove, feeling Aiden's presence as strongly as if he were standing right behind me. I knew it was stupid, but I turned around anyway, half expecting to see him standing there with that amused look in his eyes. He wasn't, of course, but I felt as if the air was thick with his spirit and I gripped the edge of the sink to steady myself.

Damn, this is even harder than I thought.

I built a fire in the living room, trying not to think of the times I'd sat watching him do just that, relishing the way his kilt moved over his legs. Memories bubbled to the surface but I tamped them down, afraid that if I were to open up the floodgates entirely, I might not make it. I concentrated instead on remembering the cabin as a child, when it was my dad who was making the fire. Of how he taught me to bait a hook with a worm while I made girly noises of disgust. Dad loved to go fishing and got so excited whenever he caught something. He'd make us eat the little fish with barely a flake of meat on them and he'd sigh contentedly with the first forkful like it was manna from heaven. The thought of my dad reminded me of why I had come.

I headed outside and walked down the hill to the lake. The beautiful June sunshine reflected off the water with dazzling brightness. Across the lake, I could see a handful of boats with people enjoying their summer at the lake. It was different than when I was here with Aiden, and I was thankful for that. Fingering the ring I wore around my neck, I thought of the emotion on his face as he'd asked me to be his bride. I held my head in my hands and allowed the tears to come.

Oh Aiden, I miss you so much. I see you everywhere I look. It's so hard.

I told myself I should stop talking to him in my head, that doing so only made it harder to move on, but I needed to tell him how I felt, even though I knew he couldn't hear. Still, this is why I had come, to get it all out once and for all so I could move on, so I could move past the pain. It was going to be a long couple of weeks, though.

Back at the cabin, I crept upstairs to take a nap, my heart heavy. When I woke, the fading rays of an orange and red sunset illuminated the loft. I sat on the edge of the bed for a long time, staring at the empty room. He was gone—I knew it in my bones. I'd accepted it at last, but only numbness remained. My stomach growled but I ignored it. My bladder made its own needs known and I begrudgingly obliged, finally getting off the bed and heading to the bathroom outside.

After rebuilding the fire, I spent the rest of the evening staring at the orange flames as they flickered back and forth, devouring the logs with beautiful tongues of fire. Darkness came but I didn't move to turn on a light, simply frozen in place, mesmerized by the movement of the flames. I opened my journal to the poem I'd written about Aiden that Ravi had set to music and felt a pang in my chest. I turned to a blank page and began to write in the eerie shadows of the firelight.

Dear Aiden,

I stared at the words on the page, unsure of how to say goodbye. A tear dropped on the page next to his name, the ink blurring slightly at the edge. I pressed on.

There are no words to describe how much I miss you, how much I hurt inside to be apart from you and to know I can never touch you again. Maybe in death we'll be together, whenever that comes again, but not now. I have cried until no more tears would come and I cannot cry anymore.

I have to let go. I don't want to. I want to hold on to you with every beat of my heart, but the pain is more than I can bear. This is the only way for me to heal. And I desperately need to heal. I can't go on this way. It's killing me inside.

*I love you. Oh God, I love you, Aiden, but I have to let
you go or I will never live again. I will remember you
forever, your voice, your smile, your touch. You are all I
could have ever wanted, my lover, my friend, my husband.*

My hand shook as I wrote the word 'husband' and I had
to stop. I prayed for strength and concentrated on the sound
of the fire, hissing and popping in the quiet stillness of the
room.

I have to say goodbye. I'm sorry.

The word 'goodbye' screamed at me from the page and
instead of feeling the release and closure I'd hoped for, anger
flared within me. My mind revolted at the sight of the word
and I pictured Aiden's face as if I'd said the words aloud to
him.

*I can just picture the hurt in his eyes. I could never do
that to him. Never.*

Somewhere in the hazy depth of my pain, my mind
grabbed hold of the word 'picture' and my blood froze
instantly.

"Oh, please..."

I leapt off the couch, the journal and pen spilling off my
lap onto the floor. I dashed through the dark shadows of the
room to the kitchen drawer where we kept the camera and
flung the contents onto the floor. Frantically, I yanked out the
camera, my hands shaking as I pressed the power button. The
light from the LCD screen glowed bright in the nearly black
room and I crumpled to the floor as my legs turned to jelly
beneath me. Clutching the camera tight with both hands, I
drank in the beauty of our smiling faces in the picture before
me.

The floodgate I'd been trying so hard to hold back
finally burst open. Heaving sobs racked my body, the heart

wrenching sound echoing off the walls all around me. I couldn't tear my eyes from his face for the longest time but at last pulled myself up, my legs still shaking. Wobbling back to the couch, I retrieved the journal, grabbed the pages of my letter to Aiden with my fist and ripped them out. When I tossed them into the fire, the pages scattered, sending sparks flying into the room as the flames greedily consumed this latest prey. Upstairs, I collapsed into bed with the camera cradled against my chest.

Fragmented dreams of Aiden filled my mind as I slept. My heart swelled with love as I watched him build a fire. He came over and pulled me into his arms, the smell of wood smoke clinging heavily to him. His clothing and his hair were thick with the scent and I pulled away from him, coughing a little and covering my mouth. He gave me a quizzical smile and I coughed again, coming awake.

Swirling grey fingers seeped through the floorboards in the loft and I blinked in confusion, my mind not comprehending why they were there. A hazy sheen of smoke was visible in the moonlight, the wispy tendrils silently jostling one another for space on the ceiling.

"Oh, shit!" I cried, my mind finally coming up to speed. I leapt out of bed and raced down the stairs, covering my mouth as I ran into the billowing smoke that had filled the kitchen and living room. The acrid stench filled my lungs and burned my eyes as I grabbed the fire extinguisher. I batted at the smoke with my free hand and it taunted me, moving away and then quickly circling back. The woodpile next to the fireplace had caught on fire and orange flames menacingly licked the draperies above. I pulled the pin and squeezed the handle, praying that it would work. A spray of white foam poured from the container and I swept it back and forth over the base of the flames.

My eyes watered uncontrollably and I squeezed them shut, focusing all my energies on putting out the fire. My arms and legs began to shake as the extinguisher spit out its final droplets of foam. I scrambled toward the door to the outside deck and tripped on the wooden mushroom footstool, knocking my forehead soundly against the hardwood floor. Crawling on my hands and knees, I strained to make it to the door. The smoke strangled me, gripping my lungs with its burning, acid stench. The suffocating pressure in my chest held me in place and I reached out in desperation before my arm fell limp and all strength was gone.

Aiden...

I called to him in my mind with my last conscious thought, then surrendered to the dense grey fog that consumed me.

Chapter 35

Strong arms pounded me on the back and I coughed hoarsely, feeling the cool, fresh air pulled into my lungs like water over desert sand. I gulped the air in desperate breaths and wiped my watering eyes with the palm of one hand, the blackened film of smoke residue smeared across my fingers.

"Oh, thank ye, Jesus," a voice breathed next to my ear and those strong arms pulled me into a bear-like embrace, making me cough harder as I gasped for air. "Oh sorry, lass."

My head snapped up at the sound and breath no longer mattered as my eyes flew open wide. "Aiden!" I croaked in disbelief. His arms tightened around me and his voice cracked.

"Lindsey, my love, you're all right," he whispered and I could feel his chest trembling as he held me. I pulled away so I could see his face, my heart singing with joy. My eyes and throat still stung terribly and the tears streaming down my face didn't help, but I didn't care.

"Aiden... Oh God, Aiden..." I couldn't stop saying his name and I ran my hands over his face, his arms, his back, unable to touch him enough.

"It's really you, *mo chridhe*. I can hardly believe you're in my arms again. Oh, Lord in heaven..." The words tumbled out of him as his fingertips traced my face in wonder and awe. I smiled at him and his face broke into a huge grin.

We both started laughing, overcome with emotion. He cupped my face with both hands, like he'd done so many times before, and kissed me. My heart leapt in my chest and I pressed myself against him, filled with unspeakable relief and joy at being in his arms again.

His mouth tasted like smoke and when we pulled away, I closed my eyes, imagining the cabin and our bodies restored, then waited expectantly for the familiar shimmer to pass over me, making everything new once more. Nothing happened. I frowned and tried again.

Nothing.

"Why can't I cast? What's wrong?" My stomach clenched in confusion and fear as I sought the answer in his eyes, but he just smiled.

"It's because you're not dead." I just shook my head, not understanding. He swept his thumb across my forehead to smooth my brow, his eyes full of excitement as if he had a wonderful secret to share. "And now, because of you, neither am I."

"What?" I cried.

He threw back his head and let out a full belly laugh as I stared at him, dumbfounded. "I can hardly wait to tell you the tale, but I think I'd best attend to our home before it burns down, aye?" He winked at me and I blinked back at him, awestruck.

Our home. Not dead.

My mind could not comprehend what was happening and I watched helplessly as he turned toward the cabin. Smoke spilled out the door and across the deck, its black and grey clouds hovering in the moonlight. Fear gripped me as he approached the building.

"Wait!" I shouted and he turned to look at me. "No, don't. Let it burn. I don't care. I won't lose you again." I tried to stand up but didn't have the strength, and instead sat shaking as tears started flowing over my dirty cheeks once again. He came back and held my hands, his face tender but his voice firm.

"You will not lose me again. I'll never let that happen if

it is within my power, I swear to you. I couldn't stand it myself any more than you could, trust me."

He kissed me softly and I believed him, the spark of hope lighting in my chest. He disappeared into the cabin, one hand over his mouth. One by one, he opened all of the windows and the front door, darting back out to the deck for gulps of fresh air from time to time. Finally, he came back to sit down next to me, satisfied.

"It will take a bit to air out completely, but the fire is out. 'Tis naught but smoke now." I nodded and told him about the fire extinguisher. "You're a right brave lass, more so than I even knew before. Well done, my love."

He pulled me onto his lap, holding me close. I sat there for a long time with my head on his shoulder, letting the shock and sheer happiness at being with him wash over me, restoring my soul. I finally sat up enough to look at him, his face glowing with wonder and excitement in the moonlight.

"Are you really here?" I asked. "And now?" His body seemed real enough beneath me but I was afraid to believe it.

"I know it's hard to imagine, but it's true." The corners of his eyes crinkled merrily as he grinned at me.

"But what happened? Where have you been? Here at the cabin by yourself the whole time?" The idea that he'd been a day's drive away for the last six months while I'd been agonizing over his loss was more than my mind could bear and a note of accusation crept into my voice. He shook his head, his forehead creased in a frown, his eyes reflecting the pain I'd lived through.

"Of course not. I would have done anything in my power to come to you. You cannot think…" His voice trailed off and his gaze bored into me, demanding an answer. I shook my head and he breathed a heavy sigh. He stroked my arm and continued softly, his voice wavering.

"No, when you were taken away before my very eyes, there was naught that I could do. I tore the place apart like a mad man, crazed with anger and pain. But it didn't matter."

He broke off, unable to speak for a moment, fighting for control. He squeezed my hand and swallowed hard, his face etched with the agony of that moment. "I stayed here at the cabin for the longest time, hoping that by the grace of God, somehow you'd come back."

"You didn't go back to transporting then?" I had always pictured him that way, moving on with his duties of taking souls to heaven. Surprise flickered across his face.

"No, love. Once I found you… no, I never went back. I was not fit for it any longer. My every thought was of you and you alone." He stopped then and kissed me, the desperate longing clear in his embrace. My heart ached at the thought of him living through the same kind of torment I'd known. He pulled away and gathered my hands in his own, stroking them as he continued.

"I don't know how long I stayed there. Time is not the same there as it is on earth, you remember? Since you cast the sun and the moon, it can be any time of day for as long as you want. So one day can feel like a thousand years or just an instant." I nodded, remembering that magical place. "So I don't know how long it was, but it certainly felt more like a thousand years that I stayed here in this cabin, raging like a lunatic and weeping like a child." He gave me a half-smile and I pulled him tightly to me, kissing his temple and stroking his hair.

"And then the most wonderful and horrible thing happened. An angel of the Lord appeared before me, blazing bright like white fire, filling me with the greatest sense of peace and joy that I've ever known. He said, 'Greetings, Aiden Alexander MacKenzie MacRae. God is pleased with you and has opened the way of heaven to you. Come with me.' But at that very moment, I heard your voice in my head, screaming. You said, *'Aiden, where are you? Oh please, Aiden, don't leave me!'*"

"You could hear me?" I stared at him in shock.

"Aye, I heard you, every thought that you sent me. And

every word was like a drop of water to a man dying of thirst. It kept me alive and I ached to hear your sweet voice again, but hearing your pain, your agony, and being powerless to help you... It was the worst torture I could possibly imagine."

"I'm sorry, I didn't think you could hear me. I only did it because it made me feel closer to you, to hold on. I never meant to hurt you."

"Ah love, don't be sorry." He brushed a curl off my cheek and smiled softly at me. "You don't know what it meant to me, to hear your voice, to know you were thinking of me. I only wish you could have heard me, too. But I know you didn't because of the thoughts you sent me. If only you could've heard how much I love you, and how I missed you, too." He stroked my hair and kissed me again, his lips soft and warm against mine.

"So you didn't go to heaven, then, because of me?" My chest was leaden with guilt but he smiled at me, understanding clear in his eyes.

"Oui, c'est vrai, ma chèrie. But you should not feel bad. I made it worse, no doubt, by casting memories of our time together. I listened to your sweet voice in my head while I watched us make love on the sand... your beautiful body... No, I couldn't leave you. Not even for heaven."

As he spoke, he ran his hand over my neck to my breast. My nipple stood stiff in the cool night air, pressed against my nightgown. His thumb circled it and a shiver passed down my spine, my flesh recalling the wonder of his touch. His mouth sought mine and I lost myself in his kiss, his hands roaming over my body like they were memorizing every curve once again.

When we broke away, he frowned down at me. "You're skinnier than I remember. You've not been eating well."

I barked a joyless laugh. "Yeah, grief will do that to you."

My words hung in the air between us like the smoke.

Part of me wanted to take it back because I could see that it stung him, but part of me needed him to know that I'd been in just as much pain.

I'm sorry, love. I know that I promised you I'd never leave.

My blood froze as his words formed in my head and I gaped at him, my mind struggling to figure out why I could hear his thoughts again. I held his face in my hands, trembling with emotion, and sent the message back.

You never did leave me, Aiden. You were always with me.

He crushed me against his chest and we both cried, overcome with relief at our reunion and grieving for the pain that the other had endured during our separation. "But how?" I asked. "I still don't understand. How can you be here now?"

To my surprise, his face split into a huge grin. "Oh lassie, I prayed and prayed. Oh, how I prayed to be with you again, but I didn't know how it could be, since I didn't want you to have to die again to be with me. But God is a marvelous and merciful wonder, I tell you the truth. I heard your cry there at the end and I knew you were in danger. I was worried out of my mind and I called out to God in agony to please spare you, even though I knew it meant we couldn't be together.

"Instantly, the angel reappeared before me, his peace and beauty washing over me like a river. He said, 'God has heard your prayers and has granted you new life. Go to her, Aiden. You are free.' And there I was, in the center of the room filled with smoke, with your limp body at my feet. I was worried at first, for you weren't breathing, but when you turned to look at me and called my name... I thought my heart would burst in my very chest." He shook his head in awe, his face beaming with joy.

"Thank you, God." My heart rejoiced as I breathed the prayer and Aiden squeezed my hand.

"Amen!" His voice was loud in the stillness of the dark night, but I didn't care. I wanted to shout it from the mountaintops, I was so elated with the sheer wonder of it all. I hugged him close and laughed, the grief and pain of the last six months dissipating like the smoke in the air around us. Finally whole once again, I wanted to stay in that moment forever.

He kissed me then, his lips reacquainting themselves with mine and his hands wound in my hair, his fingertips circling my temples and massaging my scalp. His mouth moved to my ear and jaw and the tingling sensation I remembered from his touch echoed all throughout my flesh.

"Mmmm…" I purred and closed my eyes, reeling in the sensation of his hot breath on my neck. He stopped and hooked a finger through my necklace, pulling it forward so that the charm and the ring rested in his palm. He stared at it for a moment, surprised, but then he smiled.

"Ah, I'd forgotten that you told me about the ring. When I heard your voice in my head, I couldn't believe it was true, but sure enough, it was gone from my sporran. I'm so glad you had it." His eyes sparkled as he unhooked the necklace and removed the ring from the chain. "But it doesn't belong on your neck, my bride."

I held out my hand and he slipped the ring on my finger, closing his hand around my own and holding it to his chest just as he'd done the first time.

"I think it's probably safe to go inside again. I don't want you to catch a chill." He kissed me lightly and tucked a strand of hair behind my ear. He lifted me off his lap and stood up, then gathered me in his arms and carried me across the threshold.

Chapter 36

A thin film of smoke lingered in the air, but the cross breeze had ventilated the cabin so that only a lightly acrid scent remained, clinging to the furniture and draperies. He set me on my feet at the base of the skinny stairwell and I pulled him up the stairs behind me, my heart hammering in my chest. A sudden wave of nervousness swept through me at the thought of being intimate with him again.

While we were apart, I'd spent a great deal of time reminiscing about the times that we'd made love, the longing for him so intense I thought it would break me. But the details had become somewhat blurry over the remainder of the school year and my memories were more like snapshots frozen in my mind. I could only clearly remember a specific look here and expression there, along with the beautiful lines of his muscled body.

Yet there was nothing blurry or frozen about him now as he stood before me next to the bed, his face glowing with the moonlight. He was very much alive and his chest was firm and warm under my hands. My stomach clenched as I envisioned his naked body against mine and I coughed to cover up my irrational anxiety. He glanced to the side, taking in my blankets and pillow on the twin sized bed under the eave, and raised one eyebrow as he stooped to remove his boots.

"I couldn't sleep on our bed without you," I explained, my voice barely more than a whisper.

"Ah, *ma chérie...*" He put one arm around my waist and pulled me close. "You're trembling. Are you cold? Or... maybe scairt?"

I shouldn't have been surprised at his observation since he could read me like an open book, but I was. I dropped my eyes to the floor and nodded slightly, feeling like an idiot. He lifted my chin with one finger until I was forced to meet his gaze.

"I understand, Lindsey. Truly, I do. But you've naught to fear from me. I would wait a thousand years for you, more if I had to. We don't have to do anything tonight if you're not ready. I am content just to be with you."

My lip quivered and he put both arms around me, holding me close to his chest. "No more tears, love. I think we've both shed more than our fair share and there isn't any need for it now. Come, let us just get some rest, aye?" But his compassion emboldened me and I shook my head, squaring my shoulders and taking a deep breath.

Do it now, before you lose your nerve. I told myself, straightening up as I stepped back from him, my face set.

"No," I whispered and pulled my nightgown up over my head in one swift motion, dropping it to the floor at my feet. A breeze was blowing through the room from the open window and I stood before him in only my panties, shivering with the chill and nerves, the silver charm on my necklace dangling between my breasts. I'd never felt more vulnerable and exposed in my life, but I trusted him implicitly and for some reason, I desperately needed him to know it.

His gaze swept over my body, his face wordlessly asking if I was sure. He took a step toward me and reached out, cupping my breast with one hand. His natural body heat was like a brand on my ice-cold skin and I twitched involuntarily when he touched me.

"Gracious, you're freezing." He stopped, concerned, but I took his hand and placed it over my heart, which was thumping like a bass drum. Conflicting emotions played

240

across his face.

"What do I do about you, lass? You stand before me here in the moonlight, your skin the palest ivory, shaking with cold and fear." I started to protest and he silenced me. "I can see it in your eyes. Don't lie to me." He gathered his thoughts for a moment and continued, his warm hands wandering over my skin.

"And part of me wants to gather you in my arms like a wee child, to protect you and keep you safe and warm. At the same time, your body is so beautiful that I want to make fierce love to you until you cry out underneath me. Honest to God, Lindsey, I want to own you, to possess you, to make my claim on you so there's never any question that you belong to me and me alone." His eyes burned with a primitive lust and his jaw clenched as he grabbed my hips firmly with his hands.

"And yet, the truth remains that the very breath in my lungs is because of you, *mon coeur*. And I know very well that I wouldn't be here now if it weren't for your love." His eyes locked onto mine, his voice steady and strong in the still room. "So as much as I want to make you my own, I'm the one who's bound to you. I belong to you, Lindsey MacRae, body, mind and soul. I am yours, if you'll have me." My heart pounded against my ribs so hard I could hardly breathe. I closed my eyes and spoke to him in my mind.

Make love to me, Aiden.

He swept me up easily in his strong arms and placed me gently on the bed. He undressed quickly and covered my body with his own. The warmth of his skin spread through me like a wildfire as he kissed me.

It's Aiden, here with me, at last. I told myself, hardly able to believe such a miracle had occurred, and the excitement grew in my chest, igniting the passion within me. I stroked his body and kissed him madly, abandoning any trepidation in my joy at being with him again. The movement of our bodies was not fluid and graceful, but filled with desperation and desire, pain and loss, need and lust. We consumed one another until the chasm that had separated us was forgotten and we could lie in each other's arms, completely exhausted and finally fulfilled.

Chapter 37

In the morning, I stirred and blinked sleepily, but then smiled, seeing Aiden lying on his back asleep next to me. I'd never awakened to find him sleeping, and his peaceful face completely mesmerized me. His eyelashes were darker at the roots and blond at the tips, his nose straight and strong, his lips slightly parted as he slept. I watched the rhythmic rise and fall of his chest and could not keep from grinning. I was sticky and sore, and I smelled like a chimney, but I'd never been happier in my life. I started to hum a tune without even realizing it, and he woke up, smiling dreamily as he turned to me.

"*Madainn mhath, mo leannan.* That means 'Good morning, my lover' in Gaelic."

I grinned at him and traced his bottom lip with my finger. "How do you say, 'You were amazing last night' in Gaelic?" He laughed heartily and provided the incredibly long and difficult translation for me, to which I just shrugged and replied, *"Peut être, je devrais rester avec le français."*

He chuckled and smoothed my hair. *"Oui, d'accord.* Maybe it would be best to learn one new language at a time. I'm happy to teach you both, though if you'd like. We have plenty of time now." I traced the line of muscle in his bicep to his forearm and he chuckled to himself, a private smile flickering on his face. I raised an eyebrow in question, wondering what he was thinking.

"I just realized that I've need of the privy and I haven't

felt that sensation in… well, three hundred years."

I took him downstairs to the bathroom and explained the workings of the toilet. He was fascinated by the 'marvelous contraption,' which made me giggle. We took a shower together after he'd relieved himself and took turns washing one another. Aiden's gaze lingered on the scars on my arm and on the side of my breast and I explained that they were from the car accident.

"One of my broken ribs pierced a lung when the car crushed me. The lung collapsed so that I couldn't really breathe and the doctors put a tube in right there," I pointed to my side, "to save my life. The one on my arm is from the broken glass of the window, I think."

"I'm sorry, love," he said as he traced the scars with his finger.

"Don't be. I wouldn't have you if I didn't have those. You were definitely worth it." I kissed him briefly and turned off the water, then dried off with a towel and handed one to him. I put on my bathrobe and headed into the kitchen to start breakfast while he went upstairs to get dressed.

I was cheerfully dicing potatoes while the butter melted in the cast iron skillet when he came downstairs. Alison Krauss was singing "Now That I've Found You" on the stereo and I joined in when I felt his arms around my waist. Turning in his embrace, I smiled up at him, hardly able to believe he was here with me again. We swayed back and forth to the music in the little kitchen.

"Taties and eggs sound okay for breakfast?" I asked and he broke into a grin.

"Aye, my love. I can't think of anything else I'd like more," he said, then brought his lips to mine.

Don't miss the exciting sequel to BETWEEN!

HELL TRANSPORTER

Aiden MacRae has been given new life after being stuck transporting souls to heaven for the last three hundred years. He doesn't know the culture, the times or the slang, but there is one thing he does know: he didn't come forward alone.

The master of hell has other plans for the Scottish Highlander and has sent a transporter of his own to get the deed done. Will Lindsey be able to save him or get caught in the crossfire?